UNSPEAKABLY
EROTIC
LESBIAN KINK

Edited by
D. L. King

CLEiS
PRESS

9030 0000 763 962

Published in the United States by Cleis Press, an imprint of Start Midnight, LLC, 101 Hudson St, Suite 3705, Jersey City, NJ 07302.

Printed in the United States.
Cover design: Scott Idleman/Blink
Cover photograph: iStock
Text design: Frank Wiedemann
First Edition.
10 9 8 7 6 5 4 3 2 1

Trade paper ISBN: 978-1-62778-250-0
E-book ISBN: 978-1-62778-251-7

Contents

INTRODUCTION

Taboo. The very word can cause you to take a step back, and then, depending on how your lizard brain works, can cause you to take two furtive steps forward with your head cocked to the side and your mouth forming a silent, questioning *Oh*.

The original idea was for an anthology all about taboo erotica but I quickly realized that 1) What's taboo for one person might be the next thing to vanilla for another, and 2) Some things really are taboo and don't belong in books of erotica—at least not in my books of erotica. So, the theme got changed from "taboo" to "edgy." But again, what's kinky or edgy to some might not make your top ten list of crazy things to do. And then again, what you find to be adrenaline-fueling edge play might be too over-the-top for other people. All things being unequal, what's an editor to do?

How should I go about gathering a collection of unspeakable stories designed to make you cringe just a bit before you come? If the book contained all stories that I, personally, found edgy, it could alienate a segment of my readership. On the other hand, if I made it too tame, it would alienate a different segment of my readership.

Now, compromising would mean that the anthology would be middle-of-the-road kink, so I decided not to compromise. Instead, I decided to give you an eclectic mix. Some stories might be out of your comfort range, but give them a chance; you might find yourself aroused by fantasies you never expected to find sexy. And, what about the less wild—less dangerous? Just because a story is a bit tamer than your favorite go-to edge play doesn't mean that, in the hands of a skilled storyteller, you might not find it just as big a turn-on.

So, let's talk just a little about the unspeakable: if we're going to do edge play, the first story has to be edgy—according to everyone's sensibilities. How about a Mercedes-driving, Rothko-owning, sexy older dyke— with a knife—who knows just which buttons to push? You may find yourself falling in love with J. Belle Lamb, and her story, "Pygmalion," just like I have.

And then there's "CBT." "CBT?" you ask. "But isn't that cock and ball torture? What's cock and ball torture have to do with a book about kinky lesbian sex?"

Well, that's exactly what I thought when I first down-loaded the story and printed it. And then I started to read it. I find Pascal Scott's story of a butch top meeting her ultimate sadistic femdom utterly charming. But then, I'm charmed by genital bondage, whips and clips and a woman who knows how to use them to her best advantage.

What about a foot fetish? Sonni de Soto's character, Reena, in her story, "Support Service," insists that she doesn't have one—a fetish, that is—after providing volunteer services, all night, in the form of foot massage, for her local club. She tells herself she doesn't have a fetish even as she lusts after an enigmatic dungeon monitor and her tiny, overworked feet, at the end of a very busy night.

Sacchi Green gives us a story about a tough-talking carney top, a horse woman and her giant Percherons, some very special Mardi Gras beads, and turnabout being fair, not to mention good, play in "Baubles and Beads."

Speaking of animals, a girl who desperately wants to be a kitten, finally gets to play out her fantasy at her first play party in Rose P. Lethe's "Private Party." Sometimes, besides courage, you need to find the *yin* to your *yang*.

And along the same animal vein, Mary Tintagel never ceases to completely freak me out. You may remember her skydiving story in *She Who Must Be Obeyed*. This time around she offers up a pony-play story. Well, it's a kind of pony-play story. "The Last of Marengo," set in The Netherlands, is completely beyond the pale. Does your local museum of sex have a hippodrome? Just asking.

While you'll find some old favorites, like Sacchi Green, Annabeth Leong, Kiki DeLovely, and B. D. Swain, you'll also find a lot of newcomers. I'm thrilled to get to know people like Pascal Scott, Sonni de Soto, Sir Manther, Elinor Zimmerman, and Robyn Nyx.

This book is designed to make you a little uncomfortable and make you squirm just a bit, but I hope it will be a good squirm. Not every story will do that for you, but I can guarantee that at least a few will. Some may be totally outside your comfort zone. After all, it's rare that you pick up an anthology and find you love every story in it. That's okay. I can bet, however, that if this book piqued your interest at all, you'll probably like most of them. I, on the other hand, like them all. Each one is unspeakable in its own right. So, sit down, relax, and enjoy.

D. L. King
New York City

PYGMALION

J. Belle Lamb

M ay I?" she says, taking the bottle from your hand. You've met most of the guests at Wallace's party, but she seems to have appeared from nowhere.

You let her take the wine. She's older, late fifties maybe, gray hair cut short and spiked. Standard dress leathers: dark-blue jeans that look starched, crisp black dress shirt under a tight-buttoned leather vest. A well-worn leather jacket hangs off the chair where she dropped it.

"Where I come from, a lady shouldn't have to fetch her own drinks," she says, deftly pulling a wineglass from the chaos on Wallace's kitchen counter. She starts to fill the glass and turns to look at you, almost asking a question, but you watch her close her mouth around it. A few moments later, she hands you the wine, golden in the glass.

"What were you going to ask?" You sip the wine. It's crisp and cold.

"That's a good wine. I wondered if you'd brought it."

Her tone is a little sharp, but you decide you hear playfulness under it. "I don't think we've met," she says, holding out a hand. "I'm Irene."

"Yes, I brought the wine. I'm Beatrice," you say, shaking her hand. Her grip is strong, almost painful. You have to look up to meet her eyes, even though you're wearing heels. "But my friends call me Trixie."

"Of course they do," Irene says, letting go of your fingers to fill her own wineglass. She reclaims her leather jacket before she takes your elbow, steering you over to the sliding glass doors at one end of the house's large living room. A fan of both opera and camp, Wallace decorated for the party with sprays of fake ivy and plastic grapes. The heap of golden breastplates that grace the coffee table look like they're made of spray-painted Styrofoam. A poster for the Seattle Opera's current production of *Pygmalion* has been tacked up above the fireplace.

Irene leaves her hand on your arm as she turns to face you. "Now, Trixie, the real question is what a lady like you is doing unattended in a crowd like this." She nods at the humming crowd dressed in interpretations of "opera best" that include at least two latex minidresses and a number of leather chest harnesses with matching bow ties.

"Trying to mingle, I suppose. I'm not great at being a social butterfly." You smile at Irene, whose light-brown eyes are doing a good job of helping you tune out the rest of the party.

"I'm going to have to have a chat with Wallace about his taste in friends if no one at this party has had the sense to keep you occupied." She sips her wine. "Or maybe I should just be glad I got lost on the way here. It looks like he's too busy to notice that I made it." Irene glances over at your host, whose cheeks are burnished pink as he flirts with a shirtless man twenty years his junior.

"You know him well?" Irene moves her hand from your elbow to rest lightly on your lower back. You shift your weight to lean slightly into it, enjoying Irene's satisfied smile around the rim of her wineglass.

"We've been friends for a long time. Came up together in New York." She looks around the room. "Lots of pretty people here. But a little noisy for my taste. How do you feel about getting a breath of air?" Irene nods toward the sliding glass doors.

You sip your wine slowly, pretending to consider her proposition. She holds your eyes over the glass, her smile letting you know that she knows that you'll say yes, but she's letting you play your little game.

"I'd like that." You enjoy the way she's watching your lips.

She opens the door silently, ushering you onto the porch. It's cold enough that you begin to regret not bringing your coat. Irene puts a hand on your goose-pimpled shoulder. Still silent, she holds up the jacket.

"How very old-fashioned," you say as you slip your arms into her jacket. Its silver snaps are scratched and the leather is soft with age.

Irene grins. "Sometimes the classics are classic for a reason." She settles next to you on the bench, her jeans rubbing against your black stockings.

You lean back into the bench and against Irene. The jacket is heavy, its leather scent mixed with hints of cigar smoke and a cologne that smells a little like oranges. You like it, and you decide that you like Irene. "And what's that reason tonight?"

"No need to make a beautiful girl shiver unnecessarily in the cold." Irene turns to look at you, your faces close enough that all she'd need to do is lean forward to kiss you. "I'd much rather have you shiver for me."

"Well, you're certainly cocky," you tell her, tipping your chin slightly toward her, hoping that she'll read the hint and kiss you.

Irene drops a hand to her crotch. "Not right now, I'm afraid," she says with a rueful expression. You laugh hard, the sound wrapping close around the two of you in the damp cold. She watches you, brown eyes sparkling in a fine webwork of laugh lines. As your giggles die away, she reaches across your lap, hand cupping the leather jacket's elbow briefly and then sliding down its arm to find your fingers. Irene traces the back of your hand. "Come home with me, Trixie," she says, smiling when you shiver as she strokes your hand.

"Now? But you've only just gotten to the party." You wonder how long she'll let you keep playing your game. She knows you're going home with her tonight; you know you're going home with her tonight. Still, it's satisfying to wonder what she'll say next.

Irene pauses, her fingers still on your hand. Her smile thins. You don't see the hand that's been draped on the back of the bench move, but you shiver again as she pulls your head back, fingers tight enough in your hair to prickle fire across your scalp.

"Oh yes, Trixie. I've just gotten to the party. And I know it's the kind of party where no one would care if I fucked you on this bench. Or even if I stripped you down and slammed you up against that window to put on a little show." Her cheek rests against yours as she speaks so that you feel the shape of her words as you hear them. "And I think you're the kind of woman who would enjoy that." She waits for a moment until you make a tiny noise of assent. "But I like to take my time. So, when I let go of you, we're going to stand up, and you're going to follow me through that party so that all of those fools see you leave with me. And then you're going to come to my place." She brushes the corner of your jaw with a light kiss. You shiver again. "And I will take my time with you."

It happens exactly as Irene has said: she lets go of your hair and you leave the porch, fingers twined in hers as you follow her back through the party, still wearing her leather jacket. She doesn't move quickly through Wallace's house, but heads turn to watch the two of you cross the living room, skirt the kitchen, and move toward the foyer. You think about documentary footage of deer tracking a predator's movement around the edge of the herd, all those eyes suddenly alert to the presence of danger. The thought makes your cunt tighten.

Irene pulls you through Wallace's door and down the front steps. She drops your fingers to hold your elbow again, steadying you as you pick your way through the muddy driveway in your heels. You let her half-guide, half-follow you to your car. You start to shrug out of her jacket.

"Leave it," she says, tugging the leather back around you. She reaches into the jacket's inner pocket to pull out a phone and her keys, hand brushing against your breast just enough to let you know that she meant to touch you. She frowns slightly as she digs into her vest to extract a pair of reading glasses. When she puts them on, you think you might as well just kneel down in the mud to lick her boots. Irene's frown eases, though you're sure she didn't hear your thought. She looks at you over the glasses. "May I have your phone number, please?"

You give it to her.

"There," she says, putting her phone in her back pocket and handing over your coat. "I've texted you my address. I'll wait for you at the bottom of the driveway, but this way, you know how to find me just in case we get separated."

Your car is cold, but inside Irene's jacket, you're quite warm. You turn off the stereo, wanting to hear if your heart is beating as loudly as you think it is. The soft creak of Irene's jacket is the only thing you hear. You tell yourself to stop being ridiculous and just enjoy the prospect of getting thoroughly laid.

Irene's car, a sleek little Mercedes, is waiting at the end of Wallace's long driveway. You flash your lights to let her know it's you, and then spend the next half hour trying to keep up with her as she leads you across the I-90 bridge into the heart of the city. When she pulls into the garage of a house tucked into the trees near Washington Park, you park in the driveway, your rust-and-red Land Cruiser looking out of place in the upscale neighborhood. You begin to wonder just what you've gotten yourself into.

But it's the canvas leaning against the living room wall that makes you gasp when she leads you into her house.

"Irene, is that a Rothko?" You can barely get the words out. The big painting, a central black bar separating stacked rectangles of marine blue and frayed white, makes you feel loose-limbed and dizzy.

Irene follows your gaze. "I take it you're an art fan."

"How do you have a Rothko sitting in your living

room?" The room also contains a stack of moving boxes and elegant modern furniture that clearly hasn't yet found its proper places. You keep staring at the painting, wishing you could dive into the canvas and swim in the colors.

You're dimly aware that Irene has moved to stand next to you, her arm on the back of the leather jacket. "My father bought it in New York years ago. I inherited it. I brought a few of my favorite pieces out to Seattle with me," she says, and you can feel her eyes on your face.

"A few of . . . there's more?" Something almost tangible has shifted between you and Irene. You were ready to fuck her five minutes after meeting her at Wallace's party; now, you don't care at all if you have sex tonight, but you desperately want to know what else is in her art collection.

"Oh yes. Quite a bit. My father was a collector. I inherited his passion along with his collection." She's still watching your face. "Would you like to sit down with the Rothko for a while?" Her hand is still on the jacket, a reassuring weight in contrast to the hurricane of emotion that the painting has evoked in you.

"I . . . don't know. Maybe. Or maybe not tonight. Can I come see it again?" You feel a little like you've run into an estranged ex in the supermarket: too shocked by the sudden interaction with the painting to be able to sort out your feelings.

Irene chuckles. "If it means I get to see that look on you again, Trixie, you can come see it whenever you like. And once I get the rest of them hung, I hope you'll let me show them to you, too. I have a Basquiat I imagine you'll love."

You manage to tear your eyes away from the Rothko,

still tasting its blue on the back of your tongue. "And a Basquiat," you say, looking at Irene, whose smile has relaxed from its sharpness at the party into something you find you like even more.

"Indeed. I only brought one with me. The others are still in New York." She's teasing you a little now. It's working—you feel woozy, electric, somewhere in between frantically turned on and wildly curious about her. "I wonder if we can get you out of this jacket," she asks, turning your body toward hers as she reaches inside the leather to ease it off your shoulders. You stand doll-like as she takes it off you, still stunned by the painting.

Irene tosses the jacket over a stack of boxes. She runs her hands down your bare arms, moving close enough to make you need to tip your head back to hold her gaze. "Do you want to talk about art some more tonight, Trixie?"

You find your voice. "I always want to talk about art, Irene." She's very close, and you know she's waiting to kiss you, though you're not sure why.

Irene curves an arm around to rest her hand on your ass. "So do I. Though I admit I had something else in mind when I asked you to come home with me."

You look deep into her brown eyes. "You know, Irene, if I were reading about this in a romance novel, I'd be pretty skeptical right now."

Her fingers curl over your ass. "And why is that?"

"Handsome older butch top picks up bored femme at a party and then turns out to be a wealthy art collector? Come on, Irene. Next thing I know, you're going to be taking me upstairs to show me a red velvet bedroom and your custom-built private dungeon."

Irene's expression flips rapidly through shocked to

delighted. "I don't do red velvet," she says between peals of laughter, "And I only bought the place a month ago, so I haven't had time to get a contractor for the private dungeon yet."

"Uh-huh. And you're sweeping me off to New York in your private plane when?"

She laughs so hard that she has to let go of your ass to wipe tears from her eyes. "No private plane, I'm sorry to say. But I can at least offer you business class."

You smile as you close the inches between you, reaching up to put your arms around her neck. "Deal," you say as you kiss her. Her laughter bubbles through the kiss for a moment before turning into a low growl as her hands find your ass and your hair again.

She kisses you long and hard enough to make sure she has your attention. When she stops, you open your eyes to find hers, warm and hungry. She holds you there for a few heartbeats, hand tight in your hair.

"Red, yellow, and green?" Irene's hand slides over the curve of your ass.

"I thought it was blue, black, and white," you murmur, flicking your gaze over to the Rothko and then back to her eyes.

She laughs again. "Is this the part where the hardened butch top finds out that the sweet blonde femme is actually a smart-assed brat?"

"A little from column A, a little from column B," you say, leaning closer so that you can grind your hips against hers, your scalp turning fiery again as she twists your hair.

"Saucy little bitch," Irene says, sounding happy about it. "Wait here."

She disappears down a short hallway, leaving you in

the living room. You want to walk over to the Rothko and touch it. It's an impulse you have in art museums and galleries: if you could just put your fingers on the paintings and sculptures, you'd be able to feel them even more deeply than you already do. Perhaps your arm would sink into Rothko's radiant blue. You are sure it would feel like plunging into warm salt water.

Irene returns carrying a wooden dining chair. A black bag is slung over her shoulder. She's taken off her leather vest and boots and untucked the black dress shirt. As she sets the chair about six feet away from the Rothko canvas and drops the bag near it, you smile. It's romantic, somehow, that she's seen how the painting makes you feel. She fiddles with the chair's placement, stepping behind it to look at the painting and then twitching it over an inch and brushing off its black leather seat. It's a beautiful scene: Irene in her loose black shirt and jeans fussing over the chair's sleek modern lines in front of Rothko's floating rectangles. She catches you watching and smiles.

"All right, Trixie," she says, stopping as she crosses the living room to flip a switch that bathes the painting in warm light. "Let's try again: I assume you know how to safeword." She reaches for your hand, turning it over to run her thumb over your palm.

"Sure. I'll call red if I need to." Irene's deep breath isn't quite a sigh of annoyance, but it pleases you anyway.

"Thank you. I don't intend to go too deep or get too exotic tonight, but is there anything I should know now about your play limits?" Her thumb keeps stroking your palm.

"I need to not have to explain any visible marks at

work. I don't play with excrement, and I don't like being gagged." You like how carefully she's watching you.

"No problem on any of those. Sex?" Her thumb's strokes grow longer, moving from your palm to the inside of your wrist.

"I'd like that," you say, watching her brown eyes grow even warmer. "Safely, please."

"Yes, ma'am." Irene's fingers encircle your wrist and her other hand moves around your waist.

"I like your style, Irene," you say, leaning forward so that your breasts brush against her shirt.

"And I like yours, Trixie." She kisses you, slow movements of tongue and lips drawing you deeper into her arms. She brushes her lips over your cheek before she says: "Over to the chair, please."

You walk over to the chair, heels clicking on hardwood floor until they're muffled by the living room's dark-gray area rug, its pile so thick that you have trouble balancing as your heels sink into it. The chair's back is cool under your hand as you reach to steady yourself.

"Stand behind it, please," Irene says from across the room. You put both hands on the chair's back as you face the painting. Closer, its colors take on more intensity. There are subtle threads of black and red in the blue rectangle, and you can see now that the background is a rich yellow-tan, the color of dried grass.

She's silent as she walks across the room to stand behind you. "Just stand, Trixie. Stand and look at the painting," she says, voice near your ear.

You stand in front of the painting. The blue rectangle hovers over the black bar, over the white rectangle, over the polished wood floor. Irene finds your dress's zipper.

The painting disappears for a moment as she lifts the black silk over your head.

"Lovely," she says, fingertips brushing down your back, over your black bra's strap, over the black lace of your panties, and down to the edges of your garters and stockings. The black bar in between the painting's two rectangles is off center. The more you look at it, the more it seems to float over the blue and white rectangles, as if it's on a separate screen overlaying them. You wonder if the blue and white touch under the black bar.

You feel Irene's breath on the back of your knee as she kneels behind you. She lifts one foot, then the other out of your heels. The rug settles under your feet. You realize you were wrong about the painting's background: it's not the color of dried grass at all. The more you look, the more it becomes a ripe wheat field in sun slanting under a thunderhead.

Irene unhooks your bra. Her fingertips ease the bra straps off your shoulders. You think about Rothko's slanting sun on that wheat field. Irene's touch becomes that light. You shiver.

Irene's beautiful house is very quiet. The blue rectangle starts to quiver as you look at it. It's not a balloon tugging on its string, not quite, nor a jellyfish, nor a cloud. Her knife's small click as it opens breaks your breath for a second.

Her knife touches the back of your neck, just where white-blonde curls tickle if you turn your head quickly. You stand very still. The white rectangle wants to break free. It's bestial. As the knife's point drags down the knobs of your spine, you watch the white rectangle twist and try to stretch. It stays pinned down by the black bar.

She doesn't speak. The knife finds the edge of your panties, blade's point just inside the elastic, tracing around your ass's upper curve. There are cracks in the white rectangle's fur. You start to see threads of a deep red trying to trickle through.

Irene reaches around to rest her hand above your cunt's swell; her palm cups over your pubic bone. Her shirt's heavy silk presses against your back. When the knife reaches from where she let it rest against your hip, its point pricks for an instant as it digs under your garter's tie. The ribbon parts. You can't stop a tiny moan from catching in your throat.

"Shh," she says against your ear. "Just look at the painting, my lovely."

The knife swims to her other hand. More garter ribbons slice open. The blue rectangle, you realize, wants to let you in while the white rectangle wants to run away. Both ache under the black bar's weight. You're sad for them, sick with desire for the blue. Tears begin to press against the back of your eyes. Her knife rips through the garter belt's lace. It falls.

She tugs your hips so that you have to bend, forearms now on the chair's back. The knife's point roams over your panties. It makes a small scratching sound as it moves over the lace. You think you can hear the white rectangle scrabbling in response.

You ache toward the blue; it aches toward you as Irene grabs the lace gathered against your cunt and pulls it away just enough to slide the knife under it. Your panties' shredding is loud enough to make you and the blue rectangle flinch away from each other. You almost let go of the chair to reach for it, but Irene's gloved hand moving over your cunt stops you. She finds your clit. Tears press harder in your eyes as she strokes you, her fingers beckoning the blue to come close again.

When you start to quake, she stops. "Not yet, my lovely. Just stay with the painting for a little while longer." You feel slippery inside as you try to hold on to any single emotion, desire fraying into sadness and a longing that spills into the golden field tethering the blue rectangle.

She lets the knife cut your panties free. It licks along your ass, drawing lines only Irene can see. It scratches down the curve of your asscheeks, first one side, then the other. The white rectangle roars, showing its red crackle, as you feel blood well hot on your skin. You want to look back at Irene, to see if she's watching the scratches as they call to the white rectangle. But you are sure if you move, something will go out of true that can never again be pulled back into shape.

Irene is still for several long minutes. You start to wonder if you could walk forward and rip the black bar off the canvas. When she moves, you feel her fingers against your ass, moving over your hole, spreading you open. The blue rectangle shivers as she works lube into your asshole.

You can't see what she presses against your ass. She works it slowly into you, a roundness that asks you to open up, and then open up a little more. You don't realize you've started crying until a tear blurs the painting. The blue is howling now as the white rectangle lashes and paces. Irene reaches up to pet the back of your head, making *shhhing* sounds as she pushes the roundness farther in, filling and opening you in the same instant.

"A little farther apart, please," she says, tapping your

thigh. You shift to open your legs wider. You hear her snap on a different pair of gloves. She reaches between your legs to spread your cunt open with one hand.

When the tip of her knife touches your clit, it takes every bit of willpower you have not to jump or shiver. You feel the blue rectangle pulse toward you as you struggle to keep your breath steady and your body perfectly still. Irene makes a small sound of pleasure as she traces your inner labia with the sharp knife. Your tears patter onto the chair's leather seat.

Irene pushes your cunt open with her fingers. The sensation of being held open while feeling the pressure of the toy in your ass makes you feel like a rubber band wound too tight. You want her to fuck you, to let you come so that the feeling of being held taut, of fighting not to tremble, not to come, will stop. You want release, the wish for it pacing and lashing and storming as it builds to match the strain of the blue and white rectangles against Rothko's black bar. You're all captured, all prisoners.

The knife slips into your cunt slowly. You bite the inside of your lip, hard. If you move, she will slice you open. The blue rectangle keens in sympathy. You don't move.

"So lovely." Irene's voice is next to your ear; her body is warm against your ass. You don't know if she's talking about the painting or the knife in your cunt. She holds it there as you hear her jeans' fly unbuttoning. A moment later, the knife moves out of your cunt. You let yourself shiver then, violent tremors that aren't quite an orgasm and aren't quite panic, but which leave you feeling like you're falling. The chair is blissfully solid under your arms.

Irene's cock presses against your cunt's lips. "Let go, Trixie," she says softly as she thrusts into you, cock filling your cunt as her motion pushes the toy deeper into your ass.

You scream then. The blue rectangle funnels down your open throat, filling you completely.

CBT

Pascal Scott

I've never wanted a cock. Aesthetics are important to me and, in my view, a cock is ugly. The Ancient Greeks saw it differently. They gave Western culture the ideal of the athletic body—male, of course—and the notion that banging a youth is the apex of eroticism. Me, I would have been with Sappho, hanging with the ladies of Lesbos on that lovely isle, happily separated from the cock-and-ball population.

The first time I strapped on a dildo I felt embarrassed. It was protruding out of an old-fashioned leather harness, and I had inadvertently tightened the straps until they had cut off the circulation in my thighs. I felt uncomfortable and more than a little humiliated. This had been my girl-friend's idea, not mine; I was just being a good butch. But then, when I looked up from the strange new appendage in my crotch and saw the look in her eyes—pure *lust*—I thought, *oh. Well then*.

Sometimes I'm a slow learner.

I meet Alexa at a workshop titled "Orgasm Denial," sponsored by Altamont Femdoms. Now a femdom, in case you are one of those lesbians still licking the vanilla ice cream cone, is what we in the Leatherland of BDSM call a female dominant. If you stopped right now and had a wet dream about what a femdom would look like, you'd pretty much be picturing Alexa.

It's late winter on the evening of the workshop; Alexa is the presenter. For the occasion she has slipped her sinewy body into thigh-hugging, black vinyl pants; a blood-red blouse with flowing sleeves that make her look a little like an erotic pirate; and high-heeled, laced-up, black leather boots. The colors I see are black and red and cream. The black is her hair: short and straight with severely cut bangs that reach her brows. The cream is her skin, blushed by nature at the cheeks and neck. And the red is her lips, glossed with some come-kiss-me shade of whatever it is femdoms are using these days to seduce innocents.

Notice I don't say "innocents like me." My days of innocence are long gone. I've been playing with the fire of D/s since my twenties, many decades ago now. I once received a private message from a femme on KINK—the Facebook for kinky folk—complimenting my profile picture for its "mature butch swagger." *Mature*, I thought. *Nice way of saying it*. Checking out Alexa from my folding chair in the third row back, I'm guessing I am twice her age.

We have seated ourselves in the bourgie living room of a mountaintop home outside the city limits. The home belongs to the group's organizer, a red-haired sadist named Mistress Kate. There are about twenty of us in attendance, mostly femdoms and a few submissive men like the bald-headed husband of our hostess. I am the only lesbian of the bunch of mostly middle-aged, self-styled "heteroflexibles." The way I feel about all the labels out there these days—bisexual, pansexual, genderqueer—is what the kids used to say, *whatever*. I miss the days when straight knew it was straight, and a lesbian was a lesbian was a lesbian. But that marks me as a dinodyke so I usually keep my opinion to myself, covered by a nonchalant "cool" in response to whatever I hear.

Alexa glances up from the stack of white index cards in her hand, and our eyes meet. Her eyes are the color of dark chocolate, luscious, with long black eyelashes. One trouble with dark eyes: they're hard to read. Blue eyes like mine reveal everything, all the little lashes of pain that life whips at you that can turn blue eyes into cracked marbles if you're not careful.

There's an immediate connection. The cards are transferred to her left hand as her right arm comes up and out, extended toward me in greeting as she strides over.

"Hi," she says. "I don't believe we've met. I'm Alexa."

I stand and shake her hand. It's soft but gives a firm handshake.

"Pascal," I say.

"Pascal?" she repeats.

"Yes," I say. "It's French."

"Charming," she says.

Indeed. I miss most of what she says next because I've been pulled in by *her* charms, which are considerable.

"I'm so glad you're here," I hear when I can concentrate again.

"Me, too," I say.

It's time. I sit down as Mistress Kate welcomes the group and gives the introduction. We learn that Alexa is a pro-domme and a frequent presenter at kinky conferences like DomCon and The National Leather Association Conference. Alexa stands beside Mistress Kate, surveying the room. Her gaze stops when it reaches me. She smiles. Mistress Kate finishes. Alexa clears her lovely throat. It begins.

Two hours later I have learned more than I ever thought imaginable about the art of orgasm denial. Good student that I am, I have taken notes in my pocket-sized notepad, which I will review later. I consider myself a competent practitioner of B/D but I am the first to admit that I am a novice to S/M. For some reason I don't yet understand, my play partners have always been averse to receiving pain. That is until recently, when I happened into a relationship with an attractive masochist. It is with the deliberate intention of improving my nascent sadistic skill set that I have sought out workshops like Alexa's. Orgasm denial seems to me like *the* most sadistic practice ever devised.

But *why?* you may be asking. Why would you ever *want* to deny a woman her orgasm?

Let me put it like this. Suppose I'm a mystery writer and I'm writing a story about a murder. *I* know who did it but *you* don't. Yet. It's my little secret that I'll share with you when I'm ready. When *I'm* ready, not when *you're* ready. *You* I want to leave hanging in suspense. I'll do this by teasing you with clues.

There was a dildo found by the body. It was slick with lube and smelled like a woman's juices.

Then I'll check in with you. *Did that make you wet? Does that make you want it? It does? But no, baby, not yet. I'm in charge here, not you. You don't come until I say you can come.*

Then I'll give you another clue.

There was a red ball gag in the body's mouth, suggesting her cries for help had gone unheard.

What about now? Oh, let me check your sweet pussy. Yeah, I can feel it. It's wet for me. But not yet, baby, not until I say you can come.

And so on, until the reader is begging the writer, *please please please*, and the writer is ready to reveal who did it, who stole the body's innocence, who caused *la petite mort*. Orgasm denial. That's why. Rather, that's one reason. There are others, many others. I make a note of them all as Alexa talks; I write them down for future use.

When she has finished, I put my notepad in my back pocket and approach her. She is talking to Mistress Kate, who glances at me in a way that telegraphs her discomfort. Sometimes these heteroflexibles are flexible in name only. Somehow I missed the official announcement, but apparently at some point in the last decade or two, kinky straights got together and decided that it wasn't hip to be het anymore. Nobody wants to admit she's straight now, even when it's obvious.

Alexa shares none of Mistress Kate's discomfort. She glances at me long enough to communicate interest. Again.

"Great workshop," I say after Mistress Kate has left in search of a cigarette. "I learned a lot. It should be helpful."

"I'm so glad," she says. "I'm always a little nervous about presenting."

Her hand reaches out, touches my forearm. I'm wearing my uniform: 501s, a black T-shirt, Harley boots. I feel her fingertips on my skin. Lightly, lightly, she touches me—such a tentative touch. She's close enough that I can smell her scent. Cloves, I think; she smells like cloves and smoke and something earthy.

"Listen," I say. I have no idea what I'm going to say next. "I was wondering about something. You talked about CBT as part of orgasm denial—"

"Cock and ball torture," she says. "Yes."

"Yeah, I was wondering. Do you ever do that with women? I mean, have you ever tried CBT on a woman? On a woman wearing a dildo?"

She looks a little stunned. I'm thinking, *uh-oh, hard limit. Or soft limit. Or some kind of limit.*

"Hmmmmm," she says. "No, I haven't. Of course I've tied up the classic female parts but, no, I've never done CBT on a girl. I'm intrigued."

"Good," I say.

Sometimes I don't know what I'm thinking until I say it. I can't *begin* to tell you the trouble this has gotten me into.

"Well, would you like to try it? Sometime?"

She smiles. Nice smile. White teeth, very straight. And those lips. She's got a tiny bit of red on a front tooth. That seems to happen sometimes, the lipstick goes there. I have the urge to lick it clean.

"On you, you mean?"

Okay, there it is. Ask for what you want. That's what they teach you. And isn't this all for continuing education?

"Yeah," I say.

Done. *Blue eyes, get ready to get hurt.* Why would a sweet young thing like Alexa want to play with an old dyke like me?

But no. No rejection today.

"Yes," she says. "I think I would like that very much."

We're at my place (her choice, not mine) one snowy afternoon in February. I have a modest one-bedroom townhouse in South Altamont, the decidedly unhip section of our little urban dyketopia. The Census Bureau reported last year that per capita, Altamont, NC, has more self-identified lesbians than any other area of the country. This fact astonishes my friends back in San Francisco, from where I drove the dull but sensible I-70 Middle-America route more than 2,800 miles and two decades ago.

Most of my neighbors are retired, like me. But I'm younger than the demographic of South Altamont. I retired early after giving twenty years to the State of North Carolina's Department of Education. Enough said.

Alexa is standing in my living room, wearing a Burberry trench coat and a pair of Ray-Bans. She removes the sunglasses now and sets them on the glass-top coffee table in front of the leather couch, across from the brick fireplace. She's brought along a leather handbag big enough to hold a small alligator. That goes on the ivory shag rug: black on white.

She turns to the fireplace.

"Does this work?" she says.

"Yeah," I say.

I figure that's a hint. I kneel to turn the knob that releases the gas stream. *Whoosh.* I'm acutely aware that I'm on my knees in front of a gorgeous femdom. The logs ignite in obedience. I pull the mesh-screen curtain closed over the dancing flames and stand to face her.

"Nice," she says.

She removes her coat and hands it to me. Good gentle-butch that I am, I walk it to the closet near the front door and hang it. When I return she's standing in front of the fireplace. I take her in. She's wearing a black leather corset, the kind that laces in the back and pushes up her breasts in the front into beautiful mounds. Black fishnet stockings with a sexy seam; high-heeled boots. *How do women walk in those things?* I wonder. She feels me watching her, tilts her head, smiles, then looks back at the flames.

"There's something hypnotizing about fire," she says. "It's so—primal."

"Yes," I agree.

She glances at the wood blinds covering the windows.

"Do those need to be open?"

I glance at them as well. It's cloudy outside but there is still sunlight filtering into the room, bouncing white off the fallen snow.

"No," I say.

I close them, one by one. When I'm done, I return to the fireplace. She turns to study me.

"Too many clothes," she says.

She circles me once, slowly, like an animal. Then she glides over to my big leather chair and sits. *Like a queen,* I think. Bends to untie first one boot, then the other. Slides them off, rubs the ball of each foot. Wiggles her toes, then she crosses her legs and composes herself. Her chin lifts slightly.

"Undress for me," she demands.

I hesitate for a moment. It's something I've never heard from a girl. I decide in an instant that I like it. I rip off my T-shirt.

"No!" she says.

I freeze.

"Not like that. Do it slowly. *Seduce* me."

I let the T-shirt fall from my hand. This leaves me in a black sports bra, my 501s, and boots. There's a black leather belt around my waist. I undo the silver buckle and pull it off in one smooth movement. *Snap.* I hold the buckle in my palm, fold my fingers over it, and wrap the leather around my hand four times, until I have leather knuckles. I hold up my fist to show her, like a boxer. Her eyes smile. Then I unfurl the belt, swinging it back toward me, four times, until it becomes a whip that I fling at her, twice. *Snap! Snap!* She doesn't flinch.

"I'll take that," she says when I'm done with my theatrics. She holds out her hand.

I wrap the belt into a coil and place it in her palm.

"Good boy," she says. "Continue."

I turn my back to her and bend over to unzip my boots. This gives her a nice view of my round ass. I ease out of the Harleys, kicking them aside. The socks go next. Then I turn around to face her.

There's nothing sexy about my bra. It goes up and over my head and onto the rug. This reveals my chest. I tense my pecs, suck in my abs. I no longer have the body of a twenty-year-old but I'm a lifelong gym rat, and it shows.

"Hmmm," she says with what I think is approval.

I place both thumbs behind the top button of my Levi's. Look her straight in the eye. I undo the top button, then the next. Slowly, the way she said she wanted it. Three more until the fly is open, revealing the black boxers underneath and the bulge inside. I ease my hand into my crotch to cup my mound. I see the light of amusement in the dark of her eyes. I slide the jeans down to my ankles and step out of them.

This is where I stop. I present myself to her.

An eyebrow lifts.

"I keep my boxers on," I say.

I have a thing about exposed pussy. It's fine for girls, but not for me.

"Take them off," she demands.

Remember what I said about hard limits? It suddenly occurs to me that when Alexa had asked me a few days ago by email to name my hard limits, I had forgotten to mention exposed pussy. *Well, too late now.* I pull my boxers down to my ankles and kick them off.

This leaves me completely naked. I have a nice-enough physique but if you were the third girl in the room, it wouldn't be my physique you'd notice. What you'd notice would be the erect, bright-blue dildo sticking out of my vagina.

Which is, indeed, what catches her eye.

"Oh my," she says.

It's the King, the ultimate Size Queen fantasy: nine inches of lifelike dick, including a bulbous, uncircumcised head and veined shaft. A study in realism except for one thing: it's *blue*. For some reason I can't imagine, the manufacturers decided blue and purple were the appropriate color choices for this phallus.

And did I mention that it's a *double*-ended dildo? The five silicone inches of the other end are tucked inside me. No straps, no harness. Just a butch and her big, blue cock.

Her smile has turned into what can only be called an evil grin. She uncrosses her long legs and bends to open her bag. From it she removes a coil of lightweight, white rope; a set of locking, leather wrist cuffs; two lengths of chain; a half-dozen red, plastic clothespins and a riding crop. She sets these on the glass tabletop.

"I'll need to restrain you," she says. "Not that I don't trust you to be still, but I like to make sure you feel good and helpless. It's important that you feel powerless to defend yourself or stop me because this will magnify the effect of even small sensations. When I'm playing with boys, I sometimes tie them up so they can see what terrible things I'm about to do to their cock. But at other times, we go with 'Surprise!'"

I'm starting to feel a little nervous. I'm suddenly more thankful than I've ever been in my life that I am not half of the population that has a real cock and balls.

"Uh, okay," I say.

She looks at the oak mantel, notices the two brass rings on either end. The rings, though decorative in purpose and original to the house, are actually very sturdy.

"These will do nicely," she says.

She wraps the leather cuffs around my wrists, securing them with two small locks. Each cuff is attached to a chain that ends with a double bolt snap. She pulls my left-hand chain up and over to one brass ring, opens the snap, and lets it shut in place. Then the right. My arms are now spread wide with my back to the fire.

"There," she says. "That's better."

The fire feels hot on the tender skin of my bare ass, but I know better than to mention this to Mistress Sadistic Pleasure.

"When I'm with a boy," she says, "I usually do genital bondage next."

She steps toward me, puts her face so close to mine

that I think she's going to kiss me. Instead, she whispers in my ear.

"You *are* a boy, aren't you?" she says.

I shiver involuntarily at the warmth of her breath.

"Yes," I say.

She steps to the table, picks up the riding crop, and returns. I hear the hiss before I feel the strike of leather on my outer thigh.

Damn!

"Yes, what?" she says.

"Yes, Mistress."

The crop is transferred to her left hand as her right hand comes up toward my face. For a moment, I think she's going to slap me. Instead, her soft fingertips gently pat my cheek.

"Good boy," she says.

I haven't bottomed since I was twenty-three when my first and only femdom tied my wrists and ankles to the posts of her bed, slipped a blindfold over my eyes, and played Truth or Dare with my body. I'm remembering how it feels to submit.

The hand slides down to the dildo.

"And what do we have here, boy?"

"Uh, my cock?" I say.

"Your cock," she repeats.

She wraps her fingers around the head and yanks in an upward motion. Inside me, I feel my end of the double dildo hit my G-spot. I gasp.

"You like that?" she says.

"Yes, Mistress," I manage.

She does it again. I gasp a second time.

"Good boy," she says.

She steps to the coffee table, sets down the riding crop, and picks up the rope. She unravels a length of the thin, white cord before returning to me. I feel my breathing quicken, my face flushing. With astonishing ease, she wraps both ends of the rope over the top of my cock and back under again, as if the dildo were a boot she is lacing. She pulls the cord tightly into a knot, then examines my face.

"Boys usually look alarmed when I do this," she comments.

I don't know how to respond. I'm wondering if I look alarmed but am afraid to ask her. What if I'm not alarmed enough? Or too alarmed? I'm acutely aware that the riding crop is only a few steps away. I decide it's safer to say nothing.

She continues wrapping my cock in cord, separating the ends around the base and then crisscrossing over the top.

"We'll end with a pretty bow," she says and does: she loops the rope into a gift-perfect adornment to my bright-blue package.

"There," she says. She seems pleased with her work. She grabs the bow and wiggles my cock back and forth. The dildo hits every on-high-alert nerve ending inside my pussy.

"Ohhh," I say.

"Oh?" she mocks.

She seems to fly to the coffee table and back like a dangerous angel. The riding crop is once again in her hand.

"Spread your legs, boy!" she snaps.

I spread them.

"Wider!"

I'm as wide as I can go without falling down into a graceless version of the splits.

She places the leather tongue midway in the air between my inner thighs, just below my cock. I feel my eyes widen in anticipation.

Whack whack whack.

The tongue stings the tender skin of my thighs.

Whack whack whack.

I try to shift positions, to move my feet, but this only makes her whip faster.

Whack whack whack. Whack whack whack.

I lower my gaze to my thighs and see the beginning of red bruises.

Whack whack whack.

Red! Red! Red! I'm thinking. The universal safeword. But I suck in a breath and keep quiet.

Whack whack whack.

"Does this hurt?"

"Yes, Mistress."

"Too much for a pussy-boy like you?"

I'm tempted, but I stay strong.

"No, Mistress."

She sets the crop down on the table and with her back to me, she bends and does something with the clothespins. When she faces me again, I see that she has clipped them into the bust of her corset. They look like six red exclamation points there, commenting on her uplifted breasts.

"I like to alternate the excruciatingly pleasurable with the exquisitely unpleasant," she says.

"Yes, Mistress." It's the only thing I feel safe in saying now.

With each hand she grabs one of my nipples between her thumb and fore- and middle fingers and pinches hard before turning them like stubborn twist-off caps. I grimace.

"Hurt?"

"Yes, Mistress."

At that she begins to massage them, circling the areolae with her thumbs. The contrast is immediate, and I feel unreasonably grateful. I am tempted to thank her but sense this would be a mistake. And, yes, before the thought has left my mind, the clothespins are up and off her corset and onto the skin of my breasts. One goes on the inside of each breast, another on the outside, while the two final clothespins go straight onto the nipples. I am a virgin to nipple clamps, a virgin to their unique pain. My new submissive says the pinching torture of nipple clamps is exquisite. Not so for me! *Get those motherfuckers off my tits!* is what I'm screaming inside. *My nipples are too sensitive, I cannot bear this pain.*

Then the crop is back and in her hand. She's got it by the handle, like a deadly snake held by the tail. The tongue comes up and finds my inner thighs again.

Whack! Whack! Whack! Whack! Whack! Whack!

I hear what sounds like a puppy yelping and realize it's coming from the back of my throat. I close my eyes and try to breathe. Evenly, slowly. I concentrate on my breath. In and out, in and out.

"Look me in the eye when I hurt you!" she demands.

I obey. The breathing has calmed me, and I'm suddenly feeling at peace. The world seems to be floating away, and I'm drifting, I'm floating on the air. *How sweet to be a cloud*, wasn't that what the character said in that children's book? What book was that, I wonder. Some book I read when I was a child. A long, long time ago.

"Open those eyes, boy!"

I try, I really do, but my lids are so heavy, I only manage to get them partway up. And I had thought they *were* open.

"Hmmm," she says.

The thrashing seems to have stopped, and I'm aware that I feel disappointed. And what were we doing? What are we doing?

"You may close your eyes," she says.

Oh thank god. I really didn't think I could keep them open much longer. But were they open? I don't remember seeing anything.

I hear the whoosh of air and feel a sting on my left breast and something pops off, tugging at my flesh as it goes. I'm curious, I'm so curious, but I can't manage to open my eyes. The next clothespin snaps off with the flick of the crop, then the two off the other breast. My nipples are still gripped by the final two, and I'm thinking, *this is gonna hurt,* and it does, but in a way that I can barely feel because it's a pain mixed with something else. I hear giggling as the clothespins go flying off my nipples, and I wonder, *Who is that giggling? And why is she giggling? That's entirely inappropriate.* And then I realize it's me.

I'm aware that I'm still standing. *That's good*, I think. *I haven't fallen down. That would be embarrassing.* My eyes are closed, and I can feel, I can really *feel*. I feel her body in front of me, and I can smell the scent of her clove cigarettes and the earthy perfume of the pussy juices she dabs on her wrists and behind her ears. I can feel her energy as she leans in and over me. And I can feel her hand on my cock, I feel her jerking me off. Inside, the dildo rubs against my G-spot while at its base, the cock rubs against my clit. I hear myself moan.

"Good boy," she says. "Good boy gonna come for Mistress Alexa?"

"Yes, Mistress," I say.

"Not yet," she says. "Not until I say you can."

"Yes, Mistress."

And my body is floating, it's flying to the edge of a cliff. It's the cliff at the end of the world—of this world of excruciating pain and exquisite pleasure. From that edge, you can leap; you can take a lover's leap into a sexual universe where everything is everything and we all are one, where there is only now and you and me and we're all in this together in one huge orgasm of release.

"Come now," she says, and I do, I explode into that orgasmic cosmos.

Every story has a lesson to be learned, and here is mine. So long as there is CBT and there are pro-dommes like Mistress Alexa, a cock—even a big, bright-blue one—is not such a bad thing after all.

THE AUCTION

Tamsin Flowers

It was my own fault. I'd signed the contract and there it was, Clause 93, clear as day. My lawyer didn't point it out to me because he was a coward. But the truth is, even if I'd seen it, I'd still have signed. Anchoring the evening news on the biggest network in the state was my dream job and the fact that they demanded the right to auction me off once a year for charity—well, it's the sort of shit that comes with the territory.

But that didn't stop me hating it. Called up on stage like a prize heifer, paraded in front of a room full of the entitled twerps who'd already paid more than seven hundred dollars a plate to come to the dinner, and then the worst part, praying silently that some idiot would bid more for an evening with me than they would for the weather girl. Most years I beat the weather girl easily. I had the experience—this year was my tenth auction. Compared to me the ever-changing rota of weather girls were mere children. But just occasionally one of them would give me a run for my money.

And then, after the humiliation of the sale, came the horror of the purchased evening. Seven out of the nine men who'd bought and paid for me so far assumed that the price included sex as well as my scintillating company over dinner. Two of them were sent home with severe bruising to the testicles, one with a slapped face, and the rest were just verbally lashed. One year a man brought his wife, which was fine with me because she was a helluva lot more interesting than he was. But, no, I never had sex with any of them. Just dinner, with me minding how much I drank and pretending to be interested in why they'd spent tens of thousands of dollars just to bore me rigid. At least I got to choose the restaurant every year.

Until this year. It's been different in nearly every respect. In fact, cut the nearly. In every respect.

To start with, it was the first year the whole shebang was going to be broadcast. Some suit up in the boardroom thought it would be a fun idea to make my annual ritual humiliation public. Ha! And, of course, if we were going out live, then yes, why not extend the bidding to the whole television audience. I was really thrilled about that, as you can imagine. Some serial killer from New Jersey would just be able to toss in his bid at the very last moment if he fancied having me for dinner.

"Relax, Lisa," said my boss. "He'd have to be so fucking rich to outbid the dinner guests—and all the rich people in town are coming."

"So, an out-of-state killer. Fantastic."

The new system made me more nervous than usual and the new weather girl was a doll. I felt twitchy all through dinner—part of me couldn't wait for the auction to start, just to get it over with, but part of me just felt sick. I really didn't eat much, so the two glasses of wine I drank were making their effects nicely felt.

Fuck the high heels. Though some people subsequently hinted that my slight stumble onto the stage could have garnered me some sympathy points when it came to the bidding. Who knows and who gives a fuck?

The weather girl was being auctioned off second to last, me last. Several pretty news boys had made reasonable sums before us but nothing like the amount we were expected to raise.

"Break a leg," I hissed to Cindy Cloud-Brain as she pushed past me to get up to the stage. Only I actually meant it.

Cindy was as pretty and as vacuous as a weather girl was supposed to be, so I wasn't surprised when the bidding quickly leapfrogged what I'd made the previous year. There were a few phone bids, early on, but pretty quickly they fell away and it came down to the wire between three guys who obviously knew each other and had each been seated at a table close to the front. The big spenders, in other words. I knew two of them and I'd been bought some years back by one of them. God, I prayed he was successful in buying Cindy because I didn't think I could stomach another dinner with him. In the end I didn't see who bought her because I was texting someone I actually would have liked to have dinner with. Cindy went for sixty-five thousand dollars—big money as far as the network and the charity were concerned—and she came off the stage flushed with pleasure as she went to shake the hand of whichever corpulent cash cow was shelling out.

Then it was my turn and, as I mentioned, there was that slight stumble as I climbed the steps to the stage. Bob

Moss, the auctioneer, caught my arm and averted a catas-trophe, but he whispered in my ear at the same time.

"How d'you rate your chances against that, Lisa?"

"I'm relying on you, Bob," I said as I strutted away from him to show off the goods.

The bidding got underway but—and maybe this was just me and my nerves—it didn't seem to be going so fast or so high as Cindy's had. There was a mixture of telephone bids and bids from the floor and it crept up agonizingly slowly. Cindy's show had been all over in ten minutes but my bids went on crawling up for fifteen minutes before they even reached fifty thousand. To give Bob his due, he was wheedling every last cent he could out of his recalci-trant audience but it didn't look like I stood a chance of equaling Cloud-Brain's total.

Damn!

I hollered at the bidders to keep it coming but it looked like it was stalling.

"Okay," yelled Bob. "Going once . . . going twice . . . "

You could have cut the silence with a knife.

"Wait . . . I have a final telephone bid." We waited, watching his smile grow wide. "Ninety-five thousand dollars. Going once. Going twice. Gone! Gone to the tele-phone bid for ninety-five thousand dollars."

Bob was screaming by the end of the sentence and the audience went crazy.

Great. My serial killer had come through for me. And so generously.

I was intrigued but all the more nervous to discover that the bidder had requested we eat dinner in a private suite in the swankiest hotel in town.

"Apparently, this person is hugely famous and doesn't want to be seen out with you in public," said my boss with a snigger.

"Do you know who it is?" I said.

"No." He shook his head. "It's all being handled by some mega PR company. Here are your instructions."

I followed them to the letter and presented myself at the door of room 3029 at the allotted time. I knocked. I waited. Eventually, when I'd knocked again, twice, the door swung open and a kid in leather pants and an AC/DC tank looked me up and down. I stepped past her into the suite.

"Hey, kid, where's your dad? I have a dinner date with him."

She closed the door and followed me into the most expensive hotel room I'd ever seen the inside of.

"My dad? He's back in Nebraska with my mum."

There was no one else in the room so I turned round and looked her up and down. It takes a lot of time and hair product to keep short hair looking that messy—that was my first thought. And I wondered if she worked at being so skinny or if it was natural.

"Maybe I'm in the wrong room," I said, heading back toward the door.

"No, Lisa, this is the right room."

I did a double take.

"And you are?"

"I'm the one who paid ninety-five thousand dollars for an evening with you." She threw herself down on an over-sized leather couch. "You don't know me, do you?"

I was looking at her hard by now and, yes, her features did seem vaguely familiar.

"You're in that vampire show, about the teenagers?"

She nodded. I knew her now—Darcy Chandler—and I knew how much she was worth. At least a hundred times what I was.

"And you paid ninety-five thousand to have dinner with me?"

This wasn't making any sense.

"Let's have a drink," she said, walking over to a well-stocked wet bar.

I followed her and climbed up onto one of the bar stools.

"You even old enough to drink?" I said.

"Twenty-five," she said easily. She was used to being asked. "I just *look* young enough to play a teen. Remember, I've been playing her for five years."

She poured red wine into two glasses and handed me one.

"Dinner with me?" I prompted.

She took a sip of her wine and I saw a slight tremble to her hand. She looked eighteen rather than twenty-five.

"It's not dinner I want."

"That's what you bought."

"Have you ever been tied up?"

I nodded, noticing my own tightened grip on my glass.

"Disciplined?"

I nodded again.

"Does ninety-five thousand buy me that?"

"You want to discipline me?"

"Nothing would give me more pleasure, Lisa."

Maybe it was the tilt of her nose or perhaps the sprinkling of freckles across its bridge. Or maybe it was the way, when she smiled, one corner of her mouth pulled up higher than the other. Or the way she said my name, slowly rolling it off her tongue. *Lisa.* I don't know. But at that moment, ninety-five thousand—to the network boss's wife's favorite charity—was enough. Hell, I would have given myself to her for nothing.

My no sex with the bidder policy appeared to be flying out the window, but that might have been because she wasn't middle-aged, paunchy, and entitled. Or it might have been because she wasn't a man. Either way, shit was going down.

I put down my glass and stood up. I pulled my black dress up over my head and draped it on the stool I'd just vacated. Darcy smiled and took my hand. She led me across the vast living room and into an equally sumptuous bedroom. But it wasn't the richness of the décor that caught my attention. This room had been set up ready for a scene. There were restraints on all four corners of the bed, there was a padded bench with a variety of steel anchor points and, on a highly polished walnut console, there was a long line of crops, paddles, canes, floggers, and whips. Carefully arranged in order of size, which spoke volumes to me about their owner.

Darcy was standing behind me and she draped a lazy arm over my shoulder. I could feel her breath on the back of my neck, warm and damp, and I pushed my head back as her hand broached the cup of my black lace bra. She nuzzled the sweet spot at the base of my jaw and the thrill of it made me grind my hips against hers. She stepped back from and slapped my ass with a flat palm. Was this going to be better than dinner? I laughed and she slapped me again, harder.

"Go to the bench." Her tone brooked no argument.

I walked over to it and stood beside it, waiting for her

next instruction. It was so unlike me to hand over the initiative to someone else. And to a young girl I didn't even know?

"Bend over," she said.

When she'd asked me those questions and I'd nodded, I'd been lying. This was way beyond the realms of my experience. I mean, yes, I'd slept with women—probably more often than men—but bondage and discipline, never. I looked at the bench, and then I looked over my shoulder at her.

"Is there a problem?" she said.

"No, no, it's fine."

I bent over the bench and blood rushed to my head as I leaned forward. My heart was racing and, though I still had my underwear on, I felt exposed. Positioned for inspection, for chastisement. At the margin, it's hard to tell fear from excitement. I heard her crossing the room, coming toward me.

"I wonder," she said as she got close, "will I need to restrain you?"

I didn't know if this was a rhetorical question.

"Well?"

"No," I said.

"Are you sure?"

I flinched at her touch as a single finger traced a straight path from the back of my neck, up over the curve of my back, across one buttock, and down the corresponding leg. As it reached my calf, she used her other hand to slap my ass, completely without warning. I yelped and bucked against the bench.

"I think you need to be restrained, Lisa. Do you agree with me?"

"Yes."

She produced a pair of leather cuffs and secured my wrists to steel anchor rings set into the legs of the bench. As she did up the second one I experienced a moment of panic.

"No . . . I . . . "

She drew back and looked up at me, and I noticed for the first time how very green her eyes were.

"I want you to enjoy this, too," she said. "You don't have to do anything you don't want to—just say and you can leave right away."

She waited while I took a couple of deep breaths. Two things held me in position—curiosity and pride. I wasn't going to let this slip of a girl intimidate me and I genuinely wanted to know what would happen next.

"I'm fine," I said, offering her my second wrist to be cuffed.

She did it up without saying another word, and then went round to the other side of the bench to secure my legs. A hand trailed across my back, making my stomach muscles clench.

Goosebumps rose on my arms, a shiver skittered down my neck. Desire blossomed low in my belly.

"Will you need to be gagged, Lisa?"

I could tell from her tone that she knew the answer to this, but this was where I had to draw the line. I suffered another moment of panic, as she approached me with a ball gag hanging from one hand.

"Why me?" I said, playing for time. "Why not Cindy, the weather girl? She's cute."

She paused.

"I'm not into cute. I'm into you. You were my first girl

crush—watching you reading the news . . . " She sighed theatrically. "Every evening, never missed it. You opened my eyes to a world of possibilities. You make a train wreck sound sexy. A budget announcement."

Now I had my in. I was on familiar territory—I'd always used my voice as a tool of seduction.

"Let me read the news to you now."

"While I . . . ?"

"Why not?"

Darcy scurried away and returned a few seconds later with a crumpled copy of the *Washington Post*. She flattened it with her hands and placed it on the floor underneath the bench.

"Okay," she said. "You read while I do my thing—let's see who can keep going longest."

I wasn't sure that was going to be very long, but I was game for this.

Darcy stood directly in front of me. My head was hanging down, so the only part of her in my line of vision was her feet, in battered black Chelsea boots. I heard the jangle of a belt buckle and raised my head to see her drawing a wide black leather belt out of the belt loops round the top of her leather pants.

"Safeword?"

"Cumulus."

"Start reading."

I took a deep breath and began reading the first story on the page.

"On Thursday, for the first time since 1987," I read, "the Supreme Court will hear arguments on whether software—or more exactly, programmer-implemented . . . "

The next sound I heard was unmistakable. The whistle

of leather through static air. Followed instantaneously by the crack of leather against my panty-clad ass. The first blow stung like crazy and I stumbled on the next word—but I carried on reading without losing my place.

" . . . in . . . inventions—can continue to be patented."

But if I thought this was going to be easy, I thought wrong. The second blow hit me in exactly the same spot and an arc of pain radiated through me, leaving a residue of after-burn on the surface of my skin. I grunted loudly and stopped reading for a second.

"The case in question focuses on . . . "

The third blow came quickly and made me yelp. The pain that radiated from the point of impact seemed to cut through me more sharply, traveling farther, and the echo on my skin was even fiercer.

"Breathe through it." Darcy's voice reached me through a haze of pain.

I gulped and refocused on the page in front of me, wondering how long it would go on for.

" . . . programs designed to increase payment security in exchange and banking transactions where cash . . . "

That was as far as I read. Darcy worked harder and faster and soon the only sounds coming from my mouth were gasps and sobs. She stopped for a moment, but that was only to hurriedly rip away the shreds of my panties. And then the next blow fell harder. I tried to bite my lip to contain my cries but each time she struck me, my body would jerk against the bench and my mouth would fly open with a yelp.

Then at some point the nature of the pain changed. My hips pushed back to meet the belt. My cries became moans as each sharp sting of pain was tempered by a surge of pleasure as the endorphins kicked in. Now I wanted it to last. I wanted Darcy to slow down so I could draw out the experience from each caress of the leather. I embraced the pain, the sensations that cut through me, and it was like nothing I'd ever known. Intense. Hot. It wasn't like sex— it wasn't about the shared experience. This was about the physical response within my own body. I forgot about Darcy and was only aware of the touch of her belt as it cut against my skin.

When her hand touched me rather than the leather, my body bucked against the restraints. Cool fingers stoked the fire, smooth against the curves of my buttocks and then pressing down to send another spasm of pain and pleasure ratcheting through me. I whimpered as she undid first the ankle restraints and then freed my wrists. She pulled me upright by my shoulders and let me lean against her chest, as I fought for breath. Her hands caressed my back and snapped open the catch of my bra. As my breasts swung free, she bent her head to catch one nipple in her mouth, nipping with her teeth, pain echoing pain and making me gasp all over again.

I was hardly aware as she led me to the bed, or of her ripping off her clothes and kicking off her boots as fast as she could. Then she was on me, pressing her naked body along the length of mine, kissing my mouth and running her tongue along my jawline. I surrendered myself to her completely and welcomed her grasping fingers into my cunt. First she finger-fucked me, then she fist-fucked me, then she tongue-fucked me—and after the thrashing I'd had, it didn't take much to send me spiraling away into a fierce orgasm. She followed me there quickly after placing my hand between her legs and showing me what she needed—she was warm and wet and her hips pushed back against my fingers. I pinched tight as I worked the hard bud between her lips and she bit back on one of my nipples as she came with a shudder. Then her head fell back with the softest sigh and I pushed my fingers up into her cunt to feel her clenching around me as her climax subsided.

We lay side by side on the bed, panting, sated and slick with each other's sweat. I rolled onto my side and studied her. Close up, it was easier to see her age, around her eyes and at the corners of her mouth. But twenty-five was still peachy from where I was viewing it.

"Will you bid for me again next year?" I said.

"Would you like me to?"

"Will I have to wait that long?"

Her lopsided smile told me everything.

SUPPORT SERVICE

Sonni de Soto

Sorry"—the big, broad, bald man laid out leather-clad and facedown in a sprawling pose on the low bed beside her, yawned as Reena Lathan stripped his feet of their heavy, black, lace-up work boots and thick, sweat-soaked socks—"they're a little gross."

Reena just smiled as she took one foot in her hand and began to tenderly wipe every inch of it with rubbing alcohol. "Don't worry about it," she told him. "I'm used to it." Truth be told, she liked it.

"You've been doing this all night?" he asked, his face half crushed into the pillow at the other end of the bed.

"It's my volunteer hours." She wiped her hands on a towel before switching feet. "I've been offering post-scene foot massages." To Dommes with tired, over-arched feet in impossibly tall stiletto boots. To bottoms with sore heels and blistered balls from standing and struggling and teetering on bare, abused feet. To Doms whose feet sweltered beneath leather and steel toes. And, as Donovan's annual fundraising celebration was coming to a close, it had been a long night.

Certainly, Reena was a fan of feet—finding the ridges and planes, the bones and veins, the arch and heel and toes a fascinating study of where a person was, had been, and was going. But, after three hours of aftercare service— three hours of bathing and rubbing and massaging feet of every kind—even her appreciation was being tested.

Even so, she thought as she watched the last few dungeon scenes dwindle down from crescendoing strikes to soothing strokes, she had a job to do. She was grateful for the discounted rates Donovan's offered to those who volunteered at the club. Lord knew, someone like her— still paying off student loans and barely brushing off the bottom of the mail-sorting, coffee-fetching office ranks— couldn't afford her loans, her rent, food, *and* the club dues.

"Three hours of feet, huh?" The Dom whistled and shook his head as much as his prone position would allow. "I couldn't do it."

Reena shrugged. "I don't mind." She flexed her hands against a raging cramp that had settled in half an hour ago that now burned along the base of her left thumb. "I'm happy to do it." She started to rub his large feet with her homemade foot oil.

"You got a thing for feet?" the man asked, bending a bit at the waist so he could curl and curve around to look at her.

"No," she said with a shake of her head, "I don't have a thing." She liked feet, sure, but it wasn't, like, a *fetish* or anything. She just liked them. That's all.

Reena closed her eyes and breathed deep, the scent of skin, sweat, and wear mixing with the oil's sweet citrus and cool mint both calming and invigorating at the same time. She inhaled, letting the scent waft up to her, as she worked it into the toughened flesh. She knew that most people hated the smell of feet, found the idea and the odor of overworked soles offensive. Knew that she ought to also. But there was something indescribably earthy about that scent that intrigued her.

"Oh god," the Dom groaned in relaxed relief as her fingers dug deep into the flesh of his foot. His feet flexed in her hand, the flesh arching deep, as the rest of his body followed suit. His back bowed and, with his head thrown back, he moaned almost ecstatically. "Thing or not, that is good."

Reena smiled and pressed her thumbs hard into the heart of his foot, eliciting more low growls of pleasure. She might not have a fetish, but she did have to admit that there was just something about feet that drew her. In the strong, sharp knuckles of his toes, the way those bones snaked like gnarled roots up the rise of his foot. In the coarse, dark hair spattering in patches—thin and sparse as ankle became arch or along each toe—that tickled her palms. In the variety of textures—smooth sole, callus-capped heels, fragile flesh that thinly covered yet securely held the bony bridge together.

"I think you're done now." Reena looked down to reach for the fluffy, thick terry cloth towel at her knees when her eye caught sight of a woman. Reena had seen her before. As the dungeon moderator on duty, the woman had been a constant presence in the room all night. One Reena couldn't help but notice every time the woman had walked about, taking stock and keeping watch over every scene in the space.

"Already?" The man pouted as he stretched his body, shifting the sheet pulled taut over the bed.

"Afraid so." Reena shook her head even as her eyes never left the woman. She confused Reena, interested her in a way she just couldn't describe—couldn't quite pinpoint or understand.

"Well," she distantly heard the man say, "you are amazing at that. If you're here again, I'll definitely take you up on another go."

"Sure." Frowning, she began to wipe the Dom's feet with the towel. The Asian woman wasn't particularly pretty; not really. Rather plain, if Reena was honest. With no makeup, the woman's very round, freckled face, that was several shades lighter than Reena's own olive complexion, seemed flat, none of her features particularly remarkable. Hers were eyes and lips that were made for liners and gloss.

Even her body wasn't terribly noteworthy. The woman wasn't overweight, but she was short. With short limbs. A short torso. A short neck that appeared even more so with her head craned constantly downward as she checked the ever-present, buzzing mobile device glowing in her hand.

But, despite all that, there was still something about her that Reena couldn't stop staring at. Maybe it was the way the woman moved around the room, with such surety and purpose. For such a small frame, this woman had a confidence and competency about her that Reena envied as the woman issued orders.

No, not orders, really; she had perfected the art of asking so that it felt perfectly matter-of-fact, somewhere between a request and a command. As Reena buffed the man's oiled feet by rote with swift, sure motions of the towel between her hands, she watched the woman's thin, pale lips speak. She couldn't hear what the woman was saying, but she could almost read her words in the pull and stretch of her mouth.

"Here." The Dom pulled out a twenty-dollar bill from his wallet.

"Oh, thank you," Reena said with a blush as her hands fisted in the towel, "but you don't have to; this is for volunteer hours."

The man just smiled, cocking his bald head as he took her hand and placed the bill into her palm. "You earned it, kid." He closed her fist around it.

"Thank you," she said, feeling a little guilty for letting her mind wander through the last part of his massage. "Really."

She pulled back out of his grasp only to have his hands hold her still. She looked at him questioningly.

"Her name's Elin Hwa," he told her.

"Excuse me?" Reena asked.

"Her." The man jutted his chin toward the Asian woman. "The girl you've been staring at all night. She volunteers here too. More hours than just about anyone. Not even for the discounted dues; god knows, she makes enough money. But, then again, she's just kinda a workaholic to begin with. Good luck to you," he said over his shoulder, adjusting his heavy bag.

Reena spared the woman one more look before bending low to clean up her space, wiping down the floor with her cleanser before moving to pick up her things.

"Need any help?"

Reena looked up from her hands and knees to see Elin squatting next to her, the bottle of oil in her hand.

Reena's eyes widened and she felt her face pale. "Um," she said as she snatched the bottle out of the woman's outstretched hand. "Thanks," she murmured nervously, clutching the glass bottle in her fist. "I'm sorry if I'm taking too long." She shrugged and looked around the now almost empty playspace as she said, "You probably want to get out of here."

"There's no rush," she said with a tilt of her head. She tucked her ever-present phone into her pants pocket so she could grab the bottle of rubbing alcohol off the floor.

Well, Reena probably ought to rush a little. Her bus would come soon enough and she still needed to pack up. She reached for her pad on the floor, but stopped when she saw Elin's shoes.

The chunky, low-heeled loafers were like the woman herself. Sturdy. Practical. Well-made. The designer shoes were fine, carefully crafted leather, treated and shaped by knowing and precise hands. Reena could just imagine Elin choosing them in the store. Holding them in her hands. Slipping them, new and crisp, on her feet. And knowing that they had to be hers. "Nice shoes," she said softly as she grabbed for her kneeling pillow.

"Thanks," Elin said. "They're the most comfortable shoes I own, but even they couldn't quite stand up to close to seven hours spent mostly on my feet."

Reena shrugged casually, not quite looking up into Elin's eyes. "I don't suppose you'd want a massage?" Gesturing to her things, she said, "I mean, I still have everything out. I could." She shrugged again, trying to curb the eagerness she felt trying to slip out into her tone. "If you want."

"Seven hours on my feet," Elin warned. "It won't be pretty."

"That's all right." Reena clenched her hands in her lap, almost imagining the feel—the scent, the taste—of her sweat-slicked flesh. The silk of her skin. The shape of her bones. The fight and eventual give of worn, tired muscles. She swallowed hard.

"If you're sure," Elin said.

Reena's eyes widened and her already kneeling legs went weak. Yeah, she was sure.

"Do I have to take off anything?" Elin asked as she kneaded the mattress with her hands testingly.

Uh. That stalled Reena. She blinked and tried not to imagine the woman saying those same words in a different context. She looked Elin up and down, picturing the other woman's supple body. Her pale, buttermilk skin, slightly freckled like cookie crumbs caught in the sweetest cream. God, what did she say to that? Reena felt her cheeks flush as she swallowed hard again. "Only if you want to."

Elin sat down on the bed and started to slip off her shoes and socks. Reena's breath caught as she watched Elin's small but capable hand cup the back of the shoe's heel before sliding it off her foot with a slight, soft moan. She watched the stockinged foot flex and point, the motion fluid as it flowed from toe to heel. Still bent on the floor, inches from Elin's foot, Reena could smell the scent of sweat, could practically feel heat coming off her sole.

Reena bit her bottom lip as the woman grabbed the tip of her stockings and pulled, shedding the sheer black from her feet like a second, silken skin, revealing pale, perfect legs.

Elin's hands paused a moment before she reached for the side clasp of her pants. "Well," she said as she slid the zipper down, "I don't want to get oil or anything on my pants, so I'd better take them off, at least."

Reena inhaled sharply while she watched Elin skim off the tailored cloth. Over sloping hips barely covered by silken, lace-trimmed pink. Sturdy thighs. Sweet, strong calves. Thin, almost fragile ankles. While short, her legs were grace in motion, made to run and dance and move. The smooth, shapely limbs were made to curl and wrap and squeeze. Reena could almost feel their warmth and strength around her hips, her waist, her shoulders.

She reached toward Elin to grab her foot, catching—cradling—her heel in the palm of her hand. The skin of her ankle was satiny soft, delicate against Reena's fingertips. But her heel was tougher, well worn. World worn. Like armor forged with every footstep she'd taken, a natural shield.

Reena breathed deep as she let her hand slide along the landscape of Elin's foot, feeling the dip of her arch, her ball's calloused cushion, the secret space between each toe. She knew that she ought to clean the sweat from Elin's skin, just as she had with the Dom earlier and all the others tonight. But the idea of wiping away the scent of her—warm and raw with just a sweet tang of sweat—made her frown. Reena worried her bottom lip between her teeth, her tongue feeling large behind the trap of her teeth, and wondered at the woman's taste.

"What is it?" Elin leaned over to look at her wiggling toes. "I hope they're not too bad."

They were beautiful. "They're fine," Reena assured her as she let go of Elin's feet so she could reach for her towels and bottles. "Just relax."

"I suppose you've probably seen worse tonight." The

Asian woman sat back a bit to lean on her arms as Reena began to cleanse her feet with the alcohol.

"Everyone deserves a little pampering after a long night." Reena shrugged and slid her soaked cloth between each delicate toe.

"A little aftercare." Elin flexed her foot to give Reena better access. "Absolutely." A soft moan hummed in the back of Elin's throat when Reena began to dry her feet, making Reena's belly tighten at the sweet, longing sound. "You know, I remember seeing your name on tonight's volunteer list and thinking that it was an amazing service to offer," she said as Reena began to pour oil into her palm, "but wondering what kind of person would sign up to do it." She leaned forward again to watch her.

Reena bit her lip, knowing Elin was looking at her—studying and analyzing her—feeling that gaze on the top of her bowed head. Trying to puzzle out the kind of person she was. Without looking up, Reena just focused on the feet in front of her. She grabbed the right one in both hands, wrapping her fingers around the bridge so she could run her thumbs over the smooth arch. Softly. Reverently. A bit nervously really.

"I remember thinking," Elin continued as Reena gently rubbed her sole, "that you must just really like feet."

Reena winced, opening her mouth to protest, as her grip reflexively tightened on Elin's foot, jamming the pad of her thumb harder against the woman's arch.

"Mmm," Elin moaned, making Reena's head pop up at the rich, melodic sound. "Right there," Elin directed with her head thrown back, flexing her foot as she forced it further on Reena's fingers. "That's good."

Tentatively, Reena pressed harder, sinking her thumb

deeper into her soft, giving skin. Her eyes widened when the woman's back bowed and a groan—thick and low—slipped gratifyingly from her throat. Wanting to hear that sound again—louder, longer—Reena gripped the foot in her hand harder and rolled her fist against the arch, her knuckles grinding into the flesh as it flexed under her hands.

"Oh god," Elin gasped as her arms bent to lower her so she rested on her elbows. "Keep doing that, please."

So Reena did, moving to her other foot to knead it with her fist as Elin moaned and tensed. Reena looked up the long length of Elin's leg, her gaze catching on the pretty pink of the woman's panties between her soft, creamy thighs. As if of their own volition, her hands crept up from Elin's feet to her ankle, from her calf to her knee. Rubbing and massaging the sweet flesh in her hands while Elin made sweeter sounds that urged her on.

Slowly, as subtly as she could manage, Reena scooted closer before her hands worked up the moaning dungeon moderator's thighs. Higher and higher. Inch by tantalizing inch. A part of her was waiting for Elin to stop her. For her to realize who was touching her and where. For her to storm off or at least tell her to stop.

But she didn't. She just leaned back as the muscles in her leg became limp and relaxed under Reena's touch while inviting sighs and demanding groans tripped off her tongue.

Swallowing hard, Reena stretched her fingers to just barely brush the lace of her panties.

"Ah-ah," Elin tsked as she pointed her foot, pushing her toes against Reena's chest to shove her a leg's-length away. Reena held her breath when Elin's foot slid up so she could grab the collar of her shirt with her toes. "Polite people ask before touching," she said, her soft, dulcet voice gaining a menacing edge as she pulled Reena closer with her toes. "Right?"

Reena gulped and nodded. "I-I'm sorry," she winced and stuttered. Her whole body froze as she was tugged toward the now steely-eyed woman. "I don't know what I was thinking. I'm so sorry."

"Hmmm." Elin narrowed her gaze, trailing her manicured big toe to tip Reena's chin up. "You know, I almost believe you." Reena felt Elin's sharp, thin toenail bite into her skin, the threat making her jaw tighten as she tried to swallow. "Almost."

Reena gasped when Elin flexed her foot and kicked her firmly in the chest. Surprised, Reena fell onto her back. She looked up to see Elin stand tall. Balling her fists on her hips, the suddenly stern woman stepped over Reena's knee pad. Stepped between her legs. Then planted her feet on either side of her waist. Reena stared up at her from the floor, feeling tiny in comparison to this short yet towering figure. "I think," Elin said, raising one foot to place it on Reena's chest again, applying pressure—just enough to make Reena sweat and her heart pound, "I need to be sure." Pressing down a bit more, Elin grinned as Reena began to squirm. "I think you should convince me."

"I'm sorry," Reena repeated. "I really am—"

"Not with words." Elin stopped her as she placed her big toe against Reena's quivering lips. With a smile, she tucked her toe between Reena's parted lips. "It'll take a little more than that to convince me now."

Reena blinked. Was she saying what she thought she was saying? Her lips frowned in confusion, letting the other woman's toe slide a bit farther.

Elin pointed her toes, touching the tip of her big toe against Reena's teeth. "What are you waiting for?" she asked, eying her daringly. "I thought you said you were sorry."

"I am," Reena said as Elin traced the curve of her mouth with her toe, "it's just—"

"Then show me." She toyed with her bottom lip. "Convince me."

Reena swallowed hard before opening her mouth to gingerly—tentatively—lick Elin's big toe. The tip of her tongue slicked up the tough but soft skin. Reena closed her eyes and moaned as Elin's taste, salty but so sweet, filled her senses.

"More," Elin ordered, her dark eyes glittering as she gazed down at Reena.

Loving the slight growl in the other woman's tone, Reena wrapped her lips around her big toe, sucking it deep into her mouth. She listened to Elin moan. Reena reached up to grab her with both hands, holding the writhing foot still as she moved from one toe to the next and the next. She gave each toe exquisite attention as she massaged Elin's foot with her eager fingers.

"Mmm," Elin purred, her eyes widening as she watched Reena. "More." Reena saw the flush of her cheeks and heat spark in her eyes as Elin stared down at her. "I want you to worship my feet." With a sharply sweet tone, she forced her foot farther against Reena's face. "Don't you want to?" she teased, obviously loving Reena's brand of service.

Yes.

God help her, in that moment, it was all Reena wanted. She wanted to make love to this woman's feet. Wanted to bow and grovel and beg at their anointed altar. Reena looked up from the woman's foot and stared into Elin's hot gaze and felt weak beneath this strong, demanding woman. The power she wielded—that she wrapped around her as sure as the clothes she wore—made the traditionally plain woman impossibly beautiful.

"Then do it," Elin urged, her voice a coaxing command.

So Reena did. She gave the woman's baby toe a final suck before nibbling down the side of her foot, making Elin squeal as she tried to jerk it away. But Reena kept her grip, soothing her skin with soft, wet kisses. She trailed her tongue down the center of her sole smoothly before closing her teeth around her heel, biting down, while she pressed her thumbs into the heart of her foot.

Reena smiled as the other woman's knees buckled. She bit back a chuckle at the woman's frown before she freed her foot. "The other one now," Elin said firmly, brooking no argument as she lifted her other foot to Reena's waiting mouth.

Without hesitation, Reena grabbed the proffered part and brought it to her lips.

"Excited," Elin laughed throatily, "aren't we?"

Reena moaned her assent around Elin's slick toe as she let the toughened pad scrape gently against her teeth before she laved it with her tongue.

"Yeah," Elin murmured, "you just love my feet, don't you?"

Reena trailed kisses from one toe to the next before sighing contentedly around the other woman's tender flesh.

Elin frowned again and flexed her foot, wrenching her toe from Reena's mouth. "Say it," she demanded.

Reena's brow furrowed as she looked up at her. "I, uh," she said before clearing her throat. "I," she began again, realizing that she'd never really said something like that—never said those words, that felt so embarrassing, aloud—before, "think you have nice feet." She'd said the words so quickly and so quietly she wasn't sure she'd really said them. Biting her traitorous lip, she tightened her grip on Elin's foot, trying to bring it close again, so she could fill her mouth with it rather than the words she'd been hiding for so long.

"Uh-uh," Elin said, pulling her foot back. "Those weren't the words I wanted." Narrowing her gaze shrewdly, she pursed her lips and repeated, "Say it."

"I," Reena said tensely, "really like your feet."

Reena winced as Elin swatted her cheek with her toes. "You *like* them?" she scolded. "Is that all?"

"I love them," Reena said quickly, the admission slipping out automatically. Almost without thought as her mind swam with the sting of the other woman's foot against her face.

It wasn't until the words were already out there that Reena realized what she'd said. They echoed loud and shameful in her head. She peeked up at Elin.

She expected to see the other woman scowl with disgust, laugh at her, or at least have all that hot desire she'd seen in her black eyes cool and dim. But, instead, if anything, that fire flared as a satisfied smile curved her pale, thin lips. "How much?" Elin challenged as she pointed her toe again to gently stroke Reena's abused cheek.

Reena felt something tight inside her—deep in the secret places she kept safe from everyone—let loose, freeing a lightness in her that she'd never felt before. She leaned her face into the Asian woman's foot while it petted her, cuddling close like a kitten. "I love them so much," she admitted as she closed her eyes and just let the sensation of the smooth skin soothe her.

"Tell me why," Elin said, her voice soft but compelling.

"They're so beautiful," Reena said as she felt them run down one side of her face and up the other. "Soft and smooth yet strong and sure. They move with such grace and poise." Reena inhaled, letting their scent, mixed with her oil and saliva, intoxicate her. "And they smell fantastic." She turned her head slightly to lick the foot's length. "And taste even better." She couldn't imagine anyone not falling for such beauty. "I just love touching and tasting them." She reached for Elin's foot again. She wanted to stroke and love them all night long.

Elin laughed, the sound rumbling sweetly with such satisfaction even as she pulled her foot back out of Reena's grasp. She turned around and stepped away, letting her weight settle—just for a second—on Reena's stomach, the pressure of her foot pushing the breath from Reena's lungs. "That'll do for now," she said as she walked away.

"What?" Reena sat up, shocked and more than a little aroused, only to see Elin seated on the bed again, reaching over for her discarded stockings.

Calmly, Elin pulled the sheer black socks back on over her toes and up her feet and legs. She stood up, grabbing her pants before digging out her phone. "Oh, wow," she said, glancing at the screen, "it's later than I thought, but at least we'll have missed any kind of traffic. The volunteer sheet said that you take the bus; I doubt there's one coming soon at this time of night." She zipped up the side of her pants and straightened her outfit, looking at Reena pointedly. "And you must be tired after working so hard tonight; I imagine you'd like to get to bed soon. Yours or mine," Elin told her as she slipped her feet once again into her sturdy loafers, "I'll let you decide." She bent down and made quick work of Reena's supplies, tucking them under her arm, and began to head toward the exit. "If you're interested, that is."

Reena's blush deepened as she nodded and quickened her steps to keep up with the completely compelling woman. Reena grinned and looked Elin up and down, letting her eyes stay a bit longer on those steadily stepping feet. "Yes," Reena said with a blush as she tucked a strand of her hair behind her ear. "I'd like that very much; thank you."

BLUE PLATE SPECIAL: YOUR BOOT ON MY CUNT

Avery Cassell

My fingers surreptitiously part the Kelly-green knit-cotton opening of my jockeys, and move quietly down over my soft belly bit by bit. I'm diligently working my way toward my cunt. It is Thursday, and so tonight's Blue Plate special is Rose's old-fashioned spaghetti with meatballs. I have a weakness for round food, so we brave the approaching dank fog to go to the comforting and ubiquitous Chow for dinner.

It is the fourth day of your two-week visit, and we've been living on chocolate kept in the nightstand by the bed, strong sweetened coffee, sharp mouse cheese, and rye crackers. The nightstand's top drawer is crammed with chocolate, and the bottom drawer with extra-large condoms and evil little binder clips. The black metal wastebasket is overflowing with used black nitrile gloves, spent condoms, and gold-foil candy wrappers. We've already gone through two bottles of lube, beating our personal best from last April. We've broken one purple silicone dick clean at the base, and the bed has started to creak and shift in the lower right corner. My chest, the back of my thighs, and the crease of my ass are covered in crop marks, bruises, and bites, while you have a dazed smile on your face, along with several bruises on your left wrist and the top of your hand. We're ready to leave the apartment in search of protein. We want sexy waitpersons serving us hot food and a meander through the streets of San Francisco.

As we venture out, we run into my neighbor, the elderly, bearded leatherman walking his slinky red dachshund, and he winks at us in the hallway. There is a George Jones song about what we are doing called "Leaving Love All Over the Place," and I hum it as we saunter toward Church and Market. Down Octavia Street to Market, then turn left right past the cruisin' Safeway to Chow.

But it had been what . . . an hour and a half? ninety minutes with our clothing on. Ninety minutes of walking side by side through the cool night air and then sitting at a table in a restaurant. Ninety minutes where I wasn't coming, screaming as your hand slid sideways inside of my cunt. Ninety minutes where you weren't slapping my face, causing me to gasp and sending hot sparks throughout my body. Ninety minutes where you weren't saying impatiently, "Spread your legs. How can I fuck you if you don't spread your legs?" as my legs trembled. Ninety minutes without resting my head on your breasts, while nestling my nose in your armpit to greedily inhale your musky scent. Ninety minutes without you murmuring "Dude, sweet," as I came while squirting on our boots, the air filled with the scent of come and chocolate.

So, here we are at Chow. You are wearing tan Carhartts,

your bright blue DYKES FIST! T-shirt, a gray hoodie, and a pair of big black boots. Blue is your favorite color. I'm in a tattered leather jacket, a long-sleeved red-striped shirt, my paint-splattered work overalls, green socks, and silver glitter Converse high-tops. After having spent four days fucking, we can't bear to not touch at all. So instead of sitting across from each other at the tiny restaurant table, we're sitting side by side on the long, worn wooden bench against the leaf-green wall. You're fingering your hand absentmindedly, realizing that you have forgotten to put your rings back on after our last bout. My ass is sore, so I perch delicately on the edge of the hard bench. Our paper napkins are neatly placed on our laps, Mott the Hoople's "All the Young Dudes" is playing, the warm air is filled with the spicy smells of cooking food, and we're overflowing with love and happiness.

We luck out and get the super-cute waitress, the voluptuous brunette burlesque one with the unfinished tattoo and dimples that we chatted up a few months ago, both of us flirting with her, passing her back and forth between us like a piece of red velvet cake. She brings us glasses of cold water, and then takes our order, winking at us as she walks away, her ass swaying in time to the music. We smile at each other contentedly. You're looking at me, and it happens. You know. I'm staring at your lips, and all I can think about is kissing you; the way your tongue slyly snakes into my mouth and the prickliness of the hair over your upper lip. Your pale breasts, your flesh so round and soft. Your strong hands as they inch their way inside of me. You're looking at me, and I'm looking at you, and suddenly we need to fuck. It has now been 105 minutes since we've been naked and sweating and yelling, with the cat hiding in the next room and the antique bed listing to one side like a sinking ship.

And that is when my hand starts sliding down, unzipping my work overall's brass zipper, wiggling through the fly in my green knit jockeys, and finding my way to my hard clit. I smile knowingly at you, cutting my eyes downward to make sure you notice what I'm doing. You notice all right. The tiny pointed tip of your pink tongue pokes out for a second, you take a drink of ice water and whisper that when we get home you are going to tie me up with strips of rubber inner-tube and beat me until my face is covered in tears and snot, and then bend me over the bed and fuck my ass from behind until I'm yelling unintelligibly. My cunt throbs at your promises. I smile at you lasciviously, ease my thumb into my mouth and slowly fuck my mouth with it without breaking our gaze. I want to be on my knees sucking your cock. One hundred and five minutes is a long time to wait. Too long.

Just then our favorite waitress returns with our food; I pop my thumb from my mouth, look at the wonderful cylindrical meatballs and the tangled pasta covered in marinara sauce, and dig in. The food is fabulous and smashing. I'd forgotten that food could even taste like anything at all; all of my senses have been concentrated on fucking. All of a sudden I notice you're looking at me with a strange expression and that you haven't taken a bite of your roasted chicken or mashed potatoes. I manage a pasta-muffled, "Humph?", as you abruptly stand up, walk around the table, and sit on the straight-backed chair opposite me. You then reach across the table to grab your plate, slide it over, and start eating. Your distance feels horrible, and I can't figure out what happened. Why did you move away from me? I don't want to say anything, but my feelings are hurt and I'm trying not to cry. I blink, tears misting my vision. I look down at my dinner to avoid meeting your eyes, and then I feel it. You've lifted your leg, stretched it out under the table, and your big black Wesco boot is now pushing up flat against my cunt. My mouth opens and a relieved sigh escapes.

Your big black boot is on my cunt. I say that sentence over and over in my head. Your big black boot is on my cunt. The toe of your boot is pressing against my clit and the heel against the rest of my cunt. Your boot is sitting there and not moving much, just a gentle rocking . . . barely enough to make sure that I know your boot is on my cunt. I take another bite of spaghetti and you lift your boot off of me, and then bring it down again slowly and gently. You exert just enough pressure to cause me to remember how two days ago you kicked my cunt over and over until I was sliding across the Persian rug in the living room groaning with how much it hurt and how much I didn't want you to stop. In remembering, I gasp. We are staring at each other across the table and you are increasing the force of your boot on my cunt. I love those words, "Your boot is on my cunt." You're starting to kick my cunt in earnest under the wooden table, and I'm thankful for the tablecloth because it hides the fact that you're viciously kicking me backward with your boot. I want to finish my dinner, because I truly do have a fondness for round food, and really can't live on fucking and chocolate. Even fancy chocolate. I take another bite of meatball and you kick my cunt.

My cunt is already sore from the kicking two days ago, and you kick it hard just now. It is difficult to swallow when I'm on the rebound from your boot, but having a mouthful of spaghetti and meatballs helps disguise my grunts. Six of one and half a dozen of the other; which is better, getting kicked with a mouthful of spaghetti or getting kicked without one? You're eating your garlic mashed potatoes and chicken dinner steadily as you pound at my cunt. Smiling as you cut the chicken. Smiling as you add extra butter to your mashed potatoes. Smiling as you stab your string beans with your fork. It is a hearty dinner for a hearty pounding. The force of your kicks drives my ass farther back onto the hard wood bench, and the pain of your boot on my cunt compounds with the soreness of the bruises on my ass. I'm breathing out soft puffy noises between bites of pasta, and deeper groans when my mouth is full. My nipples are hard and throb with the need to be twisted, but I can't touch them while in the restaurant. This pounding isn't going to make me come, but I'm not sure how we are going to walk a half a mile home without finding an alley to fuck in. My cunt is swollen and dripping through my shorts. I'm done in so many ways; I've eaten the last bite of pasta, and wiped up the stray puddles of marinara sauce with a crust of garlic bread. I pop the final bite into my mouth just as you land a particularly sadistic kick. I groan, placing both of my hands palm down and flat upon the table. You put your boot and your fork down, smirk at my obvious discomfort from holding back, and you're done too.

A few minutes later, our waitress leans over the table to ask if we want some gingerbread with pumpkin ice cream for dessert. She knows. I can tell. We quickly say "No" in unison, throw a handful of bills on the table, and thank her. She winks at the two of us as we fumble for cash to pay her, blessing us with her dimples. We need to get back home now, where we can fuck. I put on my worn leather jacket, you put on your plaid wool cap, and we walk out into the chilly San Francisco night. I'm walking a little funny, but so would you if you'd gone through two bottles of lube in four days and then had your cunt kicked over and over during dinner. You're smoking one of your fancy Cuban cigars and keep worrying your fingers for your missing rings. You hold your arm out for me, and we link arms. We are walking down Market Street, the moon is a silvery sliver and the air is heavy with possibilities. The woodsy smoke of your cigar combines with the evening fog to make the air sweetly mysterious. We talk in low voices about food, fucking, and fashion. We're both working on sewing projects, and discuss bound buttonholes, rubber gaiters, and interfacing. I adore bound buttonholes, and am attempting to make them on a plaid wool waistcoat. You're fretting that you should use black instead of white interfacing for your tiger-skin lounge jacket. It is the kind of light mummery chatter that occupies us, binds us, and fills our time.

The orange Milan F-line streetcar clatters by as we turn up Laguna, its bell clanging at every stop and into the night. Each alley off of Laguna is named for a Gold Rush–era streetwalker, and as we pass by Lily Street we scamper right. Lily is narrow, dark, and shadowy, and there is some construction about halfway down. A tall, rickety chain-link fence surrounds the worksite, but the ally is empty of people. Passing by the fence I think about fucking and shudder. Your grip on my arm tightens. My cunt is soaking wet, and it has been this way for 170 minutes. You turn toward me, growl, roughly unzip my overall fly, push my shorts aside to cup my cunt, and then shove me face first against the cold metal fence. My knees buckle so I grab the chain-link. The steel is chilly and hard against my cheek. I'm stretched out against the fence, pressed firmly between your body and the metal. The fence is flexible, and gives slightly with a creak as you start fucking me with your fingers. We bounce together as you slide two, three, and then four fingers inside my cunt. The chain-link wire presses against my clit. You reach around, under my shirt and binder, and grab my nipple, twisting it the way I like. My cunt pulses and swells even more around your hand. You're biting the back of my lower neck, snarling, and your teeth send sharp waves of pain down my back. My brain hates that kind of bitey pain, but my cunt disagrees and pulses and drips in adoration.

I'm trying not to make noise, as the alley is lined with tall Victorian homes and we don't want to cause any disturbances. I can see lights behind lace curtains being turned off, people walking from room to room getting ready for bed. You're fucking me with your fingers curved inside my cunt, and your palm cupped. I shove my cunt down on your hand as hard as I can, wanting more of you inside of me. All I want is to be filled by you. I want your hand inside of me as deep as it can go, and you oblige.

We don't say anything as our soft grunts travel into the evening darkness. Your hand in my cunt, our bodies pressed against each other, and the white moon and the night air is all we need. With your mouth on my salty skin, your hand in my cunt, and held up by the cold metal fence, I finally come. We rest for a minute pressed together, and then head home to bed.

SIMULTANEOUS

Annabeth Leong

I take one look at the way she's set the room up and frown.

Minnie catches the expression and her gaze skitters around, frantic and confused. I can see why. From one point of view, she's done an improbably great job transforming the basement into a piercing parlor. We already owned the professional table—it works well for anything involving needles, which describes a lot of our favorite activities. To go with it, she's obtained a black stand on rollers, onto which she has placed clamps, disinfectant, cotton, sharps and a disposal for one part of what we're doing, and gloves and lube for the other part. There's even an authentic-looking adjustable magnifying glass lamp.

She's put equal care into ambience. Nineties rock, leather and gunmetal melting wax, and a selection of posters of Hole, Sleater-Kinney, and Luscious Jackson.

Minnie's in a floor-length floral dress, a costume ring in her left nostril, black leather bands on her upper

arms, and wild, smeary makeup that makes me think of
Courtney Love. The look does make me want to throw
her onto the table and fuck her, but that wasn't the plan
for today, so I keep the frown.

"You need rope. You're going to have to restrain me."

"Re— restrain you, Miss?"

The way Minnie stammers is so cute. I give her my best
predatory smile. "Yes. You don't expect me to be able to
hold entirely still while I'm getting pierced and fucked at
the same time, do you? You don't want Alice to touch my
G-spot at the wrong moment, make my body jerk and
mess up my nice new nipple rings."

Her face falls as she realizes the mistake. "Of course
not."

"Go upstairs and get a bunch of rope. When you come
back, I'll punish you while we wait for Alice."

"Yes, Miss."

I wait to grin until she turns away. If I didn't know
Minnie's drive to perfection, I'd have suspected her of
making this mistake on purpose. It's such a delicious addition to an already promising session. The three sensations
I love most, in order, are sharp, precise pain, listening
to Minnie plead for mercy, and the way an orgasm feels
when it's coaxed up from steady pressure on the G-spot.
I had planned for two out of three, and it was downright
considerate of her to add the third.

While I wait for her to get back with the rope, I brush
my fingers across my breasts, shivering as I think about
the permanent reminder I'll have of the things we do
today. We've been playing with piercing for years, but
we always let the wounds heal. This will be the first time
I keep and live with the physical results, and I've been

dreaming about this—and getting myself off to the idea of it—ever since I saw a certain blonde bad girl get her belly button pierced in an Aerosmith video.

Minnie's feet thump rapidly down the stairs, but she slows to a dignified walk before she enters my presence, lengths of colorful rope stacked in her arms, her expression half shamefaced but half excited. I love how she can't seem to prevent either reaction. I have to work to keep my lips in their stern position.

As she sets the rope down on the piercing table, I ponder various ways to make her squirm—I want to choose one we'll both enjoy. Minnie's not a masochist like me, and I learned early on that applying pain to her is cruel and grueling punishment, not fun punishment. Lucky for us, I've learned a lot of tricks over the years.

"Do you know what you did wrong, girl?" I ask, my voice as sharp as one of our needles.

She takes a quick breath in, her back muscles rippling. "Yes. I didn't think enough about the things you'd need today."

"Do you think you deserve to be punished for that?"

Minnie spins to face me, her mouth determined, eyes bright. "Yes, Miss." There's nothing improper in her tone or expression—she never purposely gives me any reason to criticize her—but I know her body language well enough to see she's eager for what I'm about to do to her.

"Get up on the table and pull your dress up to your armpits."

She does what I ask. It's a real struggle to keep my attitude severe when she hikes the dress up and reveals the abundant brown flesh I love. I put my hands on her hips and have to remind myself that I have a purpose here—administering a punishment—and I can't just start making out with her.

I peel her panties slowly down her legs, listening for the way her breathing changes as she gets excited. Letting them fall to the floor, I sink to my knees and put my face between her thighs.

"This . . . doesn't seem much like a punishment, Miss."

I arch an eyebrow. Minnie doesn't usually get mouthy with me. It's really starting to seem like she's angling for something harsher.

I kiss her clit, picking up wetness from her pubic hair as I do. "The punishment," I tell her, as I begin to explore, "is that you don't get to come." I place the tip of my finger at her entrance, very gently teasing her open. "I'm going to do all your favorite things, but you're going to have to be careful not to enjoy them too much."

Something has Minnie really excited. Her pussy is already trying to suck my finger in, and her hips are rocking toward my mouth in tiny, rapid jerks.

"I know you're a good girl," I say, giving her my finger, but my words are almost drowned out by her groan of pleasure as I slide in. "You know better than to come when I've told you not to. You don't want to be punished even worse."

Then I fall to, licking her with the slow, heavy strokes she loves most. Her pussy spasms around my finger from the first moment—she's clearly in the throes of that magical paradox where telling someone they can't come brings them straight to the verge of a fast, strong orgasm.

If I were in a different mood, I might ease off, helping her obey my command. Today is meant to be intense, though. Soon, Minnie's hands are clutching at air, lighting on the back of my head only to tear away a moment later, accompanied by her anguished cry. Her pussy gushes for me.

"Miss! Please, Miss! You have to stop. I want to come. I need to come. Oh fuck, I'm gonna come. Oh fuck. Please stop. I can't—"

I'm a little surprised—given the way she started, it's a wonder she held on more than a few minutes. She keeps up the begging while I ponder how long I ought to keep this up. It would be a lot of fun if Alice walked into the middle of this, but if that doesn't happen in the next thirty seconds, I really don't think Minnie will make it.

"Miss!" Minnie's halfway between a whine and a scream. The sound makes a shiver run down my back. It's so delicious and desperate, so unmistakably sexual.

A different voice echoes down the basement stairs. "Do you two need time alone? I can go get a coffee and come back later."

I grin into Minnie's pussy, happy to have gotten my wish. "Come on down," I call out, not entirely pulling away. I relish the way Minnie gasps as the breath behind my words stimulates her clit and labia. "I was just punishing Minnie while we were waiting for you."

"Punishing, huh? Shit, I wish someone would punish *me* like that."

Easing my hand out of Minnie's cunt, I rise to my feet, grinning at the shock in her expression. "Don't we all. Our Minnie's a lucky, lucky girl, getting to enjoy having her pussy licked without being distracted by an orgasm."

Minnie moans, and Alice laughs, walking into my view. "Is that the game?" Her outfit reminds me of nine-ties-era k.d. lang, all slick butch appeal and cleverly gelled hair. Her toy bag is a black leather briefcase. She wears swagger well on her tiny frame, and I have a moment of raw lust looking at her.

I love making appointments to get fucked by someone. It strikes me as dirty in all the right ways, and it has undeniable planning benefits.

I pull Minnie against my side and kiss the top of her head. I may have said she was lucky, but I know I'm the lucky one.

I hug Alice hello, and she touches a spot of wetness on my cheek with a smirk.

"You smell good today," Alice tells Minnie, making her brown cheeks redden.

"You should help me punish her some more after our scene."

She pats her stomach. "I ate a big breakfast this morning. I think I'll have the energy."

Out of the corner of my eye, I spot Minnie's hand traveling toward her pussy and catch her wrist. "Ah-ah-ah. You need to get your head into the game and focus on the scene we planned for."

"Yes, Miss." Minnie hangs her head as if ashamed, but she smells strongly of arousal. I notice that the blush extends all the way down her neck. If the dress weren't bunched up around her armpits, I'd probably see her chest flushed as well. I grin at the thought of how completely I've gotten to her.

Then I coax her off the table. "I think that's going to be *my* spot."

Minnie nods, still looking dazed. She rights her clothes, finger-combs her hair, and generally tries to come back from near-orgasm. I enjoy watching her struggle to focus her eyes—nothing makes me feel like a better lover than seeing Minnie fuzzy and uncoordinated after I go down on her.

I strip off my clothes while she gets herself together. Both Minnie and Alice have seen me naked plenty of times at parties, so I don't feel there's a need for a big reveal. I stretch out on the table. For an awkward moment, nothing happens, and then Alice takes a step closer to me, putting a hand on my ankle as if she's afraid to touch me anywhere more interesting. "So, are we going to just start?"

I chuckle. "There's something Minnie keeps forgetting to do. She definitely seems to want more punishment. We'll have to work on her together."

Minnie stiffens. "I'm sorry, Miss." She grabs a handful of rope, and I take the opportunity to order her around just enough to fluster her.

"Not spread-eagled," I tell her. "I want my pussy right up by the bottom edge of the table, so Alice has good access to it. Feet on the edge of the table, calves folded against thighs. Lots of wraps. Really tight. I want to feel like I can't move, and can't quite take a full breath in."

The rope feels great—restrictive yet comforting, exactly the way I want it.

Alice leans against one wall, watching, a smile playing over her lips. "I don't know why more people haven't caught on to your racket," she says. "Given the number of rope bottoms I know who wish they could find a top, it's fucking genius to order your sub to learn how to tie you up."

Minnie and I exchange a glance. She'd thought what I wanted was weird at first, and had even questioned whether I was really a dominant. In the past, her preferred role as a service submissive had caused her to spend a lot of time folding laundry precisely, washing dishes, and organizing shoes. Eventually, I'd made her understand that learning the specialized topping skills I wanted to receive was the most valuable service she could possibly perform for me, and we've never looked back.

"Minnie's special," I say. "She deserves most of the credit."

"Mmm, that's obvious."

If I weren't in the middle of getting tied up, I'd have tossed something at Alice. Instead, I stick out my tongue.

Alice returns the gesture. "Remember, you don't get to order *me* around."

"That's okay. When you can't get a submissive, the next best choice is a perfectionist. I know you'll pay close attention when I tell you what I want."

"You ought to find a submissive perfectionist."

"I already said Minnie's special." My girl flashes a grin at that, then quickly composes her face back to the helpful, expectant look she uses while we play.

"Ha. Cute." Alice swaggers closer.

Minnie is nearly finished with the tying. I tilt my head back so I can look her in the eye. "Give me a kiss, babe, and then you can get the needles ready while Alice works on getting me going."

Minnie leans forward obediently, but the kiss she lays on me is anything but passive. It's brain-melting, laced with fast-acting temptation and sharp with dirty promise. It ought to come with a warning label and an antidote.

"Now that you've got me ready, Alice can just stick her

hand right in my cunt," I joke, gasping, as soon as Minnie lets up.

All three of us crack up at that.

Alice grabs a glove off the stand and snaps it on, then sets a bottle of lube on the table near my open cunt. "Surprise fisting? That's the plan?"

I raise an eyebrow. "You can surprise me, but maybe don't go quite that far."

Alice's ungloved hand returns to my ankle. "I thought you were going to be precise with your instructions," she teases. "I thought you were going to tell me exactly what you want."

Her fingers trail a few inches up my leg, just to the base of my calf muscle, but the touch makes me shiver. While Alice and I have exchanged friendly hugs plenty of times, and even touched incidentally in kinky settings, we've never focused on each other before, and it's never been sexual like this.

I glance at Minnie, who looks up from her preparations with the needles and offers a brief, reassuring smile. We've played with others plenty of times, both together and alone, but I always have a moment of panic when things get started, when I feel guilty and worried that it isn't actually okay. Minnie's calm attitude sets me free to return my attention to Alice.

She looks a little smug, as if she knows exactly what she did to me with a slight touch to my lower leg. She shifts up to my knee, nimbly plucking at Minnie's ropes as she moves, then comes to rest on my inner thigh. Her expression changes to something almost bloodthirsty. I have a feeling I'm going to be screaming at the top of my lungs once she gets started on me.

"I want to come and get pierced at the same moment,"
I say, returning to my mission statement for this encounter
to keep from losing my bearings in the intensity of Alice's
expression.

"I know that, darling. *How* do you want me to make
you come?"

I can tell she's about to launch into a list of questions,
but teasing is one thing and giving up control is another.
Especially in a scene where Minnie is supposed to be
submitting, I like to stay in the driver's seat. "No toys.
No tongue. Just fingers. Don't warm me up. Cram me full
right away, and make it hurt a little—or a lot. Then work
up to—"

My sentence cuts off because Alice takes me at my
word. She administers a cursory amount of lube, and then
shoves several fingers roughly into me. Once inside, she
spreads them apart, making the invasion feel even bigger.

Seeing I'm speechless, she grins, and forces another
finger in to join the others.

Wrapping her free arm around one of my thighs
for leverage, she begins to fuck me, hard, her forearms
flexing, grimacing from the force of it.

For several minutes I just moan. Then I realize Minnie
needs instructions. This is the problem with trying to be
dominant while bottoming. It can be hard to maintain
appropriate dignity and a minimum of protocol while
screaming with ecstasy or begging for mercy.

"Minnie, are you close?" I manage to ask.

"You're the one who's close," Alice retorts.

"Very funny."

She's not making it easy for me. Her wrist begins to
twist as she fucks me. Soon, she's flipped her hand all the

way over from its initial position, so her fingers curl up toward my G-spot. She took me seriously about making it hurt, too. She pushes and drags against that spot, never slowing, and the feeling takes me right to the edge. It's not that pain feels like pleasure to me, it's that it's a sensation I can't back away from, at least not when it's strong enough. That's what really makes me come—sensations that grab me by the throat and don't let go.

Alice, with all her smug swagger, is dead right. She's already got me on the verge of orgasm.

"Minnie, tell me how your setup is—oh, *fuck*—progressing." Pulling my brain back into a place where I can speak is good. It fills me with a sense of power, makes me sharper and more aware of what's happening to me. Sensations are nice, but I don't actually like to disappear into them. I taste them better when my mind's alert, and when I'm focused on the situation as a whole instead of crawling inside my own consciousness.

"Almost ready. Everything is sterilized. I'm just getting organized."

I feel her moving just beyond my field of vision. For a second, I wish I could have two Minnies. She knows how to fuck me just right. She knows how to make me feel split open in the best way, how to fill me more than I thought possible, how to push just past the point where I think I can't take it anymore, and how to tell the difference between a desperate scream of pleasure and an incoherent cry for a break.

On the other hand, if I'm going to get nipple rings in a situation like this, and I'm planning to make them permanent, it has to be Minnie who gives them to me. She's got the sense of timing required to make this work just the way I fantasized, she learned to pierce for me and I want her to mark my body for life the way she has my heart and mind.

Besides, I've got no complaints about Alice's technique. She's spearing me enthusiastically with four fingers, and Minnie must have done a good job with the rope, because I'm shocked I'm not sliding all over the place under the force of her assault. Braced this way, I can't do anything but absorb each of Alice's thrusts, and I indulge in a long whimper before forcing myself back to saying words.

"All right. Alice, ease off just a little so Minnie can set up."

She gives it to me hard a couple more times, a challenging expression on her face, and then does as I've requested.

"Just stroke the G-spot lightly. Tickle it, almost."

"Tickle, tickle." Alice smirks.

It doesn't tickle.

I take a deep breath, letting the pleasure surround me and press at the edges of me, without surrendering to it.

"Minnie, if you're ready, come here."

The stand's wheels roll closer. Minnie puts a hand on my head. Her cool touch makes me realize how hot and sweaty Alice has gotten me.

"Make your marks now."

"Yes, Miss."

I'm so sensitive that I gasp when Minnie's pen touches down on one side of my left nipple, marking a spot to guide how she inserts the needle. My cunt clutches around Alice's fingers.

"Down, girl," Alice teases. "I'll get back to the good stuff in a minute."

I acknowledge Alice with another squeeze, but most of my attention is on Minnie. She looks gorgeous above me, a cute wrinkle of concentration marking the bridge of her nose, curly, dark hair hanging down, breasts swaying under the floral dress as she moves.

She presses the tip of the pen once more on my left nipple, then touches twice on the right. I can tell she's doing her job well. I glow with pride to think about how good she's gotten at this, at how much she's learned for me, at how skilled and beautiful she is—and that she's mine.

"Would you like lidocaine, Miss?"

Minnie grins slyly. I snort.

"Painkillers aren't the point. You know that. You realize more punishment means you *won't* get to come, don't you?"

"Alice looks like she'd be quite competent at punishing me."

I feign outrage while Minnie smears sterile solution over my nipples. "And I wouldn't?"

She only smiles in reply, but I think I see her game. If Alice and I wind up trying to outdo each other—well, that's a recipe for exquisite torture if I've ever heard one.

"Once I have the clamps on, I'll be ready to put the needle in as soon as you give the signal," Minnie informs me.

I hiss as she pulls the skin taut. "Okay, Alice, you can go back to what you were doing before. No more holding back. Make me come."

Alice grins and ups her intensity—to what it was before, and beyond. The woman is strong. She gets her whole arm and body behind each thrust. I half expect the table to collapse.

"Keep fucking me through the orgasm when it hits," I instruct. "Don't let up until I say."

"You got it. Unless my arm gives out." She winks.

I'm not worried. Alice seems to have way too much pride to give up for anything short of an emergency.

What she's doing feels painful and good, but I always need more than that. Often, when reaching for orgasm, I think about a moment exactly like the one we're in now, dwell on the idea of being penetrated by fingers and a needle at the same time, imagine myself totally unable to move, caught between two excruciating sensations.

I look at Minnie, who's holding the needle less than a centimeter away from my nipple. A thrill of fear and anticipation shoots through me. Based on our temporary piercing play, I know just how it will feel, but I'm never quite prepared for what hits me when I look at a needle, a complex combination of fascination, compulsion, revulsion, and desire. I want Minnie inside me this way. I want to feel the odd, dull pain that comes from inside, combined with the sharp, crystalline hit of endorphins that punches my chest when needle breaks skin.

And there's no forgetting Alice. Her hand feels so big, so inescapable. Her thumb tickles my entrance, and I feel her knuckles hitting hard every time she presses in. I don't think I could take her whole fist this way, but I love the image of opening.

Fuck.

"Now, Minnie. Put the needle in. I'm gonna— *Fuck*, I'm— Good job, Alice. I'm about to—"

The needle parts my flesh just as I begin to ripple around Alice's hand. I can't breathe. There's no room for anything. My body wants to squirm away, but Minnie's rope has made it so I can't. My too-full cunt aches as its muscles struggle to move while impeded by Alice's thrusting fingers. My nipple is a bright spot in my mind, lit with sensation.

I cry out. Just as I've instructed, my orgasm stops nothing. Alice is still fucking me just as hard. Minnie is tugging the cannula through the opening she's made, the tugging on the inside of my nipple weird and unsettling and inescapable, just the way I wanted the pain to be.

I can't leave the moment. Both Alice and Minnie are forcing me to stay with them. So my orgasm can't make me fall off the edge of the universe, or whatever the old euphemisms were. Instead, it fills me up, overwhelms me, gathers at the base of my skull, makes my breathing feel like I'm running in a thin atmosphere. I've got nowhere to go, but this feeling needs to go somewhere. I'm stuck for a second, but then Minnie reaches the end of the cannula and begins to tug the thicker nipple ring through.

I've got no choice but to accommodate—uncompromising metal, and Alice's equally uncompromising hand.

It feels like there's not enough room inside me, but then my body *makes* the room. Parts of me are moving that I didn't know could move. My cunt finds buried centers of pleasure, and my orgasm starts within them and spreads down to my toes and up to my now-aching nipple. My body gives way before Minnie's jewelry. I feel the finality of her snapping it into place with a twist of her fingers.

I'm pumped full of endorphins. I feel amazing, like I could lift this table off the basement floor and bring both Minnie and Alice with me for the ride.

"Keep going," I shout. "This is fucking awesome. Keep

going. Minnie, second nipple. Alice, see if you can make me squirt."

Alice barks out a laugh, but she also presses hard on my G-spot. She grabs a second glove with her free hand and uses her teeth to help it on. Then she brings the bony heel of her hand into contact with my clit, sandwiching me between two excruciating forms of pleasure.

"Oh, that works," I tell her. "Minnie, I'm ready for the second nipple."

The sharp, the ache, the bruise, the bone-on-flesh rub . . . The sensations mix together into something I can't sort out anymore. Still, I've never felt so in control.

White spots appear behind my eyes. The sensations of my newly pierced left nipple press at my consciousness while Minnie works on the right. It feels like Alice is squeezing the orgasm out of me. I don't know exactly what noises I make, or exactly what my body does. I do know this feels just the way I pictured it.

And I haven't let go. I haven't forgotten that after this moment ends, after I've had a moment to catch my breath again, Alice and I will need to punish my girlfriend. Probably a lot.

It's fucking perfect.

PRIVATE PARTY

Rose P. Lethe

Taylor arrived well after eight. The tiny parking lot outside the square two-story brick building that David and Vanessa rented was full, so she had to park on the street instead, her car becoming another in a row of neutral-colored sedans. The air outside was cool, with a breeze that rustled Taylor's hair as she climbed out and slung her handbag over her shoulder.

She would have to text to be let in. That was one of the rules.

Breathing shakily, Taylor fished her phone from her bag and found David's name in her contacts. *Hey, it's Taylor. I'm here. Sorry I'm late.*

David's response came seconds later: *Anna will open the door for you.*

Anna? Taylor cast her mind back to the two munches she had been to, but she couldn't recall ever meeting an Anna. So there would be at least one person here she'd never met before.

Her nerves, already in a poor state, began to wear and fray like a cut wire, hurling sparks of panic through her. She inhaled deeply, trying to mend the damage before it worsened.

Taylor would enjoy herself. She refused to even consider the possibility that she wouldn't. She'd been dreaming about this for years, after all. First only in brief but poignant flashes, a silent yearning she couldn't quite put her finger on, and then as she learned the language she'd been lacking—submission, role-play, pet-play—a near-constant ache, a fantasy she played over and over.

Her new job had been a boon in more ways than one. New town, new friends, even a new therapist with a new approach. Dr. Browne encouraged her to step out of her comfort zone, to push herself to do things that would trigger her anxiety—although he probably hadn't had something like this in mind.

My first play party, Taylor thought. But rather than the shiver of excitement she should have felt, panic flooded anew.

She closed her eyes and talked it down, reminded herself that it would get better—just like the grocery store and the bank, both unavoidable parts of life, and now the munches and play parties, both fundamental to being kinky.

Over an hour she'd spent in the bathroom, taming her thick ash-brown hair and brushing a rosy glow onto her pale cheeks. Even her street clothes had been chosen with care: a black sweater dress that clung beautifully to her hips and tits and masked the little paunch she'd gained during the stress of the cross-state move.

Beneath the dress was her real outfit: a black see-through camisole over a black lace halter bra and matching hip-huggers. Black was Taylor's best color, according to more than one of her ex-girlfriends. It contrasted nicely with her pale skin.

The accessories were in her handbag: a narrow leather collar and a pair of cat ears. There was also a long, fluffy black faux-fur tail, attached to a slender steel plug. She didn't know if she'd want to go that far tonight, but she'd brought it just in case.

Taylor gripped the straps of her handbag, adjusting them on her shoulder. *This could be so good*, she thought. *Please don't let me freak out.*

The front door opened as she approached and shut promptly behind her, revealing a woman standing behind it. They were in an entryway, small and overly bright, with another closed door straight ahead and a set of narrow wooden stairs to the left. From behind the door, which was marked with a gold *A*, Taylor could hear the muffled beat of music and the rhythmic, telltale thudding of a flogger hitting skin.

She paid the noise little attention, too focused on the woman, who stood with her hands on her hips as though relishing the attention. Even with a pair of tall scarlet pumps, she was an inch or two shorter than Taylor, and her skin was a golden brown, her hair a dark brunette and pulled into a neat ponytail. She wore a pair of tight leather pants—so tight Taylor couldn't imagine how she'd managed to put them on—a black push-up bra, and a corset that matched her pumps in color and satiny-looking material. Her nails were neatly manicured and painted the same shade of scarlet as her shoes and corset.

She was gorgeous, and so confident. Taylor swallowed thickly, struck with the urge to bow her head in reverence.

The woman's lips, which were soft and plump but free of lipstick, as far as Taylor could tell, curved into a smile.

"Hello. I'm Anna. David and Vanessa's backup DM for the night." She offered her hand.

Taylor took it. Anna's hand was warm and smooth, a sharp difference from Taylor's clammy ones, and her handshake was gentle but firm. "Taylor. Um. Hi, nice to meet you."

Anna's hand lingered a moment, her gaze sweeping over Taylor's features, before she let go. "Welcome. Come on in."

She opened the door marked with the gold *A* and waved Taylor into a short, empty hallway. Inside, the lights were dimmed and the walls painted a deep burgundy. There were two open doorways on the right, one dark and the other with light spilling out. At the very end of the hallway, an even brighter glow came from a room to the left. The music was louder here, and the flogging sounds were accompanied by the distant murmur of conversation.

Taylor's anxiety surged. It felt like she was shaking on the inside, something thrashing under her skin to be let loose.

You want to be here, she reminded herself. *You want to be kinky. This is how you do it.*

"If you want to change or freshen up first, the bathroom is right there." Anna pointed to the darkened doorway. "When you're finished, I'll give you a tour of the dungeon."

Taylor went, still clutching her handbag straps like they could keep her from rattling out of her bones.

The bathroom was small, decorated with unlit candles and a vase of real, freshly picked flowers.

This isn't what I expected, she thought, setting her bag on the white marble countertop.

Although when she tried to conjure an image of what she had expected, she couldn't. She hadn't considered much beyond the people and the weight of everyone's scrutiny as she tried (and surely failed) to behave like she wasn't a hopeless amateur.

Her stomach twisted at the thought, so she tried to sweep it away, busying herself with undressing and removing the collar and cat ears from her bag.

The collar jingled incessantly as she lifted it, and the noise echoed as loudly as a drum in the quiet room. It was a simple collar, only a plain leather band with a silver bell in the center, but it struck her as quintessentially catlike. She'd loved it when she'd bought it.

Now, the sound of the bell made her chest feel tight. It would ring with every move she made; it would call attention to her.

That's what pets do. Is this your kink or isn't it?

It was. She knew it was.

Heart pounding and stomach still twisting, she wound the collar around her neck and picked up the ears. Fastened to a thin wire headband, the cat ears were made of black faux fur and pale-pink felt. She slipped the headband on, arranged her hair so that it hid the metal wire, and then stood back, peering at herself in the mirror above the sink.

She looked . . . childish. Like a teenager straight out of Hot Topic, trying to look edgy and cool, trying to stand out.

Pathetic. What are they going to think of you?

Panic closed in on her, covering her like a sheet and bearing down, trying to snuff her like a cigarette. Her

heart throbbed in her ears and sweat beaded on her forehead, her temples, and her nape.

She closed her eyes, clutching the countertop, and tried
to breathe. In through her nose, out through her mouth,
just like her therapist had taught her. In through her nose,
out through her mouth.

The panic didn't wane. Her limbs began to shake.

Push through it, she thought. *Remember the munches.
It always gets better.*

Still shaking, Taylor stuffed her dress and ballet flats
into her handbag. Her trembling fingers slipped twice on
the zipper before she managed to zip it shut. Then she
looked herself in the mirror one last time. Her eyes were
deer-in-headlights wide, her cheeks pale. As soon as she'd
wiped the sheen of sweat from her face, even more had
come to replace it.

It would have to do. She gathered her handbag and
left, her legs weak and wobbly.

Anna was waiting for her, leaning against the wall
and looking poised, self-assured, and lovely. A far cry
from Taylor, whose head went light and spinny. She had
to grasp the door frame to keep herself from stumbling.
Why had she thought she could handle this? The people,
the strangers, watching and judging her—

"Hey," said Anna. "All right? You look . . . not well."

Understatement. Taylor'd had enough panic attacks
to recognize that she wasn't really dying, but god, it felt
like it. Her lungs burned; her heart pounded even harder.
"I—" was all she managed.

"That's a no." Then Anna was there, her hand on
Taylor's bare arm. "Let's get you some air."

Anna led her down the hallway, not dragging or

pushing but guiding gently and with clear authority. It felt nice, somehow. Soothing. Anna's hand proved a warm, grounding presence. She gave Taylor a single, simple path that she didn't have to think about to follow.

Taylor let herself be led into the entryway. Anna gestured for her to sit on the bottom stair and then squatted in front of her. It must have been murder in her tall pumps and tight pants, but if it was, she gave no sign of it. Her expression was open and kind.

She said nothing, only remained a strangely safe and comforting presence as Taylor fought to breathe in through her nose, out through her mouth. She concentrated on the slow rise and fall of Anna's breasts, trying to match the rhythm. Slowly, the worst of the panic abated, although it lingered at the edge of Taylor's consciousness, waiting.

"We've got a kind of cool-down area in there," Anna said, jerking her head toward the door to the dungeon. "But it's past the main room. I didn't think you'd want to go through that."

No, Taylor wouldn't have. She swiped her hand across her forehead. The sweat was already beginning to dry on her skin, not just on her face but her back and chest as well, making her camisole cling uncomfortably.

"If you need more space, there's the apartment upstairs too," said Anna.

Taylor peered up the narrow switchback staircase. This was it for the play party, she supposed. Through the dwindling fog of anxiety, she felt a pang of disappointment. This was backing down, confining kink to fantasy for the foreseeable future.

Anna stood, moving toward the dungeon door. "Be right back."

She was gone less than two minutes, and when she returned, she had a set of keys in her hand. Although Taylor took up nearly the full width of the stair, Anna was able to step around her easily. Taylor caught a whiff of cocoa butter and aerosol hairspray that faded as Anna climbed the staircase.

"Come on up."

Unsteadily, the bell on her collar ringing, Taylor heaved herself to her feet and followed until they reached a door marked with a gold *B*, which Anna unlocked, opened, and waved Taylor through.

The door opened into a room that was distinctly broke-college-student in its atmosphere and decor. Two mismatched couches, one black vinyl and the other covered in a brown floral pattern straight from the 1970s, were pushed together into a *T* at one corner and covered in books, clothes, and other clutter. The coffee table was stained. There was nothing on any of the walls but a single black streak to the left of the door.

"Terrible, isn't it?" said Anna. "David and Vanessa spend all their time and money on the dungeon. Have a seat."

Taylor shuffled to the vinyl sofa and sat. She realized suddenly that she still had her handbag over her shoulder, and she shrugged it off, letting it sag next to her on the sofa.

"Thanks," she said. Her voice sounded foreign to her own ears, quavery and weak. She cleared her throat and tried to speak louder. "You didn't have to leave."

Shrugging one shoulder, Anna went to the other sofa. "I'm only the backup DM." As soon as she'd sat, she kicked off her heels one at a time with a sigh like she'd just settled into a relaxing bath. "And spending time with a pretty kitten is more my style anyway."

Taylor's chest seized so suddenly she thought at first it might've been another attack, but it was followed by a rush of warmth and a bright, bone-deep feeling of pleasure. *She thinks I'm a pretty kitten.*

"Do you want to talk about what happened?"

The pleasure faded and Taylor drooped. "Not really. I just, um. Groups of people make me . . . anxious."

"Then why are you here?"

Anna's tone wasn't harsh or accusatory, but Taylor felt her cheeks heat with shame anyway. She ducked her head. "It's . . . I mean, it's what you do, isn't it? When you're . . . kinky."

"Ahh. You're new to the scene," said Anna.

It wasn't a question, but Taylor nodded anyway. Then she heard the sofa rustle and creak, and lifted her head to find Anna standing and coming closer. Taylor scooted toward the armrest so that Anna could fall into the seat beside her.

"Can I give you some advice?" Anna said. "When it comes to kink, worry about you. Not what other people do. What do you want to do?"

Taylor didn't even have to think about it. She'd been imagining it for so long, dreaming about it, even practicing it when she was alone: dressing in her collar and ears and getting down on her knees, crawling around the apartment, thinking about how she would—

"Be a pet," Taylor said. "I want to lie in someone's lap while they pet me and scratch me and call me a . . . a good girl."

It was the first time she'd said any of it out loud. She'd

thought it countless times, even typed it more than once, but to hear herself say it, to feel her mouth forming the words was . . . it was freeing, somehow. It melted some of the lingering tension from her shoulders and quieted the last of the anxious rattle inside her.

Anna didn't even blink. "You don't need a play party for that. You just need to find someone who wants a pet."

But how? Taylor thought. The longing in her yawned wide, threatening to swallow her whole; suddenly she was seventeen again, her anxiety untreated and even more crippling, constantly wondering, *How do normal people do this?*

Then she breathed, and she was twenty-six and here, in an apartment above a dungeon with a gorgeous woman in a textbook Domme outfit who had called her a pretty kitten and led her upstairs and made her feel safe. Groups of people were a problem, obviously, but one familiar person—that was doable.

Taylor steeled herself. Her voice wavered slightly when she asked, "Are you offering?"

For a long moment, Anna only looked at her with a thoughtful expression. Then she laughed, a short breathy huff of amusement. "I didn't bring you up here to take advantage."

Something deep in Taylor cringed and shriveled, and commanded that she do the same. But she didn't. She wouldn't. "That's—that's not what I asked."

Anna considered her a moment longer, then lifted her arm, extending one of her elegant hands in a clear invitation. "Come here."

Taylor's face burned, her chest so tight it almost felt like her rib cage would crack and crumble. Still, she obliged.

The sofa was too small for her to lie with her legs and spine straight, so she folded her body instead: bringing her knees close to her chest and resting her right cheek on Anna's thigh. Her collar jingled, and her cat ears were jostled. Several strands of hair fell into her face, although Anna immediately brushed them back into place, dragging her fingertips along Taylor's scalp. Taylor shivered and pushed her head instinctively into the touch.

"That's a good girl," Anna murmured, repeating the motion. "Such a good, pretty kitty."

Taylor felt the impact of the praise throughout her whole body, from the Jell-O-y sensation in her legs to the tingling in her scalp as Anna raked her fingers again through Taylor's hair. *Yes,* she thought fervently. *Yes, I am.* She turned her head, burying her face in Anna's leather pants and urging Anna to explore even more of her.

Generously, Anna indulged her. She followed the slope of Taylor's scalp to her crown, where she rubbed in firm but gentle circles, gathering strands of Taylor's hair around her fingers. Taylor moaned softly when Anna eventually moved on, although she quieted when Anna only strayed to her nape. She squeezed once and then stroked lower, skimming over the leather collar and trailing between Taylor's shoulder blades and along the curve of her spine before reversing.

It went on like that, Anna stroking up and down her back while Taylor breathed and let her. She tried to remain still, not wanting to risk interrupting Anna's petting, but she couldn't stop from occasionally arching into Anna's hand and relishing the faint pressure against her skin.

"That's it, sweetheart," Anna said every time she did. "Such a good kitty."

Taylor felt warm and safe. She floated, calm and
contented as a cat in the sunlight until eventually Anna's
hand veered from its path and ventured up to the wire
band at the top of Taylor's head.

"I like these," she said, caressing one of the cat ears.
"They're cute."

Cute, not childish. Taylor's toes curled in pleasure and
she turned, stretching, onto her back, cuddling even closer
to Anna.

"Also this." Anna flicked the bell of Taylor's collar,
making it ring loudly. "Are these all your accessories?"

Are good kitties meant to talk? Taylor wondered
drowsily. But Anna clearly expected an answer, so Taylor
licked her lips and obeyed. "No. I have a tail, one of the
plug things, in—"

She gestured vaguely to where her handbag was now
half-sunken behind the cushion and armrest. Anna
reached for it, jostling Taylor and making her grumble in
protest. When she had the handbag in hand, Anna paused.

"Do you mind?"

Taylor didn't, so Anna unzipped the bag and pulled
out the tail plug while Taylor watched. The sight of her
hands, so gentle and graceful, stroking the length of
the thick black fur just as she'd stroked Taylor's back,
was distinctly erotic in a way that the petting somehow
hadn't been.

Then Anna touched the plug, circled it with her thumb
and index finger as though measuring the size, and
Taylor's cunt clenched. That had been in her, once. She'd
cleaned it since then, obviously, but still. She remembered
the hard, unrelenting weight of it in her ass, how strange
it had felt and how wet she'd gotten.

She summoned her voice again. "You can . . . put it in me. If you want."

Anna gazed down at her. There was an intensity in her expression, a heat in her eyes, that Taylor hadn't seen before. *She's turned on*, Taylor thought. *This is turning her on.*

"Yeah," said Anna. "All right. Can you move for me, sweetheart? I'm gonna need to pop back downstairs for a sec."

As soon as Taylor moved, Anna was up and out the door. Taylor listened to the sound of her footfalls on the staircase, brisk and light. Eager.

She removed her panties while she waited, then positioned herself on her hands and knees, facing the door.

When Anna returned, she had a box of black latex gloves and a bottle of lubricant. Her cheeks were flushed, her breasts heaving from exertion. Taylor rose onto her knees for as long as it took for Anna to sit, and then she lowered her hands to the cushion on the opposite side of Anna's legs.

Anna balanced the gloves and lube on the armrest, along with the tail, which she draped over the sofa, smoothing her hand over the fur.

"Good girl."

Anna's voice was warm and thick with affection. She cupped one hand under Taylor's chin and rested the other on the back of Taylor's head, petting her hair. Pleasure bloomed in Taylor's chest and spread its tendrils throughout her body.

"Not quite what I had in mind though. Can you move for me, you pretty thing?"

With a gentle pressure on her nape, Anna drew her

head down and down until her elbows bent, her arms folded completely, and her cheek was flat against the sofa cushion, her bottom still up.

"Perfect," said Anna.

Self-consciousness reared its head, reminding Taylor that she'd only trimmed the hair on her vulva, that she hadn't used an enema earlier, that—

But no. She was a pet now. She was less than human. No one would judge her, any more than they would judge a cat for meowing for table scraps or napping on a pile of freshly folded clothes.

She settled, remaining in place even when Anna let go and reached for the supplies on the armrest. Taylor heard the snap of a glove being put on, and then the snick of a lid being opened. There was a hand on the small of her back, where her camisole had ridden up, and another between her asscheeks. One slick finger circled her hole, making Taylor shudder, before pressing inside.

It felt strange, unnatural. Taylor's muscles threatened to tense, her body insisting that nothing was supposed to be going up that way. She shushed it silently. She was a pet now. What did she know about how things were supposed to be?

Eventually, the feeling of awkwardness subsided. Anna probed deeper, her knuckles digging into the sensitive skin around Taylor's hole, and Taylor moaned, her hips jerking. Immediately, the finger slipped out, and Taylor moaned again at how open she felt, how dirty.

"Shh," said Anna. "You're doing so good. Just a little more, sweetheart."

There was another soft snick, followed by a quiet rustling, and then Anna was touching her again, this time pushing two fingers into Taylor's hole. They were so wet that they made a soft squidging sound as they slipped inside, and Taylor felt a bit of lube leak out and dribble down her perineum. Anna wiped it away with her thumb just before it could reach Taylor's pussy.

"Needy thing," Anna murmured. "I hardly even have to stretch you. You just open right up for me."

Her fingers plunged deep and twisted, rubbing the front wall of Taylor's ass, and Taylor felt the pressure and the movement in her cunt. She couldn't stop herself from thrusting back, shoving Anna's fingers deeper while she buried her face in the vinyl sofa cushion and moaned.

This time, when Anna's fingers slipped free, they left Taylor bereft and desperate. In seconds, they were replaced with the cold, stiff metal of Taylor's plug, which slid easily into place. The tail swayed, fur brushing the backs of her thighs. She shimmied her hips and shuddered as the plug shifted with the motion, pressing into her from a new angle.

Taylor lifted her face, blinking at Anna, who was removing her gloves and setting them aside.

"Go on," Anna said. When both hands were bare, she reached for the box and pulled out a fresh pair. "You can sit up now. You've been so good."

Although her limbs were shaky, Taylor raised herself onto her hands, her collar jingling. The tail swung again, tickling her skin and making her breath catch. Shivering, she jerked her hips in a little hitching thrust, making the tail move with her, swaying between her legs.

She felt it, then. How wet she was. Not just her ass, which was still leaking lube despite being plugged, but her cunt as well. She squeezed her thighs together and felt how swollen and sensitive her clit had become, how slick her labia were, and how sweet the tiny hint of friction was—even if her pussy was empty when it needed to be as full as her ass, or even fuller.

Taylor thrust her hips again, clenching her asshole, until it felt like the plug was almost, but not quite, fucking her.

"Good girl," said Anna. She held one gloved hand expectantly in front of Taylor's face, so Taylor butted her nose into it, parting her lips so she could lick the palm affectionately. "Slutty kitty. You've needed this so badly, haven't you?"

Taylor had. She'd wanted this so badly, and now she couldn't even imagine how she'd lived without it. She turned her face in Anna's grip, rubbing her cheek against Anna's fingertips.

Can I come? she thought. *Please let me come.* But pets couldn't ask for what they wanted, so she only blinked, helpless, as her clit throbbed and ached. While Anna watched her, her eyes dark and hungry, Taylor shuffled her knees farther apart and lifted her ass higher, begging silently.

Anna understood, reaching between Taylor's thighs with her free hand and cupping her vulva, giving her something to rub against. "You've been such a good girl," she said. "Show me how sweet you are when you come."

Taylor had to thrust only twice against the heel of Anna's hand before she was coming, tipping her head back and crying out to the ceiling. Immediately, Anna was abandoning her vulva in favor of shoving her fingers into Taylor's cunt, feeling it pulse and clench for a moment before giving in and thrusting vigorously, fucking her through her orgasm until Taylor was sobbing and shaking and coming again, soaking Anna's hand.

Afterward, Taylor sagged to the side, cuddling against Anna's chest. Anna held her, petting her head and even scratching behind the cat ears.

"See?" Anna said softly. "You're perfect. Still think you want to go to the party downstairs?"

If she could, Taylor would have purred in pleasure. Purred and stretched and pawed Anna's leg like a spoiled kitten begging for even more attention.

"No," she said. "Just keep petting."

TRAINING ZOE

Meghan O'Brien

R en stood outside her closed bedroom door and reread the text message that was sent to her cell phone thirty-seven minutes earlier, just as her shift at the bar ended.

The girl you need to train has been delivered to your bedroom. She will be confused, perhaps frightened, but do not comfort her. Your job is to bring her pleasure. Make her like it.

That was all she'd been given to prepare her for the task ahead. *Make her like it.* Ren eyed the door warily. Exactly *how* frightened might this trainee be?

There was only one way to know. Ren took a deep breath, then slipped into the softly lit bedroom. Splayed out across the center of her bed was a shapely brunette wearing a pair of modest black panties and a strapless bra. Her arms and legs were tethered to each corner of the bed by leather straps ending in fur-lined cuffs. A wide black cloth covered the woman's eyes, rendering her totally powerless against whatever Ren might decide to do.

Inhaling swiftly, Ren's trainee lifted her head to blindly scan her surroundings. "Hello? Is someone there?"

Do not comfort her. Ren closed the door loudly enough to be heard, wondering whether she could refrain from providing *some* measure of reassurance if she chose to answer. Uncertainty kept her silent as she crept closer to admire the luscious curves on display. The woman's chest heaved as Ren drew nearer, her ample breasts nearly spilling over the top of her bra. Pleased, Ren sank onto the edge of the mattress and lightly traced her fingertips over a defined clavicle.

The woman gasped and tried to pull away. "Who are you? Why did you bring me here?"

"You'll call me *Mistress*—or *Ma'am*." Ren caressed the woman's flushed cheek, then rubbed her thumb over the blindfold without removing it. Unable to resist the lure of deeper verbal engagement, she murmured, "To clarify, I didn't bring you here—*you* were brought to *me*."

"Why?" The woman jerked when Ren tried to slip a finger into her mouth, past full lips that were painted a deep, decadent red to contrast brilliantly with her straight, white teeth. "What are you going to do to me?"

Ren grasped her chin roughly. "What's your name?" When her trainee hesitated, Ren used her free hand to tap firmly between her legs. After she'd elicited a surprised yelp, Ren repeated, "Your *name*."

"Zoe." She writhed next to Ren, no doubt trying in vain to work her way free of the restraints and close her legs. "Please, don't do this."

"Sweet, sweet Zoe." Settling into the role, Ren stretched out alongside Zoe's trembling body and stroked her tense stomach. "I promise you'll enjoy everything I do to you tonight."

"What?" Zoe pulled on her restraints, but the solid oak headboard held strong. "No!"

"Shh." Ren smoothed her hand up the center of Zoe's chest, coming to rest between her breasts.

"Please, Mistress . . . " Zoe quaked when Ren cradled a heavy breast in each hand. "May I at least see your face? *Please?*"

That final plea broke Ren's heart, softening her resolve. Worried that her next action could be construed as offering comfort, but not worried enough to ignore Zoe's distress, Ren tugged the cups of the other woman's brassiere down until both fleshy mounds spilled out. Then she did the same to Zoe's blindfold, leaving it bunched around the base of her throat. Anxious brown eyes sought out Ren's face and locked on, probably hunting for a hint of empathy.

"Thank you." Zoe's voice wavered. "Please, why am I here?"

"To be trained." Ren slipped a hand beneath Zoe's back and unclasped her bra with ease. She removed the garment and tossed it onto the floor, then appraised the nearly nude form of the woman bound to her bed.

"Trained to do *what*?" Zoe asked, even as Ren returned her hands to her recently bared breasts. Beneath Ren's palms, her heart pounded like a heavy-metal drummer.

"To give and receive pleasure with another woman." Ren squeezed Zoe's breasts before twisting both nipples sharply. "Ever done that before?"

Crinkling her nose in apparent denial of the gratification Ren's touch could bring, Zoe rasped, "*No.*"

"Well, you're about to." Ren retrieved a pair of scissors from her nightstand that she showed to Zoe with a sober look of warning. "Fight me and you could get hurt. I don't want that to happen—so it won't be my fault if it does. Understand?"

Zoe swallowed, eyes shimmering as she stared at the sharp blades. "Yes, Ma'am."

Ren angled a single blade beneath the elastic waistband of the cotton panties, pressed against Zoe's hip. "I'm going to lick your pussy until you come all over my face." She brought the scissors together at the tail end of Zoe's shocked whimper, then followed up with a second slice that allowed her to peel the fabric back and reveal a neatly trimmed pubic area. "After that, you'll demonstrate everything you've learned."

Zoe remained frozen as Ren moved the scissors to her other hip. Her pebbled nipples jutted up from the center of her plump breasts like miniature boulders—betraying, perhaps, a hint of arousal? Ren hoped so, even if her curriculum wouldn't change otherwise. Slicing away the last of Zoe's modesty, she discarded the ruined panties, then returned the scissors to the nightstand.

Ren ran her hand between Zoe's legs. Her fingers glided along the slick labia, coated instantly with thick, hot juices that flowed with such abundance that Ren's instinctive reaction was a peal of shocked laughter. Once the surprise subsided, she said, simply, "You little, lying *slut*."

Zoe flinched, panic rippling across her already conflicted expression. "What? No, Mistress . . . "

Ren raised her shiny fingers as evidence, then brought her wet hand down onto Zoe's pubic mound. "Pretending you don't want this." In a surge of dominance, Ren awarded her another smack, then moved lower to penetrate her defenseless vagina with a single finger. Zoe whined, arching off the mattress in a way that only drew Ren deeper inside. "But you *do* want it . . . don't you?"

Zoe dug her heels into the mattress and tried to scoot away, off Ren's finger. Moving with her, Ren plunged in and out, wriggling the digit to ensure that Zoe stayed focused on the invasive act. Zoe moaned when Ren pushed another finger in, then surrendered, collapsing bonelessly onto the mattress as the fight left her body.

Ren fingered her pussy a bit longer, then slapped the hard tip of Zoe's breast with her other hand. "Tell me the truth. Do you want this, or not?"

Tears leaked from Zoe's eyes and tracked slowly down her rosy cheeks. "I . . . don't know, Ma'am."

Withdrawing, Ren made sure that Zoe was watching before she licked her hand clean then offered an approving nod. "Yummy." Impatient for more, she spread Zoe's swollen labia open with her left hand and bent to take a long, leisurely lick of her fragrant flesh. Upon hearing an obviously begrudging sigh of pleasure, Ren straightened to meet Zoe's stormy eyes. "No worries, slut. What you want or don't want won't change a damn thing about what happens to you tonight."

A visibly throbbing pulse point in Zoe's neck begged for a kiss from Ren's lips. Her voice, however, was hard as steel. "I'm *not* a slut."

"No?" Ren climbed over Zoe's right leg to settle onto her stomach between trembling, lewdly spread thighs. "We'll see about that."

The belly beneath Ren's palm fluttered as she held Zoe steady while lowering her mouth to the puffy labia exposed by her spread-eagled pose. Zoe whimpered at the first touch of Ren's tongue to her clit, a brief tease that Ren quickly ended. Zoe's hips canted upward, seeking her out, but Ren grabbed them tightly, pinning Zoe to the mattress before diving in for more. Delving into Zoe's cunt with her tongue, Ren triggered a breathless cry that left her just as soaked as the pussy she feasted upon. Pausing to breathe some time later, she flashed a wolfish grin.

"You hate this, huh?" With a smug wink, Ren dragged her tongue from Zoe's narrow opening to her prominent clit. She latched onto the erect nub, sucking lazily as she gazed up the length of Zoe's body, into hooded eyes. By the time she pulled away, Zoe was panting heavily. "Like, you hate it a *lot*. That what you want me to believe?"

Zoe squirmed within Ren's tight grip, no longer trying to get away. "I don't *know*."

"*Maybe* you like it," Ren suggested, giving the distended ridge of flesh another languorous suck. "Maybe your pussy wouldn't be *quite* this wet if you didn't love the way I suck on it." She returned her lips and tongue to their task, thrilled when Zoe rocked harder against her face in response. As soon as Zoe again neared the peak, Ren eased back with a cruel smirk. "Tell me the truth. Do you like how my mouth feels on your cunt?"

Zoe shuddered, a tortured look on her anguished face. "I never wanted—"

"I don't care what you *wanted*." Ren slid her hands along Zoe's sides, up to squeeze her breasts possessively. "I asked if you *liked* being eaten by another woman." She tweaked Zoe's nipples so hard she yelped. "Lie and I won't let you come tonight."

Zoe clamped her eyes tightly shut, quivering under

Ren's authoritative touch. "Of course it feels *good*," she whispered. "But that doesn't—"

"Do you want to come?"

Zoe sniffled, causing fresh tears to track down her face. She nodded.

Dissatisfied with the response, Ren clamped down on Zoe's nipples until she made eye contact. "Then say the words," Ren demanded.

Zoe caught her wobbling lower lip in her teeth, visibly tamping down on her emotion. After a beat, she whispered, "I want to come."

Ren brought a hand up to cup her ear. "Louder, please—and with the proper level of respect, which you sorely lack, by the way."

Red-cheeked, Zoe managed to raise her volume by a few degrees. "Mistress . . . I want to come. Please."

"All right," Ren said in a mildly condescending tone. "But if I do that for you, you'll need to do something for me. Understand?"

Zoe's gaze flitted away as humiliation passed over her tortured expression. "Yes, Ma'am."

"Ask me to continue, then."

Zoe exhaled before meeting Ren's expectant gaze. "Please, Mistress, make me come. I promise I'll . . . reciprocate."

"Don't worry. I have a feeling you'll love that part, too." Ren winked. "Won't you, *slut?*"

Zoe released a loud sob when Ren touched her tongue to her clit—then didn't stop sobbing the entire time it took Ren to work her up to a shattering climax, one that left Ren's face slick with come and Zoe's pussy pulsing against her lips. Gratified by both the strength and messiness of

Zoe's orgasm, Ren sat up and swiped the back of her hand over a wide, cocky grin. She crawled up Zoe's sweat-slicked body until they were face-to-face and ground her denim-clad hips against Zoe's slippery, still contracting pussy, leaning in until their lips were millimeters apart. "Did you enjoy that?"

Despite the fresh tears that welled in Zoe's eyes, she nodded with enthusiasm. "Yes, Mistress. Very much."

"And now you want to show me what an accomplished student you are?"

Zoe nodded even more vigorously. "*Yes*, Ma'am. Please . . . let me."

Unsure how to interpret her trainee's newfound dedication, Ren decided *not* to untie Zoe for what came next. "Excellent, slut. That's what I like to hear . . . " She paused for effect. "*Almost.*" Twirling her hand lazily, she elaborated. "You can do better than that, can't you? Use more of your words, slut . . . *dirtier* words."

Zoe's eyes threatened to spill over. "Mistress, please let me lick your pussy."

"Eat my cunt?" Ren asked mildly, again placing a cupped hand behind her ear.

Zoe exhaled, then mumbled, "Mistress, may I please . . . eat your cunt?"

"You certainly may," Ren replied in a bright tone, punctuating the statement by threading her fingers through Zoe's hair with a firm yank. "Once you ask a little *louder*. So I can hear."

Wincing, Zoe glared at Ren with the look of a woman both fierce and beaten. "*Ma'am*, may I please eat your cunt? So I can show you . . . what an obedient slut I am."

Thrilled to have broken Zoe to the point of describing

herself using a word she clearly despised, Ren stood and stripped off her jeans, then her boxer briefs, then finally—after a quick, internal debate—her button-down shirt as well, leaving her just as naked as her increasingly willing trainee. Zoe's gaze didn't stray from Ren as she disrobed, roving up and down her body numerous times before finally coming to rest between her bare thighs. Swallowing convulsively, Zoe appeared unable to tear her attention away from the patch of hair covering Ren's pubic mound, only briefly flicking her eyes to Ren's face once she'd climbed onto the bed to straddle Zoe's narrow shoulders.

"Remember what I did to you?" Ren nudged Zoe beneath her chin to encourage eye contact.

Zoe nodded as her focus strayed back to Ren's pussy—which had to be positively *dripping*, Ren knew. "I remember, Ma'am. Honestly, I'm pretty sure I'll . . . I'll never *forget*."

Glad of that, Ren shuffled farther up the bed on her knees, until she hovered above Zoe's pretty face. "Then you know what I want. Don't stop until you feel my orgasm. Got it?"

Zoe's breath washed over Ren's labia. "Yes, Ma'am. Please . . . "

Intrigued, Ren prompted, "Please, what?"

"Put it in my mouth," Zoe keened. "Please . . . Ma'am . . . I want to taste you."

Wetness gushed from Ren as she honored the provocative request by lowering herself onto Zoe's willing face. "Open wide," she murmured, wriggling against the muscle that immediately flattened against her sensitive folds. "I want to feel you *everywhere*."

Moaning, Zoe raised her head off the pillow to push the stiff tip of her tongue into Ren's vagina with breath-taking swiftness. Ren gasped and again threaded her fingers in Zoe's long hair, holding on tight as she bobbed up and down like a rodeo cowgirl in pursuit of a record-breaking ride. Zoe intensified the suction on her clit without withdrawing her tongue, a display of natural ability that made Ren question whether this was truly her first experience with a woman. Leaving that question for later, she tightened her hand in Zoe's hair and barked a harsh command. "Stop tongue-fucking me. Suck my clit like I sucked yours. Ungrateful little *bitch*."

Zoe flinched at the slur, as Ren had hoped she would, then complied after what sounded vaguely like a muffled *Yes, Ma'am*. Ren shifted her weight backward to allow Zoe a moment to breathe freely through her nose, then pressed forward, forcing herself even deeper into Zoe's mouth as full, eager lips skillfully latched on to her clit. Groaning at the joy of receiving hard-earned head, Ren loosened her hold on Zoe's hair and gave the silky locks a few affectionate pats.

"Much better," Ren praised. "You want to swallow my come, don't you?"

Zoe responded with an impassioned nod, tugging the distended clit in her mouth up and down until Ren's thighs shook. Turned on by the one-sided dialogue, Ren kept talking as she rocked ever more fervently against Zoe's face.

"You'll do nicely, I think. At the parties. You know, the ones we throw for our female clientele. You'll be the main attraction. The *entertainment*." By now Ren was making shit up as she went along, but the visceral surge of Zoe's body beneath hers made her wish she could organize a real gang bang in her trainee's honor. Zoe lapped the tip of Ren's clit even faster, while her diligent, rhythmic lips increased their suction against both it and her tender labia. Ren drove herself deeper into Zoe's hot mouth, taking charge to ensure that she received exactly what she needed to come. "But first I need to break you in. To make sure you've got what it takes to satisfy up to ten women at once." Ren reached back and slapped Zoe's left breast, making her jolt, then suck harder. "So far you're off to a promising start."

When Zoe faltered, Ren instinctively eased off her face so she could breathe. Zoe gulped for air, then whispered, nervously, "No, Ma'am, *please* . . . I can't—"

"Back to work." Cutting off her pleas, Ren sat back down—just as Zoe turned her face to the side in protest. Aware that her clit was now smashed against one of Zoe's tear-stained cheeks, Ren rolled her hips crudely, smearing her juices across every inch of soft skin she could find. "I said *back to work*," Ren repeated, then ground her clit against Zoe's clenched jaw. "*Damn it*." Frustrated by the sudden lack of response after being so very close, Ren swiveled to face the opposite direction and reached between Zoe's spread thighs to position three fingertips at her unprotected entrance. "Suck me off right the fuck now, or I'll shove all three of my fingers into your tight, innocent hole. To be clear, they're going in no matter what, but . . . don't you want it to be at least *somewhat* pleasant for you?"

With a defeated cry, Zoe enveloped Ren with her mouth and resumed her magnificent service. Ren sighed in contentment at the blissful slide of Zoe's tongue against her most sensitive spots. A renewed flood of wetness gushed out of Zoe to coat Ren's fingertips, coaxing her to press in deeper, until she'd breached the slick opening to sink nearly an inch inside. Zoe cried out against Ren's labia, but never stopped sucking.

"That's right." Parking her butt on Zoe's face and her clit even more firmly within the tight circle of her lips, Ren waggled each finger independently, eliciting a tortured moan from Zoe that sent delicious vibrations directly into her own throbbing clit. Hating to be so close, this soon, Ren tried and failed to find the willpower necessary to cease her increasingly urgent movements against Zoe's prodigious tongue. Though she wanted to stretch this lesson out as long as humanly possible, it seemed her once reluctant protégé had decided to ace her first real test. Recalling her earlier musings, Ren lobbed a casually brutal accusation in a voice roughened by desire. "Only a genuine, grade-A slut gives head *this* nice."

Zoe sucked even harder, so that Ren had to brace herself on her free hand while she forced all three fingers even deeper. Zoe's next loud moan undid Ren completely. She cursed under her breath, spasming helplessly into Zoe's hot mouth as a thunderous wave of pure ecstasy swept her away. The pleasure grew in intensity for what felt like forever—until Ren feared she might pass out cold before it slowly ebbed away. Moving off Zoe's mouth only when she was certain she couldn't take any more, Ren collapsed next to her heaving trainee for only a moment before she sat up to reach for the open drawer of her nightstand.

Careful not to sound winded, Ren affected a placid tone. "That was . . . acceptable. Time for lesson two:

Finding pleasure in *everything* that's done to you." She withdrew a medium-sized dildo from the drawer, along with a bottle of lube, and released Zoe's wrists and ankles from the leather cuffs. Ren spent time rubbing each one, soothing the reddened imprints left by the restraints until Zoe gradually relaxed. Taking that as her cue, Ren seized Zoe's hips in a cruel grip, flipping her onto her stomach so she could climb on top. She put her mouth near Zoe's delicate right ear to issue her next command in a low, uncompromising growl. "Open your legs. It's time to take Mistress's cock."

Zoe turned her face to the side, eyes squeezed shut. "Yes, Ma'am."

Ren fit the wide head of the dildo against Zoe's relaxed opening, silently counted to ten, then drove the entire shaft into her with surprising ease. "You've done this before," Ren accused, easing out, then back in. "Haven't you?"

"No, Ma'am, I swear."

Ren rewarded Zoe with a sharp slap on her round butt. "Spread your buttcheeks apart for me, sweetheart. With your hands."

Despite body language that betrayed her growing reluctance, Zoe continued to obey. She pulled her plump buttocks open to show Ren the tiny, puckered hole concealed within. "Mistress . . . " Zoe's voice quavered. "Please, not *there*."

Leaving the dildo lodged inside Zoe's pussy, Ren slathered her finger with a generous amount of lube, then touched Zoe's anus gently, giving her a chance to adjust to the sensation. "I'll make you like it." She massaged the tense circle of muscle without attempting to press inside. "Promise." Indeed, Zoe had already started to moan.

Eager to complete her initiation, Ren said, "Play with your clit. It'll help."

Zoe hurried to obey, shoving her right hand beneath her stomach, then lower to fondle her sopping folds. "Thanks, Mistress."

"You're welcome." With that, Ren pushed her index finger inside Zoe's formerly untouched ass. Zoe let out a high-pitched squeal and tried to wriggle away, but Ren corrected her with a sharp reprimand. "*Wrong.* Lie there like a good slut while I fuck both your holes." She twisted the finger buried in Zoe's butt, then jammed the dildo deeper into her cunt. "It stops when you make yourself come."

She'd barely finished laying out the terms when Zoe surrendered and did exactly that. Shouting, she stiffened before convulsing again and again in what felt to Ren like a tremendously satisfying orgasm. Her climax lasted long, glorious minutes, during which time Ren kept up her two-handed fucking, determined to wring everything she could from Zoe's exhausted body. Finally, after multiple attempts to speak, Zoe gasped, "Bananas!"

At the sound of the familiar safeword, Ren stilled. "You want me out?"

"Of my ass, *definitely.* My pussy, too, but no big rush."

Chuckling, Ren withdrew from her wife's long-past-virgin-status butt, then swirled the cock in tiny, lascivious circles to tease her impending departure from Zoe's still-contracting pussy. "Total slut."

"Busted." Zoe giggle-whimpered when Ren started fucking her again. "Wait. Not yet."

Ren sighed. "Sorry, you've got me pretty worked up."

Zoe tossed her a flirty, over-the-shoulder smile. "You're forgiven. Also, that was *incredible*."

"I'll say." Ren extracted the dildo from Zoe, tilting her head to watch the come leak out after it. "You're pretty amazing at this role-playing thing."

"You, too." Zoe rolled onto her back, then opened her arms in invitation.

"And you've got a *filthy* fucking imagination." Ren gathered Zoe close, welcoming back the woman who'd shared her bed for the past decade with a loving kiss. "You should be ashamed."

"Funny, you seemed into it."

"Oh, I was *definitely* into it . . . but you're still a dirty, dirty slut." Grinning, Ren reflected on how fresh their sex life always felt . . . and how lucky she was to have such an adventurous lover in her life. Then she frowned, her curiosity piqued by a stray thought. "May I ask how you managed to restrain yourself like that? Both wrists, I mean."

Zoe gave her a guilty smile. "Shuree helped."

Ren groaned. "Your best friend *prepared* you for me?"

"You can thank her tomorrow."

Laughing, Ren decided that was the least she could do.

USE ME

Kiki DeLovely

S he knows that I can't get off with direct finger-to-clit stimulation. Somehow too electrically charged, my body leaps and spasms with the shock of any such contact. I'm far too sensitive. Fucking is fun and all but it doesn't do much for me. And vibrators? Forget it. Their sensation may be intriguing on other body parts, but they don't come anywhere near to making me come. Singular and specific in my tastes, there's only one way for me to get off.

My life has been a journey of discovering various textiles, fibers, and the like that will satisfy my need. I'm forever seeking out various types of barriers to serve as a buffer from overwhelming intensity such that I can stroke myself to orgasm. Panties (my earliest, most obvious choice) have long since begun to bore me. I started with those made of silk and satin (too slippery), made my way to lace (just slightly too textured), and couldn't bear the sensibility of ever donning anything made of cotton. The clothing of my lovers had its thrill but even that doesn't excite me as it once did. A necktie, the sash from a robe, the edging of a sheet or pillowcase, they (and many others) have been easily accessible in times of need and have served me well over the years. But it's time for something new. Something . . . different. I've been itching for it; she senses this in me. And now she's studying me with a curious look. One that's never before graced her angelic face.

"I want you to use *me*." This not being her usual emphasis on the word "use," I'm slightly confused as she glances down at her naked body. My eyes follow hers . . . and that's when precisely what she's getting at finally hits me. Her inner lips, significantly longer than her outer, are exposed. Brilliant. She's absolutely fucking brilliant. All my years, all my various lovers, all my searching for something new, and the thought had never crossed my mind.

My excitement increases exponentially. "You know I rub hard. It's going to hurt. A lot. Perhaps excruciatingly so."

Her gaze gets glossy, deep pools of submission surfacing. "It would be an honor."

"And you must remain completely dry so that there's sufficient friction." Already anticipating my highly specific demands, she hands me a come rag with a coy smile and spreads her legs.

This is all the consent I need. She knows her safeword well—one I'm not entirely convinced she won't be using this evening, despite her obvious convictions. As I shove the end of the come rag inside of her to sop up inevitable wetness, she lets out a moan. This idea, this genius idea, is obviously turning her on as much as it is me.

"Please, Mistress, I want you on top of me. All your

weight pinning me down as you use me for your pleasure." And before I can even ask, she assures me, "I can
take it. I want to. And I know I can."

I contemplate just how painful using her labia as
my own personal sex toy might be, in addition to the
mechanics of such positioning.

"Let me prove myself to you."

Prior to her coming into my life, I had never known
a submissive whose desire to prove herself so heavily
outweighed all other acts of altruism. I've learned to never
doubt her determination. So I hike one of her impossibly bendy legs up to the headboard and fasten a leather
restraint around her ankle. Paying for her yoga classes
throughout the last seven years is probably the best invest-
ment I've ever made.

"Mmmmm . . . Thank you, Mistress." The slightest
hint of a lisp on each of her *S*'s always gets me. My
preferred honorific somehow sparkles even sweeter when
it rolls off of her tongue.

Admiring her gorgeous body splayed out like this, I'm
almost tempted to giggle at the ridiculousness of a come
rag hanging out of her cunt. But I don't want to break
the mood. So instead I position myself atop her offering,
barely able to squeeze my hand down between us, hungry
as ever to christen a new toy. Undoubtedly awkward, it
takes a bit of wriggling in order to situate myself just so.
But I always manage to find a way. She gasps just slightly
as I grab hold of my new favored barrier, elongating
her already magnificently lengthy labia. The soft, fleshy
feel up against my clit is instantaneously satisfying. Just
textured enough to provide the traction I crave. Just thick
enough to satisfy my need for indirect stimulation.

"Mmmmmm . . . yesssss . . . yes, Mistress, ohhhhh . . . " I'm unsure whose pleasure is greater as she tenses underneath me. So I focus solely, brutally, on my own as her moans of pleasure morph into groans of pain.

I must constantly keep in the forefront of my mind that this particular barrier is more delicate than the others I've made use of in the past. Not to mention the fact that if this one tears, I'll be devastated. Substantially more so than even the time I ripped my favorite La Perla panties. And I adored those panties. Despite these factors of grave consideration, there's one thing I don't hold back on in the slightest: just how hard I'm needing to stroke myself. After all, she insisted that she can take it. So I plan to see this through, to see just how far I can push her. She's never had to safeword on me before—I tend to push her right up to her edge, hover there for a while, then only proceed when I sense she's ready for more. A natural edge-player, her limits are constantly evolving, expanding, never static. But I sense we're progressing closer to her threshold of pain the nearer I inch toward getting off. For the first time, I don't back off, don't even bother to slow down as her edge draws nearer.

My clit is throbbing in time with her own racing heartbeat. The depth of such painful sensation causes her breath to catch in her throat, a fine sheen of sweat glistening all over her body. Squeezing her eyes shut tightly, she forces them open every so often to gaze into mine, her pupils wide, a wild expression across her face that gets me even harder. I feel a bit of come drip down onto her as my moans syncopate to her grunts. A cacophonous symphony of salaciousness.

"Use me . . . use me . . . use me, use me, use me,

use*meuseme*use*me* . . . ." Her cries like a mantra, growing more ecstatic, playing their part in my swiftly mounting orgasm. I suspect they also serve to keep her from hitting her limit, a meditation of sorts that helps her to focus on something other than just how much it hurts.

Now persistently dripping onto her come rag, I grind my hips ever so slightly between hers, careful in my excitement to not give in to the frenzy of my cunt's desires. My mouth is not quite so cautious, however, as I leave a trail of bite marks across her chest. I sink my teeth in, beginning at one tit and meandering haphazardly toward the other. This new pain momentarily distracts her from that below. Her gaze rolls up to the headboard and then somewhere beyond. She arches her back, one final offering of her body to mine. Screaming into the hollow of her chest, I come harder than I have in years.

I allow myself the indulgence of collapsing atop her completely, each of us breathing heavily, our sweat mingling, pooling between us. After I've recovered sufficiently, I kiss her forehead just once before hoisting myself up and yanking the sopping rag from her pussy. A motion met with yet another gasp. Between both her secretions and mine, we've soaked the cloth through with all kinds of juices. Much to her delight, I wring it out over her chest. Pride radiating from every pore, she knows she's done well, proving herself many times over. She has aced the test.

I may only be able to orgasm one very specific way physically, but all sorts of other sadistic activities get me off mentally. Dominating her brings me an entirely unique form of pleasure, most especially because she'll go anywhere I lead her. She's always game. So I decide to take our play to another level. There's a fantasy I've been toying with for some time now. Something that I know will surprise her almost as much as the offering of her labia delighted me.

"Such a good little toy, letting me use you like that. I do believe you deserve to be rewarded for thinking so expansively outside of the box." Unhitching her ankle, I rub the life back into her slightly chilled foot. Satisfied with her circulation, I flip her over, commanding, "Touch yourself for me."

She needs no further encouragement, greedily getting to work.

"Yes, Mistress." With her face buried in the pillow, those lispy *S*'s are all the more exaggerated, pleasing me to no end.

It takes only a matter of seconds before I take note of the fact that she's obviously close to orgasming. Our previous activities have left her so ready . . . but I have other plans. I can't ever make it too easy on her.

"Don't you dare come until I grant my permission."

"I-I-I-I'm getting . . . so . . . . close . . . ."

"You know how to ask."

"Please, Mistress . . . may I please come?"

"I'm not convinced. I need to hear you beg."

"Please, Mistress, I'm about to explode! Please! I can't wait much longer . . . please, please!"

"How bad do you need it?"

"Sooo . . . unghhh . . . So*fucking*bad. P . . . p . . . pl . . . please!"

She can barely get it out, the poor thing, as worked up as she is. And I can tell how badly she wants this. This orgasm is going to taste so sweet. Which is precisely why

I'm not about to let her have it. At least not in any conventional manner.

"I-I'm . . . uh . . . I can't . . . uh . . . .pl-ease . . . ."

"No."

"But . . . ."

"You heard me." I grab her hand away from her clit, pinning her wrist above her head, pressing my body firmly against her, extending the torture just a bit more by shoving my cunt hard against her ass. I hold her—one hand wrapped around hers above and one hand below, gripping her hip firmly. "Now I want you to take a deep breath and feel the tension disperse throughout your entire body." She inhales perhaps as deeply as humanly possible in that moment, nevertheless, she's not going to get off that easily.

I delight in pushing her and this will indeed be quite the demanding task. Nothing seems to excite her more than a challenge. And nothing gets me hotter than her living up to it. An endlessly licentious cycle.

"Deeper," I whisper, with an intentional hot breath in her ear, reveling in its effect on her body as all her little hairs stand on end and every inch of her skin prickles with goose bumps. "I want you to use the energy of that orgasm . . . " (so close to the surface, we can both still nearly taste it) " . . . and push it into the farthest reaches of your body. Feel it pulsating down your legs, all the way into each toe, sensing the tingle and intensity of all that fervor."

She's still shaking, working hard against her body's natural inclinations in order to fulfill my orders.

"Good girl. Now take another deep breath, sucking the oxygen deep into your lungs, filling them as full as possible. Hold it there for a second before releasing it to thrum across your chest, traversing your arms, down into your fingertips. Feel it spark there before you let go and relax into the release of that breath."

She looks so gorgeous, her face crushed into a pillow, her expression ever obedient and needy.

"Experience that orgasm pulsing through every last pore, every last molecule of your being. Feel it pour over you, racing through your body, and let yourself go as you sink in deeper than you ever have before."

I know exactly what she's feeling. As I was fantasizing about what to do with her several weeks ago, this little scene came to mind and I played it out with myself in her place. I know the power behind an unfulfilled orgasm and what it can do, where it can take you, if you let it. But the more common option is sometimes too tempting, for both doms and subs alike. Who among us has the restraint to deny ourselves or our lovers that type of gratification?

Turns out I do.

Pressed up against her skin like that, I know she's doing beautifully. Following my every command to the nth degree, as she continues to prove herself to me. Proving herself of use to me. I can feel the energy pass into my body, that's just how exquisitely she's excelling at this task. Inhaling all she has to offer, I set the pace for her breath. She exhales into me. Our connection continues to unfurl in unnamed spaces like these. Her earlier offering may have brought me to orgasm, but it also left me wanting. Wanting to use her up completely. And then leave that taste in her mouth for a good, long while.

Hesitantly, once the energy dies down and we're just a pile of dewy, sticky flesh, she's the first to speak. "Whoa. That was . . . intense."

I grin into her shoulder, kiss her there.

"Mistress?"

"Yes?"

"Did I do well?" Holding her breath, she already knows that she did, but she needs to hear me say the words.

"Exceptionally so. I couldn't be more proud."

She relaxes into the pillow and I can hear the corners of her lips turning up, the creases around her eyes crinkling. "Do you think that maybe . . . I mean . . . perhaps . . . is there a chance . . . ?"

"Is there a complete sentence somewhere in there?"

She composes herself and tries again. "Mistress, do I deserve to come?" Doubt, expectation, and longing tangled on her tongue.

"That's something I'm willing to consider." I jump up and begin to dress as she sighs, pushing herself halfway up. While I slip my dress over my head, she cranes her neck to watch me. "We can definitely discuss it . . . " Looking back over my shoulder before exiting the room, I finish, " . . . next week."

I hear the thud of her body hitting the mattress from the hallway as her entire person, along with her hope, deflates.

Oh, how I do so love toying with her.

CUCKOLD

B. D. Swain

Tell me it isn't true that at the heart of every young butch is a balled-up, wet hankie. Prove it. The butches I know are always coming up short, feeling insecure and unsatisfied when what they've got is so right. I'm not pointing fingers. I'm talking about me; me and every goddamn butch I ever met. I'm here to tell you I needed to change. Things were no good. I was no good. But all that was going to be set straight. I was sure of it.

I never cared about being short like some of my friends. I never minded if my date insisted on paying for dinner or could drink me under the table. It wasn't the day-to-day bullshit that ate me up inside. It was a matter of degree. It was that I grew up soft, educated, rich enough to never think much about money. It was that I never worked a job with my hands. I hadn't earned the leather boots I wore. I'd bought them without thinking twice about the money. Every time I saw a hard butch pull wadded-up singles out of her front pocket and count them before ordering her beer, I hated myself.

It didn't matter that I picked a girl up at the bar. I was never butch enough. I spent the next couple of hours fucking her angry, pounding into her to make up for what I wasn't. A real butch. A hard one. I fucked her until she curled her fingers around the back of my neck and told me she couldn't take any more. I growled in her ear. She fell asleep in my bed and I kneeled next to her, staring in wonder. Why would she come home with me? How could I ever keep a girl like this after she found out I was a phony? I might look tough at the bar, but she'd find out how soft I was soon enough. It ate me up inside. I could never be the butch I longed to be.

I get what this sounds like. Poor little rich asshole. Yeah, that's me. That's all you need to know for now. But let me tell you the rest of the story. Let me tell you how I kept going back to the bars. Kept playing the part. Me with crumpled dollar bills soaking up beer on the bar. There I am with a bottle of Bud in the corner. I don't smoke but it would have been a soft pack of Marlboros if I did. I wore my jeans tight and kept a ring of keys in my front right pocket, wearing away a hole toward my inner thigh. I looked the part in those bars. I knew enough to make eye contact. I knew enough to smile and chat and get a little drunk and press my hand against the small of her back. "Baby, let's get out of here," I'd say and more times than you'd think, we'd go. That's how it played out until this one night, this one girl. She laughed and turned away and bought herself another round.

I don't know if it was the night or the girl. It wasn't as if I'd never had a girl laugh in my face before. But this time it lit a fuse somewhere deep inside. A fuse that burned so imperceptibly slowly it took me a few minutes to realize what had happened. I was on fire. This girl had set me on fire. When she laughed, she looked at me in this way that said, "Stay right here and watch me, you fucking asshole." And I obeyed. I wanted to learn, and I knew she could teach me something. I stayed right there. I stood with my beer in my hand until it was too warm to be any good. I stood there with a wet cunt and a stupid look on my face, staring at the soft edges of her shoulder blades that moved under her shirt when she lifted her drink or pushed her hair behind one ear.

She ignored the next butch who tried to buy her a drink. Didn't even shrug her off and just sat there like she hadn't heard the question. I'd seen that butch around. I knew her face but we'd never met. She wore a T-shirt that said SIT ON MY FACE in giant letters. I never saw her without some shirt like that, usually something crude about eating pussy like VAGITARIAN or something about taco night. A shirt that tells everyone you're a big fucking dyke, as if there was any question. She gave me a look that said, *Fuck this bitch, right?* I didn't take the bait. I gave her a blank look and went back to my reverent staring at this woman with her back turned to me. I was supposed to stay put. I felt sure of it. I was supposed to wait and watch. So I did. I watched. I watched as someone I would later come to know as JR got her attention.

I'd seen JR come in that night. She was amazing. A bright and shining butch with unruly, closely cropped, gray hair that looked like she shaved herself without paying much attention. Her face was weather worn and a little sunburned with white crevices in the wrinkles around her eyes. She had a sparse row of coarse hair above her lip just dark enough to be noticeable. She was tall with a big ass and heavy thighs. Her belly hung over her belt. She had big tits and didn't strap them down.

JR came in and played pool with some of the younger butches, taking their money without much effort. I loved to watch her. JR didn't give a shit. JR was too cool to try to look cool. I imagined myself in her boots with my own fat fingers wrapped around a pool cue as if I'd grown up with it. I pictured myself sinking one ball after another with a dirty grin on my face. JR won one game and then another, winning enough to buy a few beers later. She collected the dollars by pinching them between her fingers and smoothing them out before folding them up in her wallet. I lost track of her as the bar filled up that night. There were other girls to watch.

I'd forgotten about JR even being there, forgotten about everything as I sat there staring at the girl who had laughed me off. Something broke inside me as I watched her look around the room, passing over each butch one at a time before landing on JR. Something broke in the best way. Broke down. Broke through. JR was perfect. Of course she wanted JR. Someone to pin her down completely, someone who wouldn't worry about being too rough, someone who could do anything without ever thinking it over too much.

JR played pinball with her back to us. A stack of quarters on the machine, her legs spread wide, her shoulders hunched. We watched her slap the glass, grab her quarters, and move over to the jukebox. The girl at the bar, the girl with her back to me, the girl I was bound together with now, stood up. "Hey," I said, as if she were my date, as if she owed me an explanation, but shut my mouth fast and watched her go. I put my hand protectively on her bar stool and the warm vinyl made me shiver.

I watched the tips of her fingers reach out and touch JR's thick forearm. She smiled up at JR, saying something. She took a couple of dollars out of her back pocket and fed the jukebox. I watched them pick out songs together. They barely spoke, but JR followed her back to the bar. Knowing, but looking like the cat that ate the canary nonetheless.

The girl looked at my hand on her seat and, without looking me in the face, waited for me to move and let her sit. She looked at my belt as she thanked me politely for saving her spot. I felt my cheeks burn red. JR pulled at her chin and nodded to me with a slow, wide smile. I bought myself another drink and stood there listening to them, hovering too close to be respectful. JR called her "Sherry." I couldn't tell if they knew each other already or if they had just met that night. JR looked at me but no one asked my name.

I drank my whiskey fast. I felt it hit me deep in my chest the way booze opens you up and makes you bigger, thicker. My chest felt expansive. My head spun a little. I was drunk, more than a little. They flirted in front of me, JR leaning one elbow on the bar and cocking her head while they talked. All you need is a touch or two. Something simple. A finger pointing to a belt buckle strays and slides an inch or two across a belly. JR looked down at that pretty little hand, those sweet fingers. Something got said in a serious tone. Some question asked that had an unintended reaction. JR reached a thick hand to Sherry's arm and gave it a squeeze before sliding those rough fingers up to her shoulder. There was a silence before they started to move toward the door. Sherry looked back at me, and then JR. I'd already started to follow. She whispered something in JR's ear. JR looked back over her shoulder at me and didn't answer, just grinned.

It smelled like beer on the sidewalk. I can tell you a lot about that walk, the street, the garbage, stray dogs, the cigarette smoke, and giggling fags a couple of blocks over. I have a clear memory of that walk because I was paying close attention as if my life depended on remembering every detail. The way they walked together, JR with her hand riding just above Sherry's hip, sliding a little toward her ass with each step. The clicks and the thuds of their shoes. Sherry bent over to adjust a heel and hung on to JR's shoulder to keep steady. We walked past a car with sheets covering all the windows. I noticed the gum, the candy wrappers, and thought about how it used to be drug vials crunching under my boots just a few years ago. I didn't know where we were going.

It was JR who pulled out keys. JR's apartment building we stood outside. JR's living room we walked into that was tidied up in the hope of having company that night. I noticed the dirty rings on the coffee table where her drinks had been. JR pointed me toward the fridge. I pulled out three beers but by the time I turned around Sherry's fingers were on JR's buckle. My eyes traveled up JR's gut to her face, glistening with sweat, staring straight at me. It was that look from a shitty teenage sex movie. That look that says, "You're next, boy," directed at the skinny nerd who will not be next, not yet, not until the end of the movie, maybe, if he's lucky.

I opened a beer. JR reached a hand out for it and

nodded at Sherry to keep going. Sherry rubbed JR through her jeans. I could see the shape of the cock, her bulge. I opened a beer for myself. I needed something in my hand, something to do. I was here to watch JR be exactly who I wanted to be and do exactly what I wanted to be doing. I was here to watch JR take my place. JR's belt was only half unbuckled. She took Sherry's hand inside her own and rubbed it harder against the fly of her jeans. "Get it," she grunted out and drained half the bottle of beer. I felt ridiculous. Perfect.

They started fucking immediately. There was no slow make out; no long buildup. JR grunted orders at her, "Get it out. Get it wet." She slapped her quick across the face when she didn't drop to her knees fast enough. "Get it," JR said under her breath a few more times sounding like a guy cheering his favorite football team on from the couch. "Get it," I heard myself whisper, not even moving my lips, "Get it wet." Sherry had her lips on JR's jeans. Her hands were up by her forehead, undoing the buckle while her open mouth sucked on the bulge behind JR's fly. She sucked that cock out of JR's jeans. Drool dripped down her chin.

JR bent her knees and shifted her weight. One hand moved down to Sherry's face and pushed her hair back. "You look good," she said and pushed Sherry's mouth open with her thumb before sliding her cock deep inside. "I like a pretty girl on my cock," JR said. I put my beer down and gripped the countertop to steady myself. I didn't know where to look. My head was fuzzy, too caught up in what was in front of me to name my own desire. I found myself watching JR's throat. The way her veins bulged when she held her breath and grunted. Her voice sounded heavy now, her tongue thick in the back of her throat. She bit her lower lip. With my eyes on her neck, I saw her shoulders flex and hunch. She was loosening up. Relaxing.

Sherry had her hands wrapped around JR's thighs. Her mouth was filled, her cheeks sucked in. JR jerked her cock out and held it. "Keep your mouth open," she said and rubbed the tip against Sherry's lips, pushing her mouth open even wider, pushing her chin down. A thick rope of saliva slid over her lips and I stared, mesmerized, as it pooled on the floor. "Up," JR said and grabbed her as she rose, turning her around to face me. JR wrapped an arm around her chest and held her tight with one hand while the other jerked her jeans open. I saw cream-colored, lace panties covering a dark shock of hair. JR's fingers looked thick and calloused as they shoved inside those panties. She grinned and put her mouth to Sherry's ear, "Did sucking my cock get your pussy all wet?" Sherry nodded and JR's eyes flashed at mine, *Want to see something?*

I didn't need to respond before JR had Sherry's shirt balled up in a fist, pulling it over her head. Her bra matched her panties. Creamy lace you could see the shadow of her nipples through. JR brought her hand up to her nose, "You have a sweet cunt," she said and then shoved her wet fingers under the lacy bra. Sherry's stomach quivered. I could see her coming undone with the feel of those rough hands on her soft skin. The gruffness of JR's touch. I could feel it, both sides of it. JR's scratchy fingers on my thighs. Sherry's soft tits in my hands. I stood frozen near the kitchen counter. JR had her mouth on Sherry's neck, sucking loud enough for me to hear.

"Girl, I want these off!" JR said, and tugged at Sherry's jeans. "Leave the panties," she demanded, swatting

Sherry's ass as she bent over. She stood there between us in her bra and panties and for the first time I noticed the stark light in JR's apartment. The overhead lights were too bright, with a bluish tint. Bright like a doctor's office, but somehow the glare made everything more real, more intimate. Both of JR's hands were on Sherry's tits, rubbing her hard and squeezing her over and under the lace bra. "Do you feel my dick between your legs?" JR asked. "Come on." JR shoved Sherry forward, toward me. I backed away and watched JR bend Sherry over the counter. JR leaned over her and positioned Sherry's arms out in front of her on the counter. "Hold on," JR said and I wasn't sure which one of us she meant.

Sherry's face told me when JR's cock was inside her. She never looked at me. Her eyes were closed or looking down at the countertop. JR fucked her hard, holding her hips in both hands. For a long time, JR just watched her cock pounding into Sherry. I pictured Sherry's ass bouncing up and down, her panties tight around her thighs. I moved to the side when JR leaned over and pressed Sherry down against the counter with a forearm across her shoulder blades. Sherry's hands pressed flat against the Formica, her eyes were squeezed shut. JR didn't break. She fucked her long and hard. Sherry's moaning sounded meditative. JR was huffing, sweating, red faced.

They moved to the couch. JR sat back and Sherry climbed on top, hooking her hands around JR's neck. JR held Sherry's ass in her hands and lifted her like a doll. Her arms looked huge, her muscles bulging. Sherry bounced on and off. My eyes moved to her panties on the floor near JR's boot. "I want to see you come," JR said. Sherry left one hand on JR's shoulder and moved the other to her clit. JR leaned forward and sucked on a tit. Sherry's hips moved in circles on JR's cock. JR lifted her hips off the couch, holding Sherry hard against her thighs, digging deep. JR looked over at me and jerked her head, calling me closer. I almost stumbled as I moved toward them. I stood watching them from the side of the couch.

JR thought I wanted to watch Sherry come, but I couldn't. I watched JR. I watched her eyes. The stupid grin on her face. Suddenly JR showed me everything—all her vulnerability, like a little kid. Innocent.

I sat down in the corner and held my knees to my chest. I wasn't hiding. I was trying to keep everything rushing through me held tight. I am never that grinning kid. I am never exposed and innocent. I'm on the outside looking in when I fuck. I see the whole room and how I'm positioned in it. I lay the tracks out in front of me one at a time as I go, but there are still tracks. I'm not free to roam. That look I saw on JR's face is exactly what I crave. And I felt it there that night. I felt it and knew what I was missing, what I wanted. Watching them fuck, watching their freedom, the simplicity of it, I wanted out of my goddamn head. I wanted to feel alive, fully in the moment. Animal. Instinctive.

Sherry came, groaning long and low. JR made her come again and then jerked off on top of her, coming hard and pounding the couch with her fist. I didn't even watch at the end. I stayed in the corner, listening with a lump in my throat. Not crying, but feeling on the verge of tears. Feeling too turned on. Frustrated. Exhausted.

Sherry got up, collected her things, and went to wash up. JR stayed on the couch when Sherry walked to the door. "I don't like it when a butch tries too hard," she said with her back to us. We both knew she was talking to me. JR laughed. I could still hear her heels in the hall when JR leaned back and muttered, "You gotta go now, too." I made my way to the door.

That night in bed I pressed my face into the mattress, barely able to breathe while I jerked off. I came again and again. I came until I ached. I needed to move on. I wanted to force it. But it only made me sore.

THE LAST KINK

Cecilia Duvalle

Camilla watched the two women on the corner from her fifth-story terrace. They went through the same ritual every week, and, though she couldn't hear them from this distance, she knew exactly what they were saying.

A tall blonde wrapped her arms around Mora. "Are you sure you need to do this?"

"Yes," Mora said. She squeezed the other woman's shoulders as she slipped out of her embrace.

"I'll be waiting."

Mora, as always, kissed the other woman on the lips, turned toward Camilla's apartment building, and hobbled her way through the throngs overflowing the crosswalk, her knuckles white against her cane. Camilla watched until she was safely on her side of the street before waving to the blonde who had watched Mora's progress as well. The blonde touched her open palm to her lips and dropped it in her direction. Camilla signed back "welcome" with a delicate flourish and watched the other woman settle onto a bench and pull out a book. Last week's had been something thick and heavy with an orange background and white letters. This week it was something dark and thin with an invisible font from this distance.

If things were different, Camilla thought she might have liked this woman. Even be friends. As it was, she didn't even know her name. A twinge of jealousy sent her back inside. The blonde loved Mora enough to bring her to Camilla week after week. That was enough.

Camilla made a few last-minute adjustments to the items she'd set out for their session as she waited for the doorbell to ring. She'd had a removable perch custom-made to use with her St. Andrew's cross. She double-checked to make sure she'd attached it securely.

"Well, look at you," Camilla said as she opened the door and ushered her in. "You look fabulous today."

Mora flushed and looked down at her shoes. "Thank you, Mistress."

She took her by the arm to lead her into the living room. "How are you feeling today? I want to make sure we can continue with our plan."

Mora met Camilla's eyes briefly before turning her attention to the cross. "Oh, Mistress, you got it. You did this for me?" She had moved faster than Camilla had seen her do in months and placed her hand on the small bit of wood. "It's perfect."

Camilla reached out and grasped Mora's shoulders, squeezed. "I couldn't have you falling, now could I? Not on my watch, my sweet."

Mora placed a hand over one of Camilla's. "Thank

you, thank you so much. I . . . I don't know what to say."

Camilla leaned in and kissed her gently on the neck, released her, and stepped back. "You don't have to say anything. But, I do think it is time for you to get naked."

Mora spun around on her good foot and handed Camilla her cane. "Yes, Ma'am." Her eyes were bright with tears and expectation.

Mora lifted the turtleneck over her head. Her wig came off with it and she caught it as it tumbled downward. "Damn. I didn't want you to see that," she hissed as she fumbled to get it straight on her head.

Camilla hadn't been aware that she'd lost her hair. How long had she hidden that from her?

"I bet you shaved your head in the nineties, just to show it could be done. You have a nicely shaped head, Mora." Camilla's own head looked horrible shaved. She'd done it once for a cancer awareness gig ten years prior. Hers was lumpy and was stained with a birthmark she had never known about. Never again.

"Please, Mistress. Pretend I have all my hair. You'll allow me that won't you?" Her hands shook a little as she removed the lacy bra she wore beneath to release her breasts.

"Of course" Camilla could easily give her that.

Mora shoved her jeans and underwear down to her ankles. She threatened to topple over with the effort to get them off, but Camilla steadied her as she stepped out of them.

"Beautiful, as always," Camilla cooed at the now-naked woman. *Thinner. Much thinner.*

Mora laughed. Giggled really. "Oh, Mistress. You should have seen me when I was twenty."

I did see you when you were twenty. Have you really forgotten? "I see you now."

There was no need to lie. The woman was still gorgeous. Even with the lines on her face and her slightly sagging breasts, she had a glow about her. A glow that comes from within and radiates out into the world. Camilla always felt a profound sense of calm when in Mora's presence.

Mora looked away, her lips pulled together into her mouth for a second before whispering, "Thank you, Mistress."

Camilla had closed the small gap between them to grasp her nipples. Pinching them between her thumb and forefinger, she squeezed and twisted. Mora breathed into the pain and let out a contented sigh.

Camilla had set the perch at the perfect height for Mora. She could put most of her weight on it while still being spread eagle on the cross. The *U*-shaped cutout would give Camilla complete access to the other woman's pussy and ass. That part had been Mora's suggestion when Camilla had talked about it. Beautiful and brilliant.

"I'll keep the ropes simple. So I can get you down faster if I need to." Camilla wound a purple silk rope around Mora's right wrist. With each twist, she paused, ran her hand down Mora's side and up to her breast. With each caress, she paused to tease her nipple into full erection. When she was done with the tie on that side, she switched to Mora's left and repeated the actions exactly. Knot, caress, twist. Knot, caress, twist.

Camilla dropped to her haunches to tie Mora's legs to the cross. She started with her weaker leg and wrapped the rope carefully around the fleshiest part of her calf. Holding the unfastened rope in place, Camilla leaned in and nibbled at Mora's inner thigh. Traced her tongue along the path up to Mora's spread-open pussy, but stopped a few inches shy of it.

"Tease."

"Shhhhh. Do you want a ball gag in your mouth today?"

"No, Ma'am."

Camilla continued with a slightly more elaborate tie down to Mora's ankle. Spreading the pressure across the greater part of her leg would prevent swelling and issues from edema. The only part of Mora that looked old was this leg—the sole testament to her stroke three years prior. Her other leg could pass for fifty, easily. Camilla turned her attention to the last limb, continuing with her nibbling, teasing bites.

Mora moaned, but didn't speak again.

Camilla stepped back a few paces to appreciate the simple yet attractive knot-work. "Yes. This will do." She turned her attention to the small table of toys she'd set out. She chose a set of nipple clamps with a chain between them and held them up as if she were examining them.

With her back to Mora, she breathed in deeply several times and switched herself into full "Mistress mode." It took a certain force of will to do what she was going to do with Mora. Mora—the woman she'd loved for fifty years, the woman who had left her for the blonde waiting outside thirty years ago, the woman who had returned to her—finally returned to her!—cancer-ridden, dying, and needing her. *She needs me for this.*

She spun around, draping the chain of the nipple clamps over her fingers. "Look what I have for you today."

Mora's eyes were trained on the dangling clamps,

watching them sway back and forth in the air, mesmerizing her. Her nipples were already erect in response. Camilla sucked Mora's nipple into her mouth and swirled her tongue around until it was hard, and then let it pop out, glistening. She held the clamp open over the tip and blew on it as she slowly let the metal bite into the skin.

Mora sucked in a quick breath between her teeth.

Camilla slid her hand across Mora's stomach and down to her pussy. As she expected, her hand came back drenched.

"Look at you. Hungry little cunt. Dripping wet. Wanting to be fucked." *Some things never change.*

Camilla pushed her coated fingers into Mora's mouth as she drew the other nipple into her own mouth. She sucked hard, giving miniature head to the hard little nub while Mora sucked her fingers as hungrily as if they were a cock.

Camilla let the other clamp snap shut. Mora grunted louder and her lower body jerked against the ropes in response.

Camilla dropped to her knees and spread Mora's pussy open wide, pushing the fleshy outer lips toward her thighs, until her hole gaped and dripped onto the floor. She pressed the flat of her tongue against the other woman's clit and held it there until they were the same temperature before lapping at it. Mora groaned and tried to writhe, but the cross and ropes held her still.

Camilla stopped just before Mora could come. She took the engorged head between her teeth and bit down hard enough to hurt without breaking skin.

"No. Please don't stop," Mora begged. Her head fell back in frustration.

"Baby, we're just getting started."

Camilla retreated to the tray of toys and chose a flogger with dozens of soft leather tails and a butt plug with eight stops on it, the largest being the size of a large apricot. Camilla kissed her, letting their tongues share the sweet taste of Mora as she slid the butt plug into her pussy. She turned it round and round, getting it covered in Mora's own slick juices.

Dropping to her knees, she inserted the first ball of the plug into Mora's ass.

"There's a good girl, keep it in, or you'll pay."

Mora closed her eyes tight and sucked in her lips together. Her *let's concentrate* face. Camilla waited until Mora had to peek, to see what was happening, before starting with the flogger. She needed to see that little spark of fearful expectation in Mora's eyes before she began.

She flicked the flogger upward, straight onto Mora's spread pussy. She counted out ten gentle strokes, nothing too hard to begin with. She dropped to lick and suck at Mora's clit, once again right to the brink of orgasm, pulled back and pushed the plug one more notch into Mora's ass.

Mora groaned.

"What a predictable cunt you are."

"I'm sorry, Mistress."

"You should be sorry. All I have to do is flog you and shove things up your ass and you're so very, very happy."

"I'm sorry, Mistress."

"Shut up. Don't speak again. I can't stand to hear your apologies."

Camilla flogged, sucked, and upped the plug until the last, large ball was in place and Mora's sweet little sphincter was closed around the base. Her pussy and upper thighs were bright pink, swelling from the flogging.

"Well, look at that. You got it all the way in without pushing it out." Camilla twisted the plug in circles.

Mora looked at her with wide, pleading eyes, not daring to speak.

"You want more, don't you, my precious?" Camilla did not expect a response.

Camilla turned back to the tray and pulled the Wartenberg wheel out of the glass of ice where it had been chilling for hours. Not wanting it to warm up, she ran the cold spikes between Mora's breasts, careful of the chain on the nipple clamp. Mora shuddered.

"Can you feel that?"

Mora nodded.

Camilla dropped the wheel back into the ice. Ran her hot tongue along the path of the wheel, licking up a couple of droplets of stray blood. She had pressed harder than intended. She ran the wheel lightly over each thigh, the icy tickling sending shivers across Mora's skin. Goose bumps covered her body by the time Camilla put the wheel down. Lightly, she ran her fingers along the raised hairs of Mora's arms, who moaned in response, a low contented happy sound.

She pressed a large piece of ice into Mora's dripping cunt and slid it around inside.

"Are you cold?"

Mora shook her head as she shivered. "Maybe a little."

"Just wait." Camilla continued with the ice play until it was melted and her own fingers felt nearly frostbitten.

Camilla lubed up her other hand, closed her fingers in tightly, and slipped her entire fist into the iced cunt with a practiced motion. The temperature differential of her hot fist against the cooled pussy was intense and Mora groaned loudly as Camilla fucked her, moving slowly at first, gaining momentum as Mora's pussy warmed back up. Her hips writhed against the perch, unable to move very far. Camilla sensed Mora was close to coming and relented. She increased the intensity, twisting her hand so that her thumb banged into Mora's G-spot with each move.

Mora keened as she came—a primordial, soulful sound, and gushed, soaking Camilla's arm to the elbow.

"My god, bitch. You really did need release." She held up her hand to Mora's mouth. "Clean your come off my cock."

Mora did as she was told. Camilla gently stroked Mora's pussy with her free hand while Mora licked her clean.

She lifted the nipple chain with a finger until Mora's breasts were taut and stretched almost to her shoulders. She unclipped them in rapid succession and delighted in their drop and pendulous sway as they settled against Mora's chest. Mora shuddered, her eyes glassy as she transcended into sub-space.

For the first time that day, Camilla's pussy throbbed with desire—a hunger she would have to tend to later. This was about Mora. *For Mora.* She pulled the plug out of her ass in one fell swoop and wrapped it in a towel for cleaning later. Camilla quickly untied Mora, making sure the other woman didn't collapse.

Camilla half-carried, half-walked Mora to the couch. She wrapped her in a thick blanket, encircled her with her arms and legs, holding her close. Mora snuggled in against her, that look of bliss still on her face. She held her until the light outside glowed a rich orange low on the horizon. Their time was almost up.

The blonde would be waiting, anxious to leave now that she could no longer stay buried in her book. Mora stretched, wakening out of her pain-pleasure-induced stupor.

"Did you feel it all, Mora?" Camilla kissed her on her ear.

"Yes, Mistress."

"Was it what you hoped it would be?"

"Yes, Mistress."

"Should we do the same next week?" *If there is a next week.*

"Yes, Mistress. Please."

IN A PINCH

Janelle Reston

Their apartment is a shoebox, but it's what they can afford on their grad school stipends, so Kendra is mostly happy with it even if it means they can't fit a full couch in the living/dining room that also serves as an office. Kendra half sits, half lies on the loveseat with a big, floppy pillow under her back and her legs bent into upside-down Vs. Her socked feet are planted firmly on the loveseat cushion, but as she turns the next page in Katherine Mansfield's *Collected Stories*, she stretches one leg out, propping her calf against the armrest and letting her foot dangle freely in the air.

She enjoys the feeling of being at her full length, even though she also knows the pressure of the armrest will eventually cut off her circulation and her ankle and foot will go pins-and-needles numb. She hates that sensation.

She keeps her leg outstretched anyway and keeps reading. The shower running in the bathroom a few feet away serves as the perfect rainy backdrop for the story in which she's immersed.

Kendra doesn't notice when the shower shuts off. The sound of Jess moving around in the bathroom—humming to herself, opening and shutting drawers, picking up and setting down lotion bottles, snapping the towel in the air before hanging it to dry—is just as familiar and soothing.

That is, until Jess's voice snaps as sharply as the towel. "Fuck!"

Kendra jolts up straight. Jess doesn't swear often outside the bedroom.

"You okay, Jess?"

There's a slight delay before Jess answers. "Um, yeah." Something metal clinks against the tile counter. Nail clippers? A barrette? "Just . . . grooming. I'm fine."

"Okay." Kendra turns back to her reading, but only gets two sentences further before a stifled hiss seeps through the bathroom door. It's similar to the sound Jess makes when she waxes her legs, but that can't be what's going on in there. Kendra hasn't heard the distinctive *rrrrriiip* that the wax-soaked cotton strips always make as Jess pulls them from her skin, like one piece of Velcro pulling away from another.

The medicine cabinet opens and closes again, followed by a silent pause and another hiss.

"Jess? Do you need help in there?"

"I don't . . . think so. No. No. I'm fine."

Kendra tries to accept the answer. Her natural tendency is to run and rescue anyone at the earliest sign of distress, but she's learned the hard way that's not always what people want or need. With Jess especially. Jess is an introvert and staunchly independent. Sharing a tiny apartment has forced them to learn how to give each other space when they need it. Jess's showering ritual is her solitary time.

Besides, Kendra got most of her caretaking urges out earlier today during her twice-weekly shift at the animal shelter. She buries her nose back in her book.

A sudden pig-squeal noise makes the hairs in Kendra's ears stand on end.

"Okay, I know it's none of my business, but what are you trying to do in there? Give yourself a tattoo?" It's a ridiculous question. Jess is one of the most vanilla people Kendra knows when it comes to . . . everything—sex, clothes, body modification. They've never gotten any kinkier than using a strap-on. Most of Jess's clothes are beige or cream. She wouldn't be caught dead in stilettos, and she doesn't even have pierced ears. She told Kendra once that she'd thought about getting them when she was twelve, but wimped out. She couldn't stop worrying about them getting caught on something and ripping her earlobes in half.

Jess chortles. "No. Definitely not a tattoo."

"Well, whatever it is doesn't sound pleasant."

"It's not, exactly. I wouldn't call it unpleasant, though." Jess's voice starts as singsong, but ends on a low note that she usually reserves for when she's seducing Kendra.

"What's that supposed to mean?"

Jess opens the bathroom door a crack—just enough to let a little of the soap-and-shampoo scent leak into the living room, but not enough that Kendra can actually see inside. "You can come in and watch if you're that curious."

Well. Kendra's not going to turn down a direct invitation. She sets the book on the loveseat and walks the three steps to the bathroom. She pushes the door open.

Jess is standing naked in front of the mirror, her wide hips and pendulous breasts on lavish display. Kendra forgets why she's there. Her eyes flit back and forth between Jess and her reflection; they're both so sexy.

It's muggy like a rainforest in there, though the mirror is no longer fogged. Kendra pushes her sleeves up past her elbows, feels sweat bloom under her arms and in the crotch of her jeans. The wetness makes her think of other kinds of wetness, and soon she's sidling up behind Jess, her hands around Jess's hips, admiring the way they look together in the mirror.

Kendra notices the pair of tweezers in Jess's hand.

"You're plucking? But your eyebrows are perfect already," Kendra says.

Jess doesn't say anything, just smiles knowingly, like she's privy to some secret.

"What?"

Jess's smile grows wider. Her cheeks flush. "It wasn't my eyebrows." She pulls her plump lower lip into her mouth, her top teeth blanching her pink skin. "It was my nipples."

Kendra involuntarily curls her fingers into her palms so hard that she can feel her nails etching half-moons into her skin. She's plucked the hairs around her areolas before and it stings like a bitch—and hers are fine and feathery, not the thick, wiry threads that sprout from Kendra's skin. "That hurts just to think about," Kendra says. "You know I like your body just as it is, right?"

"Yeah. But I'm not doing it for you. I'm doing it because it's . . . interesting."

"What do you mean, interesting?"

Jess half shrugs and turns toward the mirror. She lifts the tweezers to her breast, clasping a thick black hair between its prong tips. She holds the skin taut with her other hand as she tugs, her breath still, her cheeks growing pinker as the hair eases out of her body. She winces as it pulls free, and then gasps. It's a high, wispy noise, not unlike the ones she makes when Kendra makes that first, gentle lick across Jess's clitoris when she eats her out.

The root is white and at least twice as thick as the hair itself. "Damn," says Kendra. "That must be excruciating."

"It is. But it's also . . . intoxicating. Here, you try it." Jess holds the tweezers out for Kendra to take.

"I'd rather not."

"Not on you, silly. On me. Pull one out. I want to know what it feels like when I'm not in control."

Kendra scrunches her nose, but she doesn't see any reason not to comply with the request, even if it's against her instincts to intentionally cause Jess pain. It's not like Jess is asking to be injured or maimed.

Kendra accepts the tweezers.

Jess closes her eyes as Kendra presses the thumb and forefinger of her left hand to Jess's breast and uses them to stretch the skin tight. With the tweezers in her right hand, she carefully grips the base of a dark, curly hair on the north pole of Jess's areola. Kendra draws it out slowly but steadily, feeling the resistance, watching the skin peak like a small hill around the hair's base until Jess lets out a low hiss and the hair comes free.

"Again," Jess whispers.

Kendra moves on to the next hair, and then the next.

Jess's blush creeps down her throat and across her collarbones. Her nipples grow hard and round as cherry pits. "Another one," she pleads when Kendra's reduced the dozen or so hairs around Jess's right nipple to a handful.

Kendra goes on until the skin there is bare, then moves to Jess's left breast. Jess shifts her legs and the scent of her arousal wafts up into the air. She must be very wet for Kendra to be able to smell her so soon after a shower.

Kendra feels her own arousal grow. It starts in her clit, as solid and dense as a seed, then unfurls in warm tendrils down her mons and up into her cunt until even her cervix feels flushed and needy. She needs Jess between her legs and inside her, and needs to be inside Jess just as much. She longs to slip a finger into Jess's folds, to bury herself in Jess's slick heat.

But she has a job to finish.

Kendra grasps two neighboring hairs and pulls both at once.

"Oh fuck!" Jess gasps. Her eyes open. Her pupils are dark and wide. She grabs Kendra and kisses her hard, her teeth sharp against Kendra's lips, her tongue a force to be reckoned with.

Kendra pulls back, a smirk forming on her lips. "Does that mean you liked it?"

"It hurt so fucking much," Jess pants. "I loved it."

"Then let me try again." Kendra grasps two more hairs and pulls them out simultaneously. The rest of the hairs are spaced too far apart to repeat the trick, but Kendra has an idea—something she's never tried before with anyone, though she's read enough erotic romance to know some people are into this. Given Jess's response to pain so far, it's worth a try.

Kendra continues to hold the skin of Jess's breast taut between her thumb and forefinger, but now curls her other three fingers under so Jess's nipple is caught between the back of Kendra's middle and ring fingers. As Kendra yanks out the next hair, she squeezes the curled fingers together to give Jess's nipple a sharp tweak.

Jess's groan rumbles straight into Kendra's belly. "Good?" Kendra says, although she knows the answer already.

"So good. I had no idea—" Whatever Jess was about to say gets broken off by another moan. Jess crosses her legs, the muscles in her thighs going tense as Kendra moves on to the last hair. "I'm so turned on right now."

"You want me to fuck you when we're done?"

"Yes. I also want this to never be done."

Kendra pulls out the final hair, then pinches both of Jess's nipples hard. "It doesn't have to be." She guides Jess so that her ass is flush with the bathroom counter. Jess gets the hint. She lifts herself onto the tiles, letting her legs fall open while Kendra drops knees-first to the floor.

"Take off your shirt so I can feel you," Jess says.

Kendra licks a stripe up the center of Jess's spread labia. "That's not feeling enough?" she teases.

"Never."

Kendra pulls her shirt off over her head and tosses it to the floor, but she's too eager to eat Jess to bother with her jeans. Those stay on, the center seam applying a pleasant pressure on Kendra's cunt as she sinks her mouth back into Jess's folds.

Kendra's hand crawls up to pinch Jess's nipple.

"Oh god!" Jess's cry ricochets against the bathroom walls, urging Kendra on. Kendra licks deeper into Jess, her chin already drenched in juice, her nostrils filled with Jess's scent. She probes her tongue into Jess's hungry cunt and gives another hard squeeze.

"Fuck!" Jess's thighs quiver, her calves swinging back and forth like windshield wipers over Kendra's back as her excitement mounts. She seems just a hair's breadth away from orgasm.

Kendra draws her tongue to Jess's clit, licking tight circles around it as she works two fingers into Jess's wet cunt and then curls the fingertips against the spot that always makes Jess fall apart.

With the other hand, she twists Jess's nipple halfway around until left is right and top is bottom.

Jess doesn't cry out. She stops making any sound at all. She holds her breath as her back arches violently and her thighs shake, then suddenly go rigid. Her cunt pulses around Kendra's fingers, pushing juice out onto her waiting tongue. It always tastes slightly different when Jess is coming—more watery but also somehow headier.

Jess gasps, her spine collapsing toward the counter. She pulls Kendra up from between her thighs. "Now take off your jeans, baby. I'm not done with you yet."

They move to the bedroom. Kendra's clothes come off and Jess works one end of their double dildo into Kendra's waiting cunt.

"Can I try something?" Kendra is overcome by a sudden urge to test the extent of Jess's desire for pain.

Jess hovers over her, her hair falling around Kendra's face, shutting out the world around them. "Surprise me."

Kendra pulls Jess closer. Jess is ticklish right beneath her earlobe, and Kendra wonders—

She bites down on the skin.

"Oh!" Jess twists the dildo inside Kendra's body.

"Is that a 'do that again,' or 'never do that again'?"

"Definitely 'do that again.' But not until I get the harness on you. I need you to fuck me, babe."

Kendra chuckles. "You're insatiable."

"That's why you love me."

"Harder, harder, please, harder." Jess is on her knees, her back against Kendra's chest, her hands white-knuckling the headboard, and she's begging in the way that Kendra loves, even if Kendra's not sure what needs to be harder: the fucking, or the squeeze around Jess's nipples, or the bite of Kendra's teeth into her skin.

So Kendra goes for all three. She thrusts her hips hard and fast against Jess's ass, feels the tight pull of Jess's cunt on the dildo; pinches and twists Jess's proud nipples; bites into Jess's shoulders until her teeth leave purple marks in the skin.

"Jesus fuck, I've needed this for so long, Kendra, wanted—" Her words devolve into a sharp cry.

"For how long?" Kendra says, wrenching Jess's nipples in the other direction. Jess lets out another bark.

"Feels like forever, except I didn't know, like it was in me but I didn't know its name and—*oh Kendra god yes that*," Jess hisses in response to Kendra's teeth on her earlobe.

Kendra fucks Jess frantically; the inner end of the dildo slams against Kendra's cervix with each thrust. She feels herself turning into jelly, knows she's going to come soon if she doesn't slow down. Jess can come a million times, but Kendra's almost always done after one or two, and she can feel already that the approaching one is going to be a game-ender, hitting her so hard she won't be able to move beyond it to the next crest.

Kendra slips her right hand between the harness and her skin to hold her end of the dildo still while the other end continues to hammer Jess. It's an awkward position, making it impossible to squeeze both of Jess's nipples at once. She almost loses her balance when she tries to put her fingers on Jess's other breast.

"Here, baby, I'll take care of it." Jess plants her head into the pillows to take the weight of her upper body and squeezes her own fingers around her nipples. "Just focus on fucking me."

So Kendra does—at least at first. She pounds the strap-on into Jess, thrusting her deeper into the pillows. She makes up for her inability to twist Jess's nipples by biting hard at the base of Jess's neck like a cat in heat.

But even with holding the strap-on, she's too close to coming. Impulsively, she does the only thing she can think of to stop the wave of pleasure from cresting: she uses her free hand to grapple at her own tit, twisting its tip suddenly, mercilessly, until the pain is so intense she can barely feel anything else.

"Oh fuck, baby," Jess cries, her hips swaying over the silicone dick, making it twist inside Kendra despite her best efforts. And suddenly the pain pounding through Kendra's breast becomes hot and exhilarating. It sears Kendra to her core.

Kendra lets go of the dildo and she thrusts forward, letting it rebound inside her as she plunges into Jess. She squeezes and twists both of her own areolas as the toy slams against her cervix.

Jess mutters a string of curses and encouragements.

"You ready to come again, Jess?" Kendra pants.

"Yes, baby. Make me come."

Blood rushes back painfully into Kendra's nipples when she lets go. It's just enough discomfort to keep her aware of her surroundings and focused on Jess's rising orgasm instead of her own. She skates her hands around Jess's torso, sliding them under Jess's hands to cup her breasts and clamp down on the swollen areolas.

"Come for me," Kendra growls, nipping at Jess's ear. "Now."

Jess cries out and fucks herself on the toy with relentless force. Her earlier orgasm was quiet and still. This one is ear shattering. Jess's shout rips through the air and makes the glass in the ceiling lamp ring. Kendra's isn't much quieter. Pleasure radiates out from her cervix in steady waves. She can't remember ever coming so hard before.

They're both too sensitive to keep the dildo inside of them when they're done. Jess uses her pelvic muscles to push her end out and helps Kendra undo the harness. They throw the entire contraption on the floor to deal with later, forgetting about it as soon as it's out of sight. Jess pulls Kendra close, their sweaty breasts mashed together. The air is redolent with the smell of sex. Kendra loves it.

"That was a nice new discovery," she says. "How long have you been keeping that secret?"

Jess sighs into Kendra's neck. "Honestly, I didn't realize I was. I mean, I always knew I got an endorphin rush from waxing and tweezing, and sometimes I got a little turned on. But I didn't know if the turn-on was the pain or the smooth skin."

"And now you know?"

Jess nods and the tip of her nose rubs against Kendra's skin. "There's something empowering about feeling pain and knowing that it won't actually hurt you."

"Huh. I hadn't thought of it that way." Kendra looks down at Jess's swollen areola. "Too bad hair only grows so fast. It'll be a while until I can tweeze you again."

"Yes, but . . . " Jess says, circling the pad of her index finger softly over Kendra's irritated nipple, "we could make room in this month's budget for a pair of nipple clamps."

"Or maybe," Kendra says, wincing at the touch, "we should invest in two."

BAUBLES
AND BEADS

Sacchi Green

Garish pink, purple, and green fingers of light from the midway groped between the buildings all the way to the horse barns. Some of the fair's rides and hucksters kept on as long as cash still smoldered in the pockets of the farm boys, but Carla shut down her balloon-dart concession at the official closing time. She could've handled the lingering customers by herself, most of them on the leering side of friendly and the slurring side of drunk, but my looming six-foot-two of crop-haired farm girl didn't hurt. We rolled down the canvas, secured it, and slipped away into the shadows.

Lights just as garish had seeped through skimpy curtains from the neon sign outside her motel room last night. I'd scarcely noticed, obsessed with Carla herself, the black-haired, blue-eyed, bad girl of my dreams.

She'd bound me to the bedposts with strings of flashy Mardi Gras beads, my prizes from her game, and challenged me NOT to break them no matter what she did. I'd almost managed it. And learned, first, how it felt to give up, give in, abandon my strength, my will, all the armor built up over the years. In the beginning I'd had to struggle not to strain against apparently flimsy bonds, but the more Carla forced pleasure into pain and pain into pleasure, the more both willpower and reflexes faded away. I floated somewhere beyond thought, drowning in pure sensation. When she tipped me over at last into a thrashing orgasm I must have broken those strands of beads, but it was a long time before I noticed them sprawled limply across the bed, and longer still before I saw that they were strung on strong nylon thread, knotted between each bead, every strand only broken at a single point.

So the second thing I learned, the most important, was not to assume that just because something looks flashy and cheap it must be flimsy.

It was my first time exploring the darker pleasures of sex, at least with someone who knew what she was doing. In grad school, studying veterinary medicine, my friends and I had plenty of access to barns, and ropes, and dim spaces deserted at night. I'd been invited to some secret sessions where we played, or rather played at being players, but it was strictly amateur night. Mostly clumsy flogging, and the occasional cracking of a whip, but no real sex to speak of. I'd known how to crack a whip without touching my horses' glossy hides since I was half grown, and could control my two-ton draft team with no tools but my voice and muscles, so floundering around in a hayloft with whips and floggers just seemed silly. So did the girls who couldn't take even a fraction of what I could have delivered—or give me a fraction of what I didn't even know I needed.

I still didn't pass up any chances to learn my way around women's bodies, including my own, and had a fine time of it, but Carla . . . well, "hot" didn't begin to cover the vibes she gave off. Something in the way she moved, and the way she played to the guys ogling her in her booth, wisecracking with sultry innuendos that didn't actually promise them anything. They never caught on when she got to bantering with me and really did promise more than I could imagine. Even my muscle-bound teen-aged brothers had no clue what I was up to. They'd finally given up on hovering within range of her seductive aura when I gave them extra money and told them I'd seen a swarm of girls from their high school on the prowl over by the Tilt-A-Whirl.

In a lull while her customers' attention turned to a dramatic scene between a guy and the girlfriend who dragged him away, Carla let me know that big dumb farm boys weren't her type, but a big farm girl—no "dumb" implied—might be right up her alley.

My wrists and ankles were still raw. My tenderer parts ached when I remembered the keen torments and even keener pleasures she'd put me through. But later, after I'd demonstrated my own grasp of the basics—and of her tender parts—and taken possession of the shiny beads, Carla had offered to meet me again tonight on my own ground to face any challenge I set, even if it meant getting up close and personal with horses that looked to her "big as elephants and twice as mean!"

Whatever I thought I'd known about women, Carla was a whole different story. A story turning out to be more complicated than I'd bargained for, but worth every bit of whatever it took. Last night she'd taught me more about myself than I'd ever faced up to before; tonight it was my turn to challenge Carla. Maybe even teach her a thing or two. And find out more about myself.

The horse barns faced east, away from the chaos of the midway and the crowds. I'd signed up for the overnight security shift, so once the guy on evening duty saw me coming, waved, and took off, there was nobody else around. There'd sure better not be.

A full moon was rising. Carla gazed up at it for a minute or two while I reached around from behind and fondled her sweet round breasts. A warm late-summer breeze raised tendrils of her hair to brush against my cheek. Moonlight intensified the hint of mystery I'd already sensed about her even in the glare of neon, an impression of layer upon hidden layer. I hoped for a chance to explore them all.

"Autumn's almost here," I murmured. "Plenty more fairs coming up. I'll be bringing my team to half a dozen or so. You'll be at Fryburg in Maine?"

"Maybe." She shrugged and stepped out of my embrace. "But bring on your challenge now, Ree."

She knew it would be about the horses. Yesterday, when I'd led my team out of the pulling ring and over to meet her, she couldn't hide her terror. Molly and Stark, great black Percherons, two thousand pounds each with hooves the size of pie plates. Any city girl would be scared. I'd backed the pair off, told her I'd meet her at ten at her carnival booth and moved on toward the barns, surprised at how much that lapse in Carla's femme-top self-possession excited me. A chink in her armor.

Now I leaned against the open barn door. "First, find out where I hid the beads."

Carla relaxed, back in her own territory. "Let's see.

Maybe here?" She probed the pockets of my shirt, managing even through the flannel to tweak nipples still sore from her clamps last night. Then she reached up under the shirt to squeeze my heavy breasts, sending lightning strikes deep into my cunt. I tried hard to control my breathing. "Or here?" She worked her hands into the front pockets of my jeans, finding the same tube of horse lube I'd used with her last night, then the rear pockets, with more squeezing. My hips began to shift. The look on my face must have given me away. Or maybe the catch in my breath.

"Aha." Her fingers went between my legs to knead the thick seam of my jeans into my crotch. "Are these beads in your pants, or are you just glad to see me?"

I could barely get any words out. "See . . . for yourself!" She wriggled a hand down inside belt, jeans, and briefs, found what she was looking for, and began sliding the strands through my slippery heat. I nearly lost it. One of those strands had been nestled even deeper the night before last, when I'd been supposed to be resting up before the final round of the draft horse competition, but could think only of her. Tonight the beads had been driving me wild for half an hour. Was I really so set on being in charge tonight?

I gritted my teeth and yanked her hand, clutching its wet ruby and peacock-green prizes, out into the night air. I'd retied them securely after breaking them last night. Even in the dim light from a single bulb inside the barn they glowed like a Rajah's treasure. Or . . . what was the right term? A Ranee's?

"Mmm." Carla ran them across her tongue before draping the strands around her neck so that they swayed across her breasts.

I drew a shuddering breath and turned away. "Now find the other two strands." I stepped into the barn. Carla hesitated, then, very slowly, followed.

Molly, in a roomy box stall just inside the entrance, leaned her great black head over the gate and whuffled a greeting. Her brother Stark, just across the way, merely dozed on.

"Molly, this is Carla. Carla, Molly." Molly lowered her nose politely to be petted. Carla jerked back, braced herself, then raised a tense hand. I knew her fear of the horses wouldn't last long, but it might at least soften her up a bit.

"Hello, Molly." Her voice wavered. The black nose dipped lower, snuffling at the green and ruby beads on Carla's chest and then at her hands. Carla jerked back again, then suddenly laughed. "You're smelling Ree on me! I guess that makes us all pals." She stroked the velvety nose tentatively. "And you're wearing beads, too!" The gleaming strands twined through the mane on either side of Molly's neck, the golden on the right and the purple on the left.

"You'll have to climb on the gate to reach them," I pointed out.

She shot me a dirty look, mounted the lower bars, and reached across and upward. Even then, if Molly hadn't been nuzzling her shoulder, the beads would have been too high for her to reach.

The first strand came loose easily. Carla climbed down, dangled it in front of me, then let it go when I gripped her wrist too hard for comfort. Yes, I definitely did want to be in charge, now that she had to meet my challenge. More was at stake than a tumble in the hay. Carla's chin went up almost imperceptibly—and then she lowered it, turned, and climbed back up on Molly's other side. Molly bent her head again cooperatively, but I gave a low whistle and she moved backward so that Carla couldn't reach no matter how far she tried to stretch.

"That's how I tell her to back off," I said conversationally as I pulled Carla's skirt up and panties down. "You want me to back off any time, just whistle. You do know how to whistle, don't you?"

She stopped reaching in vain for the beads, kicked off her panties and skirt, and thrust out her bare butt. Playing along, letting me get away with something, but taunting me just the same. I let the golden beads drift gently over each round, tempting cheek, drew them along the valley between, then whipped them suddenly across each side. Carla gripped the top of the gate and didn't look around. I swung them harder twice, slashing in diagonal strokes that left an intriguing latticework pattern. I'd tried whipping my own arm with the beads that morning, though, and knew how extra painful they could be, so I switched tactics. Breaking the skin would end things too soon.

Besides, I couldn't wait any longer to touch her directly. The heat of her skin, the sound of my bare hands striking her flesh, the tremors of her body, her musky scent intensifying by the second . . . I lost count of my strokes, intoxicated, high on power and lust, all the more when she began making guttural sounds interspersed with gasps. "It's . . . it's okay, Molly!" she got out as the horse twitched and shifted nervously.

I eased off, until she grated, "More, Ree, dammit!" twitching her hips to emphasize the demand.

"My territory, my rules! I decide what you get, and

how much, and when." I made a stab at sounding stern. It felt good. More than good.

Her muttered words were barely audible. "Yes Ree, all right, whatever you want . . . " Then, even more faintly, "Please . . . "

My hand came down hard again on her rounded, tantalizing butt, over and over. I wanted her to want more of that, and to want all the kneading and squeezing of her reddened flesh my fingers indulged in between bouts of spanking. I needed her to want those things, and to want them even more because they pleased me.

I struggled to keep some control over myself. A whack on a draft horse's rump just hard enough to get his attention could do real damage to a slender girl. I tried to gentle her again with slower strokes, but she shuddered and squirmed.

"Please . . . " Carla's whisper was low and tremulous now. "Don't stop . . . don't let me drop . . . " Whatever she meant, I was dead sure playing along had nothing to do with it anymore. She wasn't enduring the pain now so much as absorbing it, consuming it.

"Trust me," was all I thought of to say. I got one boot up onto the bottom rung of the gate and one arm around her waist, supporting her, never letting up but varying the rhythm of my hand. Her dark hair hung down on either side, exposing the pale nape of her neck. After a while I gave in to temptation, bent my head, kissed that tender, vulnerable skin and felt a tremor wash through her.

Then I bit down, just hard enough to leave my mark without drawing blood. That jolted her into shuddering motion. Her breath came harder, in gulps, then hard, wracking sobs. I lifted her down and managed to get to the folding chair beside the door and sit with her cradled against my shoulder until the heaving of her body subsided. She murmured something into my shirt that might have been, "Thank you . . . " and then raised her head just a little. "If only . . . I wish . . . "

I'd have done anything for her by then. "Wish what? Just tell me what you want!"

She shook her head, wiped her tear-streaked face against my shirt, seemed to pull herself together, and sat upright on my lap. The old Carla was back, cockiness muted, playing along, but any real vulnerability well hidden.

"Whatever *you* want, Ree." She pulled off a tank top, her only remaining garment, and started to unbutton my shirt with her teeth. My tits strained toward hers, just inches away. Suddenly her mouth changed course, toward the shirt pocket where I'd clumsily stuffed the strings of beads. Loops of each still dangled outside. Carla's tongue flicked the golden strand, drew it slowly all the way out and dropped it into her hand. My cunt clenched as though the beads had undulated right through it.

"You don't want to let these go to waste, do you?" Her tone was low, smooth, sultry.

The raw marks on my wrists from last night tingled. I hesitated. What did I want most? Carla wriggled seductively on my lap, but couldn't conceal a wince of pain. I stroked what I could reach of the superheated cheeks pressed against my thighs. That backside needed a rest from friction. More sitting wasn't an option.

"Across my lap. Now. On your stomach with your hands behind your back." I lifted her just enough to ease her movement, and had her wrists bound behind her in seconds with the golden beads. Nobody's better at one-handed knots than a horse handler.

I forced myself to take it slow. Two more strands of beads slid between those lovely moon-pale, red-striped cheeks—rolled lower into the hot, wet heat between her thighs—nudged at her hardened clit—until I couldn't stand to let the beads have all the fun. I got the tube of lube from my pocket, opened it with my teeth, lubed my hand, drew out the beads, and slid two fingers deep between Carla's folds. She arched into the pressure, moving frantically at first, needing more, more depth, more force, but I still teased her with retreat and advance and retreat, over ever more wet and slippery terrain, ignoring her wriggles and pleas for more until my own need forced my hand.

Faster, deeper, harder, her sounds and movements igniting my own body. Time had no meaning, only motion. My big hand raced to give her everything she wanted, everything she could take, everything I wanted her to have, until her body tightened around my fingers, pulsed to a relentless beat, then clenched even harder as the crescendo shook her.

Carla's sobs of release dwindled gradually to whimpers. I lifted her down to the sleeping bag I'd left spread on a mound of clean straw in the empty stall next to Molly's, lay down with her, and started all over again—with the added benefit of lips, tongue, full frontal contact, hands freed from beads, and my own thundering crescendo.

Much later Carla muttered drowsily, "I didn't get the other strand yet. I failed the challenge."

"That's okay." I pulled a rough horse blanket up over us. "Just never assume that because something looks extra big and strong, it must be scary."

"Maybe I'd like it to be scary, now and then."

I let her have the last word, unless you count Molly's gentle snort, and drifted into sleep. But only for a while.

"Ree!" Carla was straddling me, her old cocky, assertive self again. She'd retrieved the purple strand of beads from Molly's mane while I slept and bound them around my wrists, and now she whapped me across the chest with golden ones. "Molly and I want to go for a ride!" Meeting my challenge in full, then topping it.

"Okay," I said. "But for the sake of Molly's unblemished reputation, I'd just as soon you kept it inside this barn and the one next door." Even with my wrists tied I could make a stirrup with my hands for Carla's foot, and toss her high onto Molly's broad back.

It was a shame, really, that no one but me got to see a dark-haired, naked Lady Godiva ride a great black mare through the horse barns that unforgettable night at the county fair. Especially since I very much doubt that the original lady rode with strands of golden and royal-purple beads coiled inside her well-seasoned cunt.

That glorious sight turned out to be a parting gift. We slept again, clinging together, but when I woke in the morning Carla was gone. Gone from my arms, from the barn, from the fairgrounds, with nothing to tell me how to find her, and no sign of her at any of the other fairs that year. All I had left was a new sense of myself, searing memories of pleasure and pain, Carla's scent on Molly's back, and a faint voice murmuring in my dreams, "If only . . . I wish . . . "

I haven't given up wishing.

APPETITE

Emily Bingham

Pulling up in front of Lou's house has become a Pavlovian turn-on. The sight of the location of so much pleasure causes the center of me to light up. So there's a giddy skip in my step as I walk up the stairs to her door. With every iota of my body alight in anticipation, I knock and wait for it to open. That is until the seconds add up and I realize that opening isn't coming. My heart sinks; I'm confused and feeling exposed on this porch that's ordinarily a portal to a land of tender hedonism. I decide to slink back to my car, only noticing the paper taped to the door at the last second.

K: It's unlocked. Come in, undress, and sit.

The handwriting isn't familiar—in the age of texts and emails we've never exchanged penmanship—but instinctively I know it belongs to Lou. My breath catches as I nervously eye the door.

My hand trembles to twist the knob, wondering at the game she's instigated, but inside the house everything is warm and familiar. To my left, the coffee table I was once bound to with Saran wrap. To my right, the couch where we cuddle and fuck with equal frequency. Beneath me, the carpet's distinct texture I know from when I've been pressed facedown in it with my ass in the air. Straight ahead, the ottoman I've been spread-eagled on more times than I can count. But the living room doesn't seem to be on the menu this evening.

The smell of spices and baking bread draws me to the kitchen. This room has many happy memories attached to it as well; however, none of them are erotic. Lou is an accomplished cook, and the meals we share are so delicious as to be nearly orgasmic, but this is the one room of Lou's house where we've never fucked.

I grin to notice the lone wooden chair resting out of place at the center of the kitchen. It sits to the side of the wheeled island with its cutting board of ingredients abandoned mid-chop. This must be where I'm meant to sit.

Removing my clothes, I drape them over the chair back, glad to be unwrapping from my autumn layers in Lou's steamy kitchen. It seems a shame to shimmy out of the lacy bra and matching panties that I bought specifically for Lou to enjoy, but the note said to undress, so I do, noticing a stirring behind me as I finish folding my clothes.

Suddenly I'm aware of having been observed during my entire unintentional striptease. This explains the half-chopped veggies; Lou must have gone into hiding when my footsteps announced my arrival. But rather than turning to look, I continue to pretend not to notice her company while setting aside my clothes and sitting to wait.

When Lou approaches the chair, putting her fingers

over my eyes, I'm momentarily startled but the texture of those rough hands and the smell of her skin soon soothe me. Then the deep voice that's the vehicle I follow into so many fantasies whispers in my ear, "Hello, sexy."

I reach to run my hands along strong arms, melting back into my lover, ready for anything. Trusting and relaxed, my body purrs with delight in this preamble to pleasure.

Soon she guides my hands to my sides and the game begins. Always thrilled to be bound, I keep still while feeling my wrists encapsulated by the buttery soft cuffs Lou and I bought years ago. We use these restraints so regularly that the leather is molded to the shape of my body. I issue a moan of delight as both my hands are cuffed and then clipped to the chair's arms. Lou stands behind me, continuing to remain hidden.

When she moves into my vision I take in the body that makes my lover so handsome, starting with the swell of her shoulders. Then there's the curve of her chest, which even while pinned down by a binder hints at the abundance of breasts that I envy and Lou loathes. And the bulge at the fly of her tight pants lets me know Lou is packing.

Running my eyes back up her body, our eyes meet; hers are shocking hazel points of intensity, mine an opposite and eager blue ringed by the beginning of the crow's feet that Lou enjoys kissing tenderly. We hold this gaze until my inability to read my future in Lou's eyes makes me shy. I gaze at the floor near her shiny black boots hearing, "Mmm, that's my lovely girl."

She's aware I love to hate being called this. It's been decades since I could reasonably pass for a girl. But the tenderness and lust I feel for Lou has made me young again. As if youth is contagious. As if each time she dives between my legs, it takes years off my age. I always leave her with a bounce in my step. And there is an intensity to our relationship that I haven't felt since college. Perhaps it's the trappings of lectures and note taking, piles of women's and gender studies books piled in the office, as well as the frequent "I can't tonight, love, gotta study," that have me acting—through osmosis—like a schoolgirl.

Her hand drifts down my face, pausing at my chin only to linger at my throat, fingers gripping the soft meat of my neck, holding my life and breath in her palm. Our pulses merge as Lou tips my head back so we're eye to eye. Predatorily she comes close; mouth open with such menace I could swear Lou has fangs. She holds eye contact, breathing me in only to back away with a suddenness that makes me gasp.

Lou smiles, voice still imbued with danger. "You stay there; I'm going to finish cooking."

My senses are turned up to eleven with excitement, so that I'm already wet and wiggling on the chair. I almost hate her knowing me so well that she's aware a hand on my neck makes my heart skip. Every damn time.

I breathe heavily while watching Lou chopping with her back to me; listening to the gas of the stove whistle as it's turned on, a pan placed over the heat at the ready. The oil sizzles over the flame, awaiting Lou, until she tosses a palm full of garlic in with a hiss. Agitating the aromatic herb, Lou fills the room with a scent that has me near drooling. Left here bound with nothing but the sight of Lou's ample curves for amusement, I melt into the chair, enjoying the view and the smells of her expert cooking.

From the oven she pulls pillows of steaming bread dappled with poppy seeds that resemble freckles. I watch the boules, set aside to cool, begin to sink slightly in the center, a sign they've been kneaded and allowed to rise properly. An image of the heels of Lou's strong hands working repeatedly through the soft dough fills my mind. In awe, I've watched her perform this essential ritual of bread-making many times. I've also been under the palms of those hands so she could knead at the muscles of my back, working out the stress of life until I writhe in pleasure-pain.

Next, a green vegetable enters the oven. Closing the door with a creak and a slam, Lou looks at me over her shoulder with a smile, "Almost done. You hungry?"

I spread my thighs exposing my cunt. If she can tease me I'll return the favor. "Ravenous."

Lou responds with a raised eyebrow while unwrapping chicken pieces from butcher's paper to add to the frying pan. The sizzle and pop of fat has my stomach rumbling. I can't tell if I'm more eager for dinner or to become Lou's meal.

Soon the stove is clicked off; she sprinkles ribbons of fresh basil over the meat, pulls the veggies from the oven, and plates the feast. The ideally browned chicken nestles next to roasted peaches, asparagus, and thick slabs of rustic bread with fresh butter, all of it plated to resemble a work of art.

Lou pours an effervescent white wine into a glass and retrieves a place setting. All this I watch with silent curiosity.

She sits at the countertop, making a show of sipping the wine, then reaching to grasp the knife and fork. Before cutting the meat, Lou glances in my direction across the room where I'm pouting, feeling left out. "Just kidding. This is all for you, darling."

Plate in hand, Lou uses the other to pull a chair in front of me. I close my thighs to make room for Lou to come nearer but she shakes her head, using a foot to wedge my thighs open.

"Stay."

I feel like a piece of meat myself as she eyes me, knife in hand. Happily, it's dinner that sharp blade is meant for; she cuts a thin slice of chicken, then a sliver of peach, spearing them together and lifting the cutlery in my direction. Parting my lips, I accept the food. Tender, juicy, and garlicky this dish feels like summer on the tongue. Moaning, I close my eyes and slowly take it in.

"You like?"

"Very much so, thank you."

Kissing my forehead Lou says, "You are quite welcome, you know how much I love to cook for you. Such a willing victim to my experiments. All of them." She winks at me before preparing another forkful. I watch her chew until her eyes light up as she makes a self-congratulatory nod of approval.

I giggle in excitement as Lou pulls apart a piece of decadently thick bread into a bite-sized morsel. She drags it through the juice of herbed peach and chicken glaze, sopping up the liquid into the white of the bread's leavened interior. Longing for a taste the moment it's offered I reach forward as far as my bonds allow. The delicate crust surrounds a soft, juice-dampened center. This crisp flake gives way to the perfectly tender crumb, all of it melting on my tongue.

"Uh, Lou, sweet Jesus that's amazing bread."

Lou portions out another piece that she pops in her mouth, and nods. "Yes it is. New recipe and it's a keeper. Just like you."

This makes me blush. Lou knows exactly what she's doing: the sweet talk, the teasing, the perfect meal, keeping me exposed to embarrass me slightly. She keeps on hitting all the buttons that make me lust for her.

Cutting the delicate length of an asparagus stalk, Lou traps it on the fork and throws me off by consuming it before creating another serving for me. This tease is so frustrating that I struggle against the cuffs, anxious to taste the next morsel of Lou's creation.

"Aw, life is tough for you." Lou guides the citrus-drizzled, salty vegetable into my mouth, placating my hunger, this greedy need she opens up in me when she's near. For now I'm trapped and at her mercy as she continues this pattern of preparing mouthfuls of delicious food, but my lust will soon be transferred to my unending desire for Lou's body. Her hands, mouth, tongue, fingers, skin: I long for them all to be mine.

She alternates between the dishes she's prepared until I'm satisfied. Then moaning, she finishes off the plate as I watch, endeared by the simple pleasure of her love for food. Lou washes the dishes, stores the leftovers, and puts everything in its place so that I'm sure it's time for me to be released. Instead Lou turns the oven on and walks to me, her lips on my ear and hands on my thighs, and whispers, "Don't go anywhere."

"Okay." My body flushes and my skin thrums, longing for more of Lou's touch.

Her boots thump across the living room and while

listening for any hint of what comes next I'm keenly aware of the wetness between my thighs. When Lou finally returns, she kneels in front of me, between my parted legs, while looking up my naked body, into my eyes. Smiling nervously, I long for her to act, unable to endure the anticipation any longer. Lou knows this: I'm a jump-and-ask-questions-later type, so it's torture for me to sit still and wait.

That sly grin returns as she runs one hand up my thigh, the other hidden behind her back. She tickles her way to my cunt and continues to tease. Rather than diving in Lou caresses my labia, causing me to buck into her hand with need.

"Stay!" Lou says as she slaps my thigh hard with a sting that forces me back into the desired position. "Understand?"

I nod and she returns to where she left off, stroking my lower lips. All the while I groan and plead wordlessly. "Someone is still hungry," she says, running a finger across my wetness, and I shake my head to the affirmative again.

Lou brings her other hand between us, revealing a small silver bullet vibrator. She slides the bullet inside me, places the control on the chair between my parted legs, and bares her teeth ferociously. I know I'm in trouble.

Gradually Lou thumbs the power switch up, the buzz of the vibrator increasing and throbbing through my cunt. When I arch my back into the chair, closing my eyes to the pleasure, Lou knows she's found the sweet spot and speed to get me going. I'm so on edge already that it's nearly enough to make me orgasm. The teasing has me crazed with lust, so that I'm thrusting my hips to encourage the pressure of the vibrator into my pleasure centers.

I'm ready to pass over the edge when I feel Lou's hand on my throat again, pulling me back to reality. "Don't you dare."

"Please?" I try. Lou tightens her grasp for emphasis.

"If you come before dessert is ready, you'll be in so much trouble."

I whimper as Lou walks to the stove. She doubles back and there's that look again. Lou turns the vibrator up just enough to drive me mad. Groaning desperately, I can't imagine resisting the urge to come much longer. Lou chuckles to watch my struggle. Dessert better be a strawberry or there's no way I'll be able to hold out.

She places two ramekins in the preheated oven. I know there's only one thing Lou makes in these dishes, my favorite treat: a decadent cake with a center of liquid chocolate. It feels cruel, her using my desires against me, pitting chocolate and orgasms in a battle of wills.

Knowing that those cakes take twelve minutes to cook, I try centering myself to muster the willpower to endure this torment as long as Lou desires. She closes the oven and leans against it, setting the timer while smiling knowingly. "Well, what shall we do to pass the time?"

I'm so focused on thinking of something, anything, other than how much I need to come that I can't respond. She watches me, sweaty and shaking, feeling as if I've run a marathon. "Aw, no smart-ass response?" I shake my head and look at her pleadingly. "You look stressed, let me help you."

Lou knows she isn't playing fair to run her fingers down my shoulders and arms. This only heightens my lust and already I'm so wet I worry the bullet will pop out of me to shoot across the room.

I look at my nemesis, the oven, hoping to make time pass faster. Lou, not to be ignored, ups the ante by running her hands down my breasts. My focus switches to admiring the contrast of her dark fingers on my moon-tan white skin, adoring the numerous differences between us: color, age, lifestyle, and attitude. Opposites do seem to attract and hard. But now that attraction is working against me.

"Is there a problem?" Lou pinches my nipple, shooting a jolt of pleasure to my cunt that nearly makes me come without warning. I dart Lou a look of disproval while panting. "What's the matter?" Her devious fingers brush my hips and angle lower, grazing my bush.

Groaning, I try to close my legs, knowing even as I do that it's not going to help. Lou slaps at my inner thighs hard, forcing them open again. "What did I say?" I whimper but she doesn't relent; instead she massages my cunt and clit expertly. I want to disappear into the chair or will away the need to orgasm but I can't, not with her touching me with such intensity.

"I can't . . . uh . . . oh fuck, Lou . . . you're gonna . . . " Lou quickens the pace. Now I'm certain she's set me up to fail and feel no remorse about letting myself go. Giving myself over to the vibration, I moan and thrust against Lou's hand. Meeting her fingers to undulate into the seat, I'm wiggling uncontrollably, my cunt muscles grasping at the vibrator as it pushes me over the edge repeatedly.

Lou continues fingering my clit while grinning. She leans in and whispers, "Naughty, naughty, now you're going to have to suck me off."

That's a punishment? I think. The promise of having Lou inside me causes another wave of orgasm.

Lou's erect cock appears for me to wrap my lips around. The head of the slick silicone member slips down my throat until much to Lou's delight I'm gagging. She grabs the back of my head to force her dick deeper. My body shudders and tears roll down my cheeks. Lou thrusts roughly, intensifying my gagging until I have to pull away to suck in a full breath. Another wave of orgasm passes through me.

"You dirty cock-sucking slut."

Lou smiles, as I lean in to once again bob against her dick. Hoping to see her get off, I push the base against Lou's crotch to transfer my movements into her body. It's like a very grown-up version of playing make-believe. If we both pretend that this cock is real then magical things happen. It certainly feels genuine, a very important part of my lover, imbued with so much pleasure-giving desire for both of us. It's not some prop.

Lou grabs my nipples to pull me forward as motivation to not pull away, not even for a breath, because the pain would be too intense. I'm sputtering and gagging, drool and tears running down my face until my chest is glistening with my own bodily fluids.

"You're so pretty right now." The look in her eyes is pure admiration as I make a disaster of my mascara. Even as I'm sniffling and sweating, I know she means it, getting off on the mess she's made of me.

When the timer goes off, Lou tweaks my nipples until I force myself to pull away and break her grasp, instinctively needing to cry out at her cruelty. Lou giggles, throws her head back, and glides her hand between her legs. She gestures for me to continue sucking and I'm more than happy to bob back and forth on her cock as the alarm sounds urgently throughout the kitchen.

Between her ministrations and my attention to her shaft, Lou comes, her knees melting in delight. The shuddering of her body is so intense she holds on to my shoulders so as to not tip over. I look up the expanse of her chest to the bliss on her face. My lover is so handsome I almost want to come again, but I'm having too much fun watching her get off so I focus on pleasing her.

As soon as the peak of her pleasure subsides, Lou pets my head and walks away to remove the cakes from the oven. At last the alarm is silenced and she waggles her cock at me salaciously from afar. "Ready for something sweet?"

I can't tell whether she means her dick or the cake, but starving for either, or both, I say, "Fuck, yes!"

BITCH SLAP

Sir Manther

As soon as we're both over the threshold, the door shut behind us, she grabs me by my tie and pulls me toward her. She holds me there for a teasing moment, a glimmer of mocking delight playing around her eyes and smile, before reeling me in all the way. The moment her mouth touches mine, it already feels like we're fucking. This isn't foreplay or some kind of introduction, it's just straight-up sex: heat, friction, penetration. Our tongues are thrust deep inside each other's throats, our teeth pressing forcefully through the flesh of our lips. There is a ferocity to our movements, as though we are snarling through our wide-open mouths, eating each other alive.

I feel one of her hands trace the front of my shirt, pulling open the buttons. She reaches inside, ignoring my tits, and grabs my waist with a forceful caress. Her fingers drift up my torso, the sides of her nails scraping as she presses into the divot between each rib. Reaching lower, she grips the curved ridges just above my pants, what most people would mistakenly call hip bones, but we both know better, these aren't joints, they're the pelvic wings, and when she touches them, I'm flying. With one arm, I circle her body, my hand finding entry between her shirt and pants, fingers grazing the top of her ass, applying a dancing pattern of pressure. As the tips of my fingers register the sensation of her skin, something begins to come alive between my legs, a liquid creature pulsing with heat.

She stops kissing me so fast it takes a moment for me to catch up, and I'm still trying to recover myself when, grinning, she hands me my tie, loose and unknotted. I didn't notice her untying it. She pushes my opened shirt off my shoulders, teasingly snaps the waistband of my trousers with one finger. I hasten to remove the rest of my clothes. Beside me, she does the same.

She doesn't look at me as we are undressing, but I can't help stealing a glance at her. It's not the first time I've seen her naked; we were friends years ago in college and spent many warm evenings skinny-dipping in the river that ran through town. I wanted her that whole time, of course. Whether she knew it or not, I can't say, and I never had the courage to ask. We're not friends anymore, but her magnificence is no less tantalizing. You won't see a body like hers in magazines, but to me, she's everything I want in a woman and more. This girl doesn't need a tight, hard body to prove she's tough as nails. She catches me looking, and I can see in her face that I will pay later for my lack of discretion.

Freed from our clothes, we stand together by the edge of the bed like swimmers poised to enter a pool. She pushes me in. I struggle for a minute, not quite able to regain my balance, but manage to grab on to her as we tumble down onto the mattress. I squirm and thrash until I'm on top, her body under mine. I'm not playing nice. One of my thighs presses between hers, and I start to move, thrusting into her, rubbing myself against her hip.

She doesn't protest or try to wrestle me down. Instead, she brings her forearms up around my back, hands gripping my shoulders. Even though we haven't moved, even though her body is still below me, she is the one setting the pace now, ensuring that I harbor no illusions of control.

I can feel her wetness and mine as we move together, gathering momentum. Tensing my quadriceps until they scream, I ride her hard, like my leg is a cock, hitting her right where I know she'll feel it most.

Her climax is silent, but her breath comes in gasps and her body arches and struggles. I dated a girl once who used to say my name when she came, or sometimes "I love you." I hated this. The girl beneath me now is thrashing and shuddering, but I'm not quite there, so I tighten my own grip and don't let up until my clit is hard as a diamond and beginning to tingle. The orgasm spreads outward through me in a kaleidoscope of colors and textures that I know she cannot see. I'm quiet too when I come. There's no way for me to share with her or anyone else these visions that fill me in the highest moments of sexual ecstasy, and right now, I am enjoying this selfishness.

We both collapse onto the mattress, sprawled haphazardly, bodies overlapping slightly. I become aware of the sensation of her hair lying against my shoulder, so fine and silky that I almost can't feel it. Her tattoos have multiplied since I saw her last, and I can make out a single word done in white ink across her collarbone, lines of black slanting script tracing her rib cage, but it's too dark in here for me to read them. The way that we are lying together, halfway intertwined, could be almost tender, but I know better. Sitting up, I look her hard in the eye, even though I know she can't see me in the dimness, and ask, "Do you trust me?"

I can tell by the way her posture changes, becoming instantly alert, that she understands exactly what I mean.

"Yes."

Standing up, I'm suddenly nervous. I've never done this before, and I'm not sure if she has either, but I vowed years ago that if I ever had the chance, I would do it to her. Scanning the room, I see my discarded clothes lying in a pile. It won't be an expert job, not even close, but hopefully she'll go with it.

I had been wearing kneesocks, and I fasten one around each of her ankles, attaching the other ends to the foot of the bed. She is resting on her back, and I use my necktie to bind her wrists together, her arms extended, hands above her head. Her eyes follow my movements, but otherwise she is still. Waiting.

Finished, I pause and evaluate my handiwork. I know she could free herself if she really wanted to, but she has agreed to this, allowed herself to be vulnerable, given me the illusion that she can be contained. The power I have over her in this moment is only that which she has explicitly granted me, for the sake of both of our pleasure.

Slowly, I lay myself over her, feeling the delicious sensation of her skin against mine, maximizing the interface of our surface areas. I run the point of my canine tooth along the edge of her clavicle, lightly at first, then harder. Moving down her body, my fingers find her nipple and dance around its perimeter before grabbing and pinching it sharply, twisting a little. She flinches, an inhale catching in her throat, and I smile.

I repeat the motion with my teeth across the raised edges of her pelvic bones. Her steely self-possession is as acute as ever, but I hear a subtle quickening in the rhythm of her breathing. Tugging hard on her other nipple, I bite her hip again, increasing the pressure until I can see the imprints of my incisors on her skin, a curved smile of marks. A drop of blood wells in one of the indentations, and I push it away with my thumb, not sure if she has noticed. Regardless, I can smell her arousal, and I know neither of us feels like waiting any longer. Grabbing her ass with both hands, I move to her center, teasing her clit with firm, relentless strokes. I can feel the energy building under my tongue, converging to a point and then expanding in forceful pulses. A ripple passes up her body, then another and another, a flagellated, whiplike motion. I don't let up until she is limp and panting.

Slowly, I untie her ankles and wrists. She moves her hands and feet slightly, readjusting to their freedom, as I sit down beside her. Pulling herself upright, she gives me a fast, hard kiss, less *thank you,* more *you're welcome.* Unable to stop myself, I lower my head to nuzzle her neck.

In a single gesture, she flips my body, shoving me down into the bed. Helpless, I stare up into her face. She's grinning, her hands on my shoulders, eyes locked into mine. I know it's my turn, though what exactly she has in mind remains a mystery. A slight shiver of fear passes through me, but it's almost fully overshadowed by my enjoyment at feeling her unapologetically substantial form pressing down on me from above.

She too asks only a single question.

"Do you want to watch?"

"No."

She blindfolds me with my tie. I lie there for a moment, adjusting to this greater darkness within darkness, not knowing what will come next.

The sting of her first slap brands me across the side of my hip, the impacted skin awakening at her touch. She continues with an onslaught of openhanded smacks all across my body, each blow forceful and intentional, the way we used to slap each other as a chaser after a long pull from a passed bottle of whiskey. The throbbing echoes of her touch crisscross and overlap across my body, and behind my blindfold I can picture the marks on my flesh, a sensory map of Technicolor sensation traversing the topography of my arms, legs, and torso. This isn't pleasure from pain or painful pleasure; rather, the two are synonymous, indistinguishable. She is an artist, stimulating every sense of my synesthetic landscape, bringing me to life, painting me from the outside inward.

Without warning, she shoves her knee into my crotch and I come at once. A small cry escapes my throat, the sound one of surprise as much as pleasure. I've never come this way before, instantaneously, without any preamble of velocity and acceleration, didn't think it was possible for my body to so drastically redefine the laws of physics. The arousal flashes across the impressions left by her hands, pulsating patterns of color and sensation. No one has ever made me feel like this before. My orgasm crashes through me in lurching waves, finally descending back into the motionless reality of my spent body sprawled across the bed.

When I have finally regained composure, I open my eyes to realize that she has removed my blindfold. She sits on one side of the bed, running her right thumb lightly across her left palm. I don't have the words to tell her my gratitude, to express how much I needed this, have always needed it I guess. To be fucked by someone who could see through the muscles, the men's clothing, the advanced degrees, someone who knew me before all of that and wasn't afraid to possess me, fully and without remorse.

Looking over at me, a smile slips across her face, and she gestures with her head toward the shower, then stands and walks in that direction. We're finished here, I understand, and it would be pointless to protest.

I follow her into the bathroom. Under the bright overhead light, I can see her body in its entirety, can finally read the verses adorning the curves of her flesh. She is exquisite, every inch a masterpiece, and I feel a momentary sadness that I will never, can never, call her my own. Nor could anyone for that matter. But the feeling passes, and we step into the shower.

Her hands trace my shoulders and sides as she admires my own ink work, which has also increased in the years we've been apart. The colorful images announce themselves from my skin, each one the signature of choice and defiance, my best attempts to claim this body as my own. I can feel her approval in the lingering caress of her fingertips, outlining each design as if to animate its static contours.

The water flows over us, less a baptism than a rainstorm, bringing relief but not clarity. I reach my hand out to trace her hair back behind one ear, wanting to feel its silky length while I still have the chance. It's longer now than I've ever seen it before, though there are still no earrings in her ears, nor the empty holes that would indicate a secondary absence. She turns to face me, one eye flashing me a mischievous wink, and then she presses me up against the shower wall, lips whispering and teeth nipping down the side of my neck as I nearly dissolve in pleasure. When we step, dripping, onto the tile floor, I catch a glimpse of myself in the mirror and see a crimson mark on my throat that would be visible from a mile away. I don't know how I'll be able to explain this one at work tomorrow, but right now I can't think past the elation of her touch.

She dries herself quickly, shaking water out of each ear. We dress in silence. As I push the last button of my shirt through its hole, she approaches, holding my tie, and I let her tie it around my throat. I want to say something, anything, everything, but my mind is oversaturated, the thoughts too densely packed to allow the linear structure of a sentence to take shape. She expertly knots the silky fabric, giving me a tug and smirk to show she's finished with it.

We walk outside into the fading afternoon, and I am instantly and profoundly disoriented, as if I'm leaving the theater after an early movie, shocked to find that out here there is still daylight. The sky looks dusty and orange, the imposing geometry of skyscrapers silhouetted in the distance. Trash blows and scuffs in the gutters.

I turn toward her. Start to speak, trying to find at least a few words to leave her with, to express how much this meant, but my lips and brain are still useless. She tilts her head, surveying me casually. Slowly, she raises one hand and then abruptly slaps me hard once more, full across the face. The moment her fingers make contact, I come again, light and electricity exploding across the hand-shaped echoes she has left all over my skin. I stumble back against a wall, my body flashing like a silent neon sign, a private fireworks finale, the climax entirely invisible to the people walking past, intent on their own journeys.

It takes me half a minute to emerge from the fog of shock and arousal to find that she has left me there alone on the sidewalk. I gape after her retreating form, and she turns her head slightly, flashing me a Cheshire cat smile, before continuing on her way.

ALOHA À TROIS

Kathleen Tudor

I might love my job, but I was still out the door at 5:03 p.m., my blazeróo tucked over my arm to let the sun kiss my shoulders. It had been three weeks since I'd moved to Hawaii, and my routine was beginning to settle. I'd drive home, change into something more suited to the island, and head straight back out again, sometimes to jog in the wet sand and cool breezes, and other days with a book in hand to find a corner of paradise in which to lose myself.

Today was different, though. I drove home and changed as usual, but where I would normally walk to one of the closest beaches, this time I drove across town to park at a familiar resort. I took a deep breath of salty air, turned my face to the warmth of the evening sun, and then started for the sand, angling away from the resort and toward a quieter stretch. Around a bend, a group of local surfers had set up camp, some lounging and chatting while others charged the waves.

It didn't take me long to spot her among them. Anani:

the Polynesian goddess who'd spent ten sun-kissed, perfect days healing my broken heart before releasing me back to real life.

I'd never really gone back, though. Or at least, a part of me had remained on the island, pinned to Hawaii by the beauty, the peace, and the gentle touch of a woman with a big heart and love to spare.

I settled in easily, sitting straight in the sand and watching the surfers bob with the gentle swells, waiting for their ride. One of the men joined me a minute later. "Hey, you new around here?" His grin was welcoming, and I smiled back.

"Sort of. I've been here before . . . I was one of Anani's lost kittens once upon a time." That's what her friends called us—the women, fragile or needy or sad, who Anani gathered to herself, comforted, and released.

"Oh." His expression hadn't exactly become cold, but it was suddenly guarded.

"Don't worry," I told him. "I don't expect anything. I just want to see." *What* exactly I wanted to see was open to interpretation. See her? See if I could persuade her to be mine? See if I'd remained trapped in a corner of her heart the way she had been in mine? "Just see."

He shrugged, granted me a small smile, and took off for the water, scooping up his board on the way. I lay back, relaxing into the sunshine like a hot bath, and let the sound of the surf lull me into a doze.

Some time passed before I heard a familiar voice. "You look more relaxed this time."

When I opened my eyes, the sun burned behind Anani like a halo, and I grinned at the image. "Much more," I agreed, sitting up. "But you look just the same."

Anani laughed and sat beside me. "Couldn't stay away?"

"Not at all. From Hawaii or from you, I guess. I hope that's okay."

She took my hand, and even though she was still wet from the sea, her hand was warm in mine. "I told you before that I'm no good at relationships, sweet girl, but that doesn't mean we can't have today."

"Today's a good start."

"Where are you staying?" she asked, her voice as thick and sweet as warm honey.

"I'll drive you."

She loaded her board into her friend's truck, pulled a loose dress on over her bathing suit, and followed me to the resort's parking lot. "I'm Rachel, by the way. I know you make a lot of friends."

"I remember," she said, but with the mischief behind her smile, I couldn't tell if it was true or not. It didn't matter.

I parked the car and we met in front of the hood, our hands coming together like they belonged entwined as I led her toward the concrete steps up to my apartment. She stepped in once I'd unlocked the door, and her eyebrows rose at the sight of boxes half unpacked.

"This isn't some Air BnB place, is it." Not quite a question.

"All mine," I replied, wondering what she'd make of it. "It's still a bit of a mess out here, but the bedroom is all finished."

She grinned. "Well, let's go see, then." She pulled the dress off on her way, and I followed, my heart starting to pound at the sight of her beautiful surfer's body. She turned the corner to step into my bedroom and I pulled my own dress off and tossed it aside as I went to meet her.

Anani had shed her top in the seconds she'd been out of sight, and she stood turning in the center of my bedroom, her small, firm breasts inviting my caress. "It's lovely," she said.

"You're lovely." Maybe even more than I had remembered. I stepped forward, one hand lifting to cup her breast as I pulled her against me with the other. I wished in that moment that I'd paused to take off my own bra, but as her salty-sweet kiss burned through my veins, I knew I couldn't have waited another moment to taste her.

She moaned into my kiss and her body swayed into mine like the palm trees outside, stroked by the wind. Her nipple beaded hard under my touch and I teased my palm across it gently before rolling it between my fingers to make her gasp. It also made her throw her head back, so I took advantage of my access to the dark, salty column of her neck, kissing my way from her jawline to the hollow of her throat. She reached around me to unclasp my bra as I journeyed down her skin, and I sighed when the bra fell away and the weight of my breasts hung free, soon caught up in her eager hands.

It was my turn to gasp and moan as Anani kneaded my breasts with a touch that alternated between firm and gentle, making heat rise in my belly. "Come to bed." I skimmed out of my panties as I stepped back and she shimmied out of her bikini bottom before eagerly pressing her body over mine. Her skin was warm against mine, soft, but not delicate. She was lithe muscle all over, and I ran my hands over her firm skin, sighing as her muscles contracted beneath my palms.

She kissed me, this time taking charge. It was like that first burst of Hawaiian afternoon after a day in the sterile air-conditioning of the office. Refreshing. Invigorating. With warmth that spreads all through your body . . .

Anani shifted so that her thigh pressed against the slick heat of my pussy and I groaned and arched into the contact. Somewhere deep inside, I felt like I had been waiting ages for just this moment, and now that it was here, it was perfect. She was perfect. She moved against me, as rhythmic and inevitable as the crashing waves, and a tide rose within me, sweeping me away. I reached between us to seek her center and found her wet folds slippery and hungry for my touch. When I found the pearl of her clit she moaned, but her rhythm didn't change. She ground against me, driving me crazy. I gasped and writhed beneath her, a soft keening caught in my throat, and I let it wash me away.

Anani soon followed, her cries high and sweet as she came. I held myself still as she rubbed gently against my fingers, slowly bringing herself down.

"That was beautiful," she said as she eased herself down beside me.

"Do you want more?" It was a loaded question, and one she evaded.

"What I want is a nap!"

I laughed, but with her tucked warmly against my side, sleep was soon irresistible. And so we dozed.

We woke at nearly nine, both of us starving and a little bemused at having slept so long. "Is it too late for me to take you to dinner?" I asked.

"Not if we go now," she said with a playful shrug. "And if you let me borrow some clothes!"

We were tucked into a local restaurant twenty minutes later. A part of me wanted to avoid the hard discussions, but they would still be there haunting me if I tried to ignore them. "We should talk about what it means. Me living here."

Anani scrunched up her face like a recalcitrant child, but what she said was only, "I told you once that I'm no good at relationships."

I wondered if she remembered because I'd made an impression on her, or because it was something she said to all of the little lost kittens she adopted on her beach-combing excursions. "All relationships? Or just monoga-mous ones?" There it was. The thing I had spent a year pondering, exploring, accepting, and even enjoying.

Anani blinked, and when her pause had extended long enough, she was granted further amnesty by the arrival of our entrees. I waited as she picked at her pork and rice, determined not to rush this. Rush her.

She surprised me by answering with, "Did you move here for me?" I could barely hear her over the live music playing at the other side of the restaurant; I couldn't read her tone.

I thought for a moment, wanting to give my most honest answer. "I thought about you a lot," I began, chewing the tip of my thumb instead of my meal. "You . . . inspired me. But you didn't drive me here. I'd like to try to find a way we could be happy together, but if that's not going to work, I hope we can at least be friends."

She stole one of my sweet potato fries. "Friends with benefits?"

"Polyamory can be like that," I agreed casually. It was hard to be so outwardly relaxed when my heart was flut-tering, but I didn't want to pressure her. "Why shouldn't we try?"

She spent the next week treating me like one of her vacation girls, lavishing me with attention in the evenings and making love to me until we were both limp with satisfaction. When her texts and invitations started to feel more rote than enthusiastic, I went to meet her at her beach.

"Go," I said, kissing her lightly and pushing her away. "Go hide away from me for a while, or find a lost kitten to heal. Take the space you need."

"You don't mean that," she said, sighing in concert with the waves.

"I mean it. I'm going home. Don't call me until you're really ready." I stepped closer again, just long enough to press her in a warm, brief hug. Then I smiled, turned my back, and walked away.

Anani called me three days later. "I met a woman," she said.

"Will you tell me about her?"

"She's a stunning black woman—her skin is even darker than mine. And she's a lawyer. She's getting a divorce and she came here to celebrate—and maybe to mourn."

I laughed. "I bet you made her vacation memorable."

Anani hesitated. "I think so." Another pause, longer. "I hope I did."

"You always do. You made my breakup feel like a beginning instead of an end. Hell, you turned it *into* a beginning."

"You're really not angry, are you?" she asked, and her voice was still so cautious that my heart caught.

"No, sweetheart," I said, lowering my voice. "I want you to enjoy making your lawyer-divorcee purr."

There was only a short pause this time, and then, "She goes home in two days. Can I see you? After?"

"Of course."

Anani had tested her bonds and found them pleasantly flexible. She spent most of the night after her lawyer went home making her pleasure very, very evident.

Soon we had a pattern: we would have a very normal week or two as a couple, and then Anani's attention would fade and she would ghost away, sometimes for as much as a week. When her temporary lovers flew home, she would find me, and the passion she unleashed would often leave me dazed and bleary at work the next day—not that I was complaining.

One afternoon my phone buzzed just as I was walking out of work. It had only been three days since I'd last spent time with her, but sometimes it was just that fast. *Can I see you tonight?*

I smiled at my phone as I walked to the car. *I'll be reading in the courtyard. Come over.*

To my surprise, she didn't show up alone. I was curled in a lounge chair in the inner courtyard of my apartment complex when Anani ushered a bronzed beauty in. The other woman had short, dark curls and her skin practically glowed, though I couldn't tell if it was sun-kissed or naturally tan.

"Rachel, this is Chloe," she said, and the breathtaking woman—Chloe—smiled brightly and put out a hand. I quickly dropped the marker into my book to take it, and was surprised when Chloe held on, stepping closer.

"I don't mean to presume," she said, and though her grip was loose enough that I could have pulled away, I didn't. "Anani told me about your arrangement, and I told her that I'd really like to meet you."

"To make sure everything is above board?" I'd met some in the poly community who were fastidious about checking in person, but I already knew deep down that that wasn't why she was here.

Chloe shifted, smiling. "Because Anani makes you sound so . . . delightful."

Anani moved toward me, stilling Chloe with a glance, and drew me a little distance away. "It's okay if you say no. We probably shouldn't have just showed up this way, I know . . . I think you'll like her, though." She grinned and turned so that only I could see the wink she shared with me. "And it's not fair that I get to have *all* the fun, now is it?"

I glanced back over at Chloe, who had picked up my book and was casually studying the back cover. She *was* pretty cute. Her dark hair curled gently down to her shoulder blades, and it fell to partially curtain her face as she gave us our moment of privacy. "Okay." It was all I needed to say. Anani squeezed my arm and we moved back together to meet her. "Would you like to come upstairs?"

Chloe smiled and handed me my book. "I'd love to."

She wasn't shy. Just a couple steps inside the door, she turned and stepped in front of me, forcing me to a stop. And then, with slow deliberation, she reached for my face and drew me gently into a kiss.

She tasted like lip gloss with just a hint of rum, and I smiled into our kiss, wondering where Anani had picked her up. But her steady, sweet pressure soon pushed distractions from my mind as her lips worked over mine, stoking low heat deep within me.

I'd almost forgotten that Anani was watching, but she didn't let herself be left out of the fun. She pressed herself against my back, her fingers teasing against my breasts as she slowly undid the buttons of my blouse. She must have been teasing at Chloe, too, because the other woman gasped and let out a low thrum of satisfaction as our kiss grew deeper and hotter.

Anani finished with my buttons and pulled my bra free, then moved to Chloe, whose dress left her easy prey. She threw back her head as Anani bent and began to gather the hem of her dress, and I took the opportunity to kiss the hollow of her throat, tracing the lines of her neck with the tip of my tongue. She gasped, and then the fabric was between us, hiding her briefly from my view as Anani pulled it over her head and tossed it aside.

She'd already skimmed out of her own dress when she was hidden behind me, so Anani stepped in, pulling Chloe against herself and kissing her deeply. I set my book aside as I stepped out of my shoes and the pencil skirt I'd worn to the office that day. Then I shrugged and did away with the underwear, too.

They were beautiful together. Chloe's powerful arms and trim legs made me wonder if she was also an athlete. She was a good match for Anani, whose naturally brown skin was contoured and muscular from the hours she spent on the waves. Even with her underwear on, I could see now that Chloe was naturally lighter, but she'd spent enough hours in the sun that her skin glowed as warmly as the gold Star of David that dangled tantalizingly above her cleavage.

I wasn't sure what she might expect from me, but Anani I could read like one of my stories. She was hungry for touch, and her hands roamed feverishly across Chloe's body as they fused close, little gasps and moans the only thing between them.

I moved behind Anani and slid one hand into her panties, cupping one of her small, firm breasts with the other. She moaned without breaking the kiss, and I hummed my own pleasure as my fingers slid through the welcoming slickness of her pussy. Her juices coated my fingers as I slid them up to find her clit, and she practically vibrated beneath my touch as I began working her toward her breaking point, quick and merciless. My other hand moved in a gentle caress, fondling the familiar curve of her breast, and also brushing curiously over Chloe's soft flesh and the satiny gloss of her bra.

Anani let out a whimper, and then another as my fingers found the rhythm that drove her insane every time. She leaned back into me, her cries slowly intensifying, and Chloe pressed close, crushing my hand between their breasts as she grabbed the back of my neck and pulled me into a kiss. The angle was slightly awkward, but I moaned into the heat of it as Anani's cries grew frantic between us. Then her whole body shook and she let out the long, low moan that meant I'd driven her over the edge, and all three of us came down together, my hand gentling to a soothing stroke between her legs as the kiss between Chloe and I tapered off in intensity.

When she released me, all three of us were flushed and breathing hard. Chloe grinned at me. "Is there a bed? Because I'd *really* like to eat you out."

Holy shit that was hot.

Anani found her legs, grabbing each of us by the hand to lead us to my bedroom. My double had never seemed insufficient before, but now I wondered how we were all going to fit. But Anani and Chloe took charge, guiding me to the head of the bed and settling Chloe between my legs. Anani perched beside me, her fingers toying with my sensitive nipples. I felt strangely exposed, my lover on one side and a strange woman between my legs, her smile beguiling as she breathed deep, taking in the sight.

Anani distracted me, leaning forward and taking one of my nipples in her mouth, and my eyes fluttered shut as she sucked hard. That was when I felt Chloe's tongue tease across my lower lips, dipping only very gently into my folds. I cried out and let my head fall back, surrendering to the glorious sensations as two mouths worked lovingly over my body.

Chloe was gentle and teasing, torturing me with the promise of paradise with each stroke of her tongue, while Anani sucked and nibbled hungrily, stirring me up and leaving me breathless with the wealth of sensations. When Chloe finally licked deep between my folds, plunging her tongue into the hot wetness at my core, I was more than ready. I cried out and spread my legs for her, urging her deeper. She flicked a couple of teasing licks across my labia before she complied, pressing her face into me to tongue my slit.

The sensation was glorious. I was kept grounded—just—by nips and tugs at my nipples, distracting me from totally losing myself and forcing me to experience everything . . . I felt so full of pleasure I could burst.

Anani, knowing exactly what my desperate pants meant, finally took pity on me. She smoothed her hand down my belly and found my clit. My whole body jolted with the sudden shock of pleasure, and then I began to tremble from head to toe as she applied the short upward strokes that were guaranteed to set me off like a firecracker.

In seconds their combined efforts sent me over the top, my consciousness tumbling and my breath coming in fevered gasps. Chloe moaned as she lapped up my juices, and when her seeking mouth found my clit, I shrieked as another orgasm swept through me.

Eventually my mind calmed and I became aware of soft hands stroking my body and warm mouths planting sweet kisses on my thighs and belly and throat. When Chloe saw me lift my head she came up to meet me, and her lips tasted of my own salty sweetness this time. I moaned as I swept my tongue through her mouth in teasing imitation of the way she'd devoured me, and she sighed contentedly into the kiss.

All too soon, we parted, and Chloe moved away from the bed and began gathering her clothes. "I had a great time," she said, glancing up as she wiggled into her panties. Anani rested against my stomach and watched her from the bed. "I'm sorry I have to cut out on you guys, but I have a really early shift and I need to get some sleep."

She came back to give us each one last kiss, and Anani rose with her to see her out.

"Early shift?" I asked when she returned. "She's local?"

Anani hummed agreement. "She's a nurse. Sexy, right?"

"Sexy," I agreed, stretching out on the bed. "But a local?"

"A local who likes me . . . " She came back to the bed and measured her length against my back, her softness pressing into my shoulder blades in a pleasant, comfortable way. "And who likes you . . . " She kissed my neck and I shivered, whimpering. "And who likes hot lesbian threesomes without messy strings attached."

I could hardly think through the haze of pleasure that was rising in me at her renewed attentions, but I thought I could see what she was driving at. "Will we see her again? Like this?"

"I was hoping you would want to," Anani said. And then she bent her will to making sure I couldn't think at all.

DATE NIGHT

Brey Willows

I take out the black dress you asked me to wear, thinking about our impending night together, and remembering the beginning of us. You've always loved that deep *V* that shows lots of cleavage. But on our fantasy date nights you usually prefer me to wear something tight and short, something you can get me out of quickly. This dress is long and flowing and it makes me wonder just which fantasy you're going to make come true.

We'd just begun the dating dance and were learning where we stood with each other. You'd brought a bottle of expensive wine to go with the homemade dinner I'd invited you over for, most of which was burnt or under-cooked. By the end of the night we were sharing some of our deepest fantasies between heavy make-out sessions and even more bottles of wine. After every kinky revela-tion, we learned just how compatible our tastes were. And damn if it didn't soak my panties just thinking about you doing those things with, and to, me. I'd confessed to you that I wanted to have sex outdoors, and I wanted to be dominated. I had watched your eyes narrow thoughtfully as you listened, and through my haze of embarrassment I had a feeling you were already working out how to make it happen.

"I'm going to make them all come true," you said. "Each and every one, and any you think up later."

"I'd like to see you try, stud." I had laughed and eventually we'd ended up in bed having a marathon sex session.

I smiled at the memory as I slid on my dress and sat down to do my makeup. I let my mind drift back to that first fantasy date night, the first of many.

"There's a box on your doorstep. Wear exactly what's inside, and nothing else."

I could hear the smile in your voice, and I felt my pulse race in response. I ran to the front door and grabbed the large box. Inside were the kind of clothes a woman only got to wear to a costume party, or for an evening's thrill to spice up the bedroom. But I get to wear them for real. A note on top of the pile of all-black material said, *I promised to make them all come true. Let's start tonight. It's date night, baby. Will you be my slave?*

I hugged the clothes to me and danced around the house, giddy with desire and excitement. I took my time getting ready, sliding every piece of clothing on, paying attention to the way it hugged me, considering the way it would feel under your hands. I wanted to look perfect, like someone out of your fantasies.

You'd picked me up. We were uncharacteristically quiet, like the anticipation required a kind of respectful silence, as though anything mundane would ruin the spell. The look in your eyes told me I didn't need to worry. You liked what you saw, and a tiny part of me was disappointed you didn't just drag me back inside and undo all my hard work. But when we got in the car, and I saw how dangerous, how sexy, you looked in your tight jeans and tank, I didn't give a damn where we were going, as long as I was with you. And when you wrapped bondage rope around my wrists, tying them together in my lap, I worried I'd leave a wet spot on your leather seat.

Minutes before midnight we were in the middle of nowhere and you were about to make one of my kinkiest dreams come true. It was dark and deserted on the long desert road that didn't seem to have an end and the only streetlamps were miles in the distance. Thousands of tall, shadowy cacti looked like a prickly army standing guard over the vast, sandy plain and scattered rock formations. Your hand rested warm and strong on my thigh. You turned off of the main road and onto a single-track dirt lane. After bumping and grinding along until the main road behind us was swallowed by darkness and even the dirt track we were using faded into the shadows, you stopped the car at the base of a hill and turned the engine off, but left the fog lights on.

"Out," you said softly and gave my knee a gentle squeeze.

I joined you at the front of the car, my head bowed and heart racing. Lifting my chin, you kissed me passionately, your tongue promising raunchy, sexy things to come.

You pressed me against the car. Unbinding my wrists, you boosted me onto the hood and pushed me down so I was on my back, the heat a welcome contrast to the cool night air. Lying on top of me, you continued to kiss me and grind against me. I could feel your hard strap-on in your jeans and I moaned into your mouth. Even if the fantasy had ended right then, it would have been more than I'd dreamed would actually happen. In the dark, miles from anywhere, under your hard, strong body, I felt safer, and sexier, than I had ever felt before.

Moving off me, you placed my wrists above me and secured them to the side mirrors with soft black rope. I tested them and smiled, secure in my bondage. You pulled my short black skirt up around my waist, exposing my lace-topped black thigh-highs and leather knee-high boots. Per your instructions, I wasn't wearing any panties. The thrill of you starting your domination before we'd even left the house had made me so hot I could hardly contain my need to come, and I had very nearly gotten myself off right then. But somehow I knew that wouldn't be playing fair.

You unzipped the leather halter-top, baring my breasts to the midnight air. With my skirt bunched around my waist and my top pulled open, I felt deliciously exposed, wanton, and hedonistic. I heard you go into the car and when you came back you put the long riding crop on the hood between my legs.

You ran your fingers down the inside of my thighs, caressing me, the calluses on your fingertips rough against my sensitive skin. You spread my legs and picked up the riding crop. I closed my eyes as the crop struck one thigh and then the other, over and over again.

Instinctively, I began to close my legs against the pain. You stopped and stroked the welts gently while I caught my breath.

"Never close your legs to me, love. Never. Do you understand?"

"Yes, Sir," I whispered, spreading my legs for you again. Nothing in the world has ever gotten to me the way simply spoken sexual commands have, and tonight was certainly no exception. I imagined my desire pooling on the hood of your car.

"Good girl."

You began again, this time on my breasts. I screamed and bucked, pulling against my bonds as the thick leather tip struck my nipples and the soft undersides of my breasts. Before I could recover, you struck my stomach, my thighs, then moved back up again. I was screaming incoherently, begging, although I wasn't sure what for. I wanted the pain to stop . . . but I didn't. I wanted my hands free . . . but I didn't. I wanted everything and nothing, but couldn't articulate anything through the haze of endorphins clouding my mind.

You stopped and your fingertips slid over the fresh welts. I jerked under your touch and heard you moan softly.

"You're so beautiful," you whispered, "and your pain is so fucking intoxicating. I want more."

Sliding two fingers through my wetness, you thrust into me and fucked me hard and fast. I rode your hand, never wanting you to pull out.

You kissed me softly, gently, deeply, like your soul was open, pooling on your lips, just waiting for me to take it from you. I couldn't get enough of your mouth, of your essence. I kissed you for all I was worth, pulling against my bonds as far as they would allow in an attempt to get closer to you. But you pulled away, took your fingers from their hot place inside me, picked up the crop, and began again, starting with my breasts and moving down my body with harder and faster strikes. I screamed, struggled, and fought not to close my legs against the pain as you beat my pussy and swollen clit. The blanket of brilliant stars in the black night sky spun above me, a whirlwind of cosmic pleasure.

You stopped and set the crop aside. Starting at my knee, you kissed a trail up my thigh, over my drenched pussy, across my stomach, between my breasts, and finally to my lips as you settled your weight on top of me. I cried out at the feel of your clothing on my welts, but you ground down on my thigh, and came within seconds. Even tied down, I felt powerful in that moment. My screams and pleas brought you to that moment, and I liked that. A lot.

You reached between us and released your black silicone cock from your jeans. I moaned when I felt the stiff length of it against me. You brought the biggest one, the one I told you I probably couldn't handle even after hours of foreplay. You jerked me to the edge of the hood, slid your hands under my ass, and entered me forcefully.

I moaned and met every deep thrust of your cock. I came, and moments later, felt it when you came, too. I begged for you to keep going, and you did. As you fucked me even deeper and faster, I screamed for you, bound to the hood of the car, my heels resting on your shoulders as you gave it everything you had. Your hand closed gently around my throat, squeezing tighter and tighter as you slammed into me harder and harder. It is that moment I remember most clearly, I think—that moment when my life and sex were in your hands, and the only thing I wanted was for it to never stop.

"Come."

I did, again. How could I not have, with that command in your voice? It was that tone, that domination I'd been looking for all my life.

"You're mine," you growled softly. "You'll take everything I have to give you." The loss I felt when you pulled out of me completely was almost unbearable. You gently touched my stomach, caressing my skin as I came down. Tears coursed slowly down my cheeks, but they were tears of relief, love, safety, desire, and acceptance. Cleansing tears. Tears that came because I knew I'd been found. Not just me, but the me I kept hidden away, the part of me I couldn't show anyone because they didn't get it, couldn't understand this intrinsic need I'd always had to be taken, used . . . owned. You kissed them away and I knew that no matter how detailed my fantasies had been, they were nothing compared to this feeling of sublime submission.

"Can you take more?"

"Anything for you."

"You may regret saying that." You smiled to show you were teasing, but there was a definite hunger in your eyes that made me wonder if it was true.

When you lifted my legs so my ankles rested on your shoulders, I moaned, begging, though for what I wasn't sure. When the cold lube hit my ass, the first edges of panic set in. I saw you rubbing lube on a smaller cock, heard the wet sounds of it as you covered it, watched as you looked me in the eye seriously and said, "I want you to take it all." You spread lube all over, pushing it inside me, around me, but never taking your eyes off mine. In that moment I knew I would take anything you wanted to give me, as long as you never stopped looking at me like I was the only thing in the world worth looking at.

I cried out when you pushed the head of your cock into me, and you reached forward and placed a wad of material in my mouth, and I remember noting it was the black bandana you had in your back pocket the night we met at the bar. You knew, I think, that I didn't want to disappoint you by crying out my safeword. Not on our first special date night.

You pushed it in, gently, slowly, taking my ass as I screamed behind my gag, shaking my head and pulling hard on my ropes. You stopped for a moment, letting me get used to it, stroking my legs and stomach and rubbing my clit in gentle, small circles.

You began to move again, and it was easier to take. You slid in and I bucked to take you more deeply. You growled and began to thrust, drove your cock to the hilt inside me, held my hips and pressed your face to the leather of my boots.

I wasn't articulate, especially with the gag in my mouth, but you seemed to know exactly what I meant when I looked at you with my eyes wide, my desperate need pouring out of me. You wrapped your arms around my thighs and began fucking me even harder.

Soon, you pulled the gag from my mouth so you could hear me scream. You tugged and twisted my nipples, fucked my ass harder and harder, until suddenly you slowed and stopped, making small circles inside me. "Look at me."

I wearily lifted my head and opened my eyes, higher than I've ever been, riding a silver wave of pain like I'd never experienced. It was like being on all the best drugs the world had to offer, and I couldn't imagine ever coming

down. I also knew I was hooked, addicted to the kind of
. . . of . . . not relationship. Not just fucking. Ownership.
That's what it was. You'd taken me and made me what I'd
always wanted to be: your slave. I looked and saw you,
my amazing, gorgeous master in your tight white tank,
your cock buried inside my ass. Then I realized you were
holding the other cock, the one you'd already fucked me
with.

With a grin you pressed it against my pussy and slid
it in slowly. I moaned and began to cry. It felt like you
were ripping me open, taking my soul in your hands and
stretching it. But there was no way in hell I was going to
use my safeword. I told you I wanted this night, and you
were making it happen just the way I'd described it after
wine and foreplay. I wasn't about to ruin it by saying I
couldn't take it. I took a deep breath and concentrated
on your face, on your strong jawline and beautiful green
eyes, on the tats on your arms and collarbone that looked
almost alive in the desert night darkness. You worked the
dildo all the way inside me.

"Breathe, baby. Breathe and let me show you a little bit
about what belonging to me means."

I came, over and over again, and you followed me over
the edge, coming in my ass as it tightened around your
cock. I've never seen anything as awe-inspiring as you at
that moment, letting go and yet in complete control at
the same time. Sometimes it's the image I fall asleep to at
night.

You lay still on top of me, pressing both cocks into me
even though you had stopped moving, my legs wrapped
around your waist. Our sweat-soaked bodies stuck
together and you kissed my face, my lips, my neck, my

eyes, as I pressed my lips to your skin and tasted your salty realness.

Slowly and carefully, talking to me the whole time, you pulled the cocks from inside me. You moaned my name when I cried out my love for you. Your eyes were closed and you looked almost like you were in pain. You told me later it was because it felt so right you wanted to start all over again. You wanted to tear me apart and put me back together again, as your very own sex toy, your new forever.

I was empty and the night air made me shiver. The stars seemed to press down on me from above and the world felt too big, too vast. You untied me quickly and grabbed a blanket from the backseat before lying beside me on the hood. You held me close, and there's never been a moment as perfect as the one we found together that night. We watched the sunrise over the desert, and on the way back, you tied my hands behind my back, lay me on the backseat, and covered me with a blanket. Without me asking, you'd known I wasn't ready to be free yet.

I'm startled from my reverie when you knock at the front door. Tonight is fantasy date night number twelve, and I have no idea what you have planned. You've made all of the fantasies I told you that first night come true, and then taken me to new places I'd never even considered once the original fantasies ran out. Sometimes, that meant it was more than just the two of us, but there was never a question about where our ultimate loyalties were. Since that first date night under the desert stars, we've belonged to each other, heart and soul. My panties are soaked through from remembering our very first fantasy night, and I quickly slide them off and tuck them under a pillow on the couch. God knows where they'd end up later anyway.

THE LAST OF MARENGO

Mary Tintagel

I'd met Fenna only a couple days before in the Vivelavie bar on Amstelstraat. She'd promised to show me Amsterdam, but so far all I'd seen was the inside of her tiny bedroom, in her tiny apartment—located above a café on the Lindengracht. The exception being when I'd had to go to meetings at Zurtech Inventure, the printing company where I was working. I'd traveled over from the States to assist with new infrastructure and hardware testing. It was Friday evening, and I was too tired to hit the bars; instead I was sitting up in her bed Googling Amsterdam attractions on my laptop, the ones I'd have to tell everyone I'd seen when I got back home.

"Do you know where you want to go tomorrow, Julia?" Fenna called from the kitchen. She opened a couple of bottles of Maibock and poured them into tall frosted glasses.

"I dunno, honey. Of course, I'll have to go and see the Anne Frank House and the Van Gogh Museum before I go home. But on a Saturday, I really want to cut loose and have some fun rather than soak up history and culture."

"Fun we can have right here," she chided, laughing, as she put the beer down on the bedside table. As I sipped at the lager I drank her in too. The long blonde hair was mussed and untidy, maybe her mouth was a little too narrow, but her eyes were the thing—a greenish blue: jade and sapphires crushed to powder. Her slim, slightly athletic build she seemed to share with practically every girl under twenty-five in this city—maybe it was all the cycling, which also accounted for the raw-looking patches of scar tissue on her elbows. This was not New York; nobody seemed to wear any kind of protective gear. Girls wore cutoff jeans, as short as possible. And skintight white T-shirts—like they might be fined by the Amsterdam Police if their clothes looked a little baggy.

I turned my laptop to show her the result of my last search.

"How about this? The Museé Du Sexe . . . " I suggested.

Fenna just laughed.

"Oh my god, are you serious? That place is such a terrible, tasteless tourist trap."

As if to underline her point, the website started to play cheesy music. I muted the audio. What was her problem though? It didn't look that bad.

"Look, if that is the sort of thing you are interested in," she began, "then there is really only one place to go—*Huis van de Praktijk van Egypte.*"

My Dutch wasn't really up to it.

"The Egyptian Practice House?" I half guessed.

"That's pretty close, actually," she admitted, still laughing.

Yeah sure, I got the reference to the Jewish Law, it's not very obscure—*Like the practice of the land of Egypt you shall not do . . .* Sounded like this place was built specifically for the purpose of flouting that injunction.

I started to type it into the search engine.

"You're not going to find it on Trip Advisor. This is something a little esoteric. There's almost like a pact . . . an unwritten rule in our community . . . it is poor taste to talk about it too openly. You don't *ever* mention it online. You don't take just anybody there. Every tour is private and it can be booked up for months in advance."

"Then how on earth are we supposed to get tickets for tomorrow?" I asked.

In response, she just reached for her phone and I heard one side of a conversation with a girl called Roos who worked night security at *Huis van de Praktijk van Egypte*. The tone meandered across the spectrum all the way from pleading and begging to extreme surprise at something Roos said, and finally to gratitude.

"Well we're not going to need tickets. Tonight, Roos can leave the fourth floor fire-escape door open and then relock it automatically after we're in."

"Wait a minute, we're going to just sneak in the back like a couple of kids?"

"Why not? It'll be fun. I've had to do it a couple of times before to get people in. It's not like we're going to get arrested . . . I guess Roos could be fired if we're caught but that's pretty unlikely. Anyway, the point is Roos says the place is under refurbishment. Lots of the galleries have been emptied of exhibits already. But the sad thing is that one of my favorite rooms isn't going to reopen after the refurb. It's kind of a hands-on area and the equipment is looking a little tired—most of it is from the 1920s or even before. And I guess it's always been a little dangerous; nowadays everyone is health and safety mad."

"Fenna, I'm a forty-seven-year-old IT consultant, I don't need a huge amount of danger in my life," I said.

"We really need to reignite your sense of adventure. Come on, get dressed. We have to go tonight, not tomorrow night. Tomorrow morning the *Atmeydani Chamber* will be taken apart for good. This is our last chance to make use of it."

I started pulling on my jeans.

"What does *Atmeydani* mean? Is that Egyptian?" I asked.

"I think it's Turkish. I'm not quite sure what the word would be in English. I guess you would borrow from the Greek—it would be *hippodrome*."

Ten minutes later, we were cycling through the night at high speed and ignoring red lights until we reached a wide and surprisingly well-lit alley off Koggestraat. Fenna abandoned her bike against the wall without even bothering to padlock it, and was up the fire escape faster than a cat. I did secure my bike—hell, it was a rental— and pretty soon Fenna was calling for me to hurry up in a ridiculously loud stage whisper. The red light on the security camera above the door winked knowingly at us; somewhere, Roos was watching us. And then we were in. We were met with darkness and a mixture of odors from the building work: brick dust, wet plaster, and the light perfume that is exuded from freshly cut wood. I could see nothing until we reached a long corridor where the soft orange sodium light of the city seeped in through the windows to illuminate glass display cases and vases standing on pedestals that might have been straight out of the Smithsonian or the British Museum.

Finally, I sensed that we had passed into a great and airy open chamber—although everything was still black as pitch. Fenna started to feel for the light switch. The overhead fluorescent tubes stuttered and strobed for a moment, and then the scene was revealed by their flat and garish light. The "chamber" was a small oval auditorium about the size of a tennis court surrounded by tiered cherrywood seating. About five feet lower than the last row of seats, the performance area was covered with a thick layer of sawdust—it could almost be a show-jumping practice arena, except I could not see how you would admit horses to it. Over the arena were a series of parallel ropes, a little looser than tightropes, with a pulley arrangement and rounded hooks on leather straps hanging from them. It was puzzling. Fenna obviously knew what the purpose of it all was—but plainly I was too dumb or naïve to recognize what this was all about. Fenna was rooting through a cabinet next to a glass display case, searching for what we would need. On the floor, she placed what looked to be age-worn brown leather basques with strategically placed brass rings attached to them (at the hips, belly, and the center point of the back).

"Okay, this one is about your size. Get your clothes off and put it on," she ordered. I complied. She had selected a basque for herself and was doing the same thing. I couldn't help watching as she stripped. Her form was supple and sinuous, her limbs long. Her breasts were small, almost too meager, but I yearned for them just as soon as I saw them. I wanted to suck and chew on the pastel-pink nipples right away, but there was no opportunity; they were partly hidden from view behind the old cracked leather of the basque. When I saw how high her tits were pushed up and how the top edges of her nipples were still in view, like the delicate crescent edge of shell that is half buried on the beach, I wanted her even more. For all the time we had spent together in the last few days, my tongue and fingers exploring every single part of her, the chain reaction of attraction and desire that had started when I first saw her had still not reached satiation. Instead it was feeding on itself. There was the potential for this lust to run out of control and start to work me like a puppet.

"Turn around," she said. Naturally, I did. I stood with my hands on the back of one of the cherrywood seats. She gently forced my legs apart, and I bent forward of my own volition. Again, she was rustling around in the cabinet. Without warning a big handful of icily cold lube was spread onto my anus. I flinched as something long went deep into me. I thought she'd slid her finger in so I reached back to grab her hand. I ached for more. There was no hand. Just hair. A coarse length of hair at least two feet long. It seemed I now had a tail. A real horse's tail. My insides clenched and shuddered spasmodically. I reached back again to feel the flange of the horse-tail-ended butt plug. It seemed much too small and I feared that the whole thing would be lost up inside me. The fear made my muscles contract even more tightly around the head of the plug. I would not know this until later, but the beeswax around the head was melting inside of me, unmasking keratinized stippling—like rounded barbs. As soon as they touched my rectal tissue there was a burning sensation followed by the most explosive sexual climax I had ever experienced. My knees locked painfully. My

G-spot felt like it was in overdrive—my inner thighs were wet from the fluid dripping out of me. I was actually drooling with pleasure, until Fenna fitted a brass bridle bit into my mouth—and I was appalled. Gagging and coughing on both the unpleasant metal cylinder between my teeth and my own saliva. Next my eyes were almost completely covered—blinkers? I could only see ahead, and even then, just a tiny slit of light. Something was bound in place over my right hand—something as heavy as a tree branch which totally enveloped it from the wrist down and made it impossible to move my fingers. Then the same happened with my left hand. There was a sudden jerking as I was elevated off my feet and left to dangle about four feet in the air. I'd been lifted by the hook attached to the back of my basque. Finally, my ankles were connected to the back of my thighs with leather straps. Now, something was tightly joined to my knees. I dipped nearer the ground just for a moment and the blinkers were yanked off me. Then the rope pulled me back up and I was swung up over the arena. In less than two minutes I had ceased to be a human being and had become a horse. The things attached to my arms and legs were my new horse limbs. Of course, it seemed obvious now, a *hippodrome* is a place where horses race.

The rope suspended above the arena was carrying most of my weight; my "hooves" were barely in contact with the sawdust. Within a minute or so I discovered that I could walk and ultimately run as a quadruped with hardly any effort. Yes, initially I stumbled and slipped on the sawdust and my legs splayed out like Bambi on ice, but I soon got the hang of it and started to find it exhilarating. I became accustomed to the bit in my mouth. It started to

seem an essential part of the spell. I also discovered that
due to the cunning arrangement of gears and pulleys I
was not restricted to a single linear path: using my weight
I could drag the rope laterally and go anywhere I wished.
I'd heard about pony-play and it had never struck me as
my kind of thing—pulling around a cart with a dominant sitting on it. This took the whole thing to an entirely
new level. I started to wonder when Fenna would join me
down here. I could hear her talking half to me and half
to herself. She stood over a long glass display case, apparently straining to open it.

"Damn! This wasn't locked the last time I was here.
Someone has locked it and I can't fucking get Marengo
out. I'm only ever Marengo," she added, as if by way of
explanation. Then without another word she picked up
one of the horse limbs she had allocated for herself and
wielding it like a club smashed open the case. At first I
thought she'd lost her mind, but to her it was all perfectly
logical. Tomorrow morning this place would cease to
exist. Everything would be in a storage bin or a dump-
ster. Either way—whatever Marengo was, this would be
its last outing.

From within the display case she removed a full-size
leather and metal framework representative of a stallion's
head. It reminded me somewhat of pictures of props I'd
seen for the stage show *War Horse*. She donned the head
and paused by the edge of the arena. I saw her insert
her own horsehair tail and wait, in anticipation of the
orgasm building inside her. When it arrived, she didn't
emit a stifled gasp, like me, but rather a throaty, braying,
inhuman whinny. This was her moment of ritual tran-
sition: woman to horse. She affixed a belt around her

narrow middle and additional leather loops about her
thighs. Into this arrangement, she locked the longest dildo
I have ever seen. It must've been over twenty inches long.
Thick girthed, chisel ended, and brownish black with the
apparent flexibility of a fencing foil.

"Let me introduce you to Marengo. They say it was
made from a cast of the erect penis of Emperor Napo-
leon's favorite horse. They say he used it on Empress Jose-
phine when he could not satisfy her with his own member.
Let's see how much of it you can take."

That sounded like insanity. The thing was long enough
to reach from my cunt to the top of my chest cavity. And
looked pointy enough to skewer plenty of my internal
organs along the way. I galloped to the far end of the
arena to avoid Fenna. Of course, she could not affix horse
forelimbs to her hands because there was no one to assist
her. She did, however, manage to strap her ankles to her
thighs and attach hind limbs and then, with a practiced
motion, lowered herself down into the arena. Like me, she
had a supportive tether line running from the midpoint
of her back to one of the ropes that ran high above the
hippodrome.

She teetered after me on the curved equine stilts of her
hind legs, looking like a rampant heraldic stallion come
to life—a priapic were-horse that would somehow have
to be satisfied with my modestly proportioned snatch. I
continued to dodge away from Fenna, but I was persistently pursued. The pursuit became, albeit in microcosm,
a courtship. Somehow it was the courtship that had been
absent from our relationship in this all-too-hasty world. I
knew that I would give in to her. And I trusted her. This
was all just theater. She would never hurt me.

The sting of the horsewhip came out of nowhere. My right shoulder burned. I turned in outrage to see a young dark-haired woman standing on the edge of the arena wielding the whip. It could only be Roos.

"Cut the bullshit. I want to see you get fucked by Marengo," she snapped.

Although I'd guessed we were being watched on camera, I did not take kindly to Roos appearing arena side, in person. I spat the bit as far as I could out of my mouth and told her so.

"Did I ask about your fucking preferences?" she sneered, her face a frozen mask.

Experimentally, I lifted up my foreleg onto the barrier wall in a vain attempt to climb out of the arena. Roos grabbed it and pulled me forward. I almost lost my balance, and as I recovered it I saw that she had obtained a belt abandoned by Fenna and tied my fetlock to the low barrier around the arena. Futilely, I swung at her with my other forelimb, but she caught and held it easily—effectively immobilizing me.

"Give it to me then, darling," I said to Fenna. "I want it, I'm just not too happy about this bitch watching."

Marengo's girth was so great I felt like I was being clamped open. Fenna didn't go at me like a pile driver, but inched in until she arrived at the median line—ten inches along the shaft. Then she stopped thrusting and made a subtle undulating motion with her hips. This is where the horse cock dildo's flexibility came to the fore. The undulations were exquisite and powerful. It was only seconds until I came. In the midst of the pleasure I had a terrifying realization: The head of the butt plug had shot up inside me as a result of the orgasm, and it felt like it had taken a good length of the horsehair tail with it. I had visions of myself trying to explain all this in an Amsterdam emergency room. The visions dissipated as the pleasure struck. The head was spiraling and whirling inside me, biting and stabbing as it went. One second it felt like a punishment from Dante's *Inferno*, the next moment it was a bliss I would barter my soul to keep, and all the time the kinetic waves from Marengo were delivered inside me. Nobody could take this for long; there was a sense of rawness and building friction. Finally, just pain and fire. But still Fenna didn't stop.

Roos untethered my forelimb and pulled me nearer. Behind me Fenna moved in closer to make up the distance. In little more than an instant Roos had pulled off her pants and underwear and lain on her back, on the ground with her legs far apart. I could see she'd recently been waxed to within an inch of her life. Fenna maneuvered me so that my head was level with Roos's crotch. The inverted *V* of her clitoral hood and the moist folds of her lips were as beautiful as rare orchids. I did not like this girl, or her presumption that I would now pleasure her, but I acted out of pure self-interest. I knew when I started to kiss and lick her it would turn me on, and I desperately needed more lubrication to stop the burning from Marengo. So, I went to work.

The next orgasm was so powerful I think I blacked out. When I came round, Fenna and I lay on our bellies in the sawdust while Roos unstrapped us and removed the horse limbs. Then she held a horse tail in each hand and tugged. Fenna's came out easily in the first split second; mine was like a tug of war that seemed to be pulling me inside out. As the stippled head was finally dragged out of my anus I came again. Roos dropped the butt plug next to my face and I saw what had been inside me.

"Oh my Jesus," was the only thing I could vocalize. It had been a surreal and savage experience here in this chamber. I wondered about those who had played this game before me in the decades since it had been built, and those who had watched them. The pleasure and pain had both been intense. But the cynical part of me wondered to what extent all this had really been spontaneous. Had I been royally screwed in more ways than one? Was this really the last night of this place or was it all just a prank that these two occasionally played? I wasn't actually sure if I was going to find out.

As I got up I looked at Roos and saw that the whole set of her face had changed. The mask had unfrozen into a pleasant and relaxed smile.

"Sorry to have acted like such a queen bitch, but it's all part of the act I put on here. Most people like it," she said.

"Well it was certainly very convincing," I assured her.

After we'd climbed up out of the arena and got dressed I surveyed the scene. There was glass everywhere from where Fenna had smashed open the display case to get at Marengo.

"There'll be trouble over that, Roos." I suggested. "We should help you clean up."

"Don't worry. There are identical cases in storage. I can swap it and sweep up before morning," said Roos.

"Can't we take Marengo with us if no one is going to use it again?" asked Fenna.

"The Board of Trustees expects exhibits to be archived and accounted for. Maybe at some point in the future it will be put out on display again. So no, you can't just steal it," said Roos, patiently. At that, Fenna made a move as if she would smash the horse cock against the floor and break it. Frankly, I doubted she had the strength to snap its metal core, but it was merely a pretense to rattle Roos, after which she dropped the dildo to the tiled floor.

"Well let me get a shot of it just for remembrance," I said. I took my phone out of my jacket pocket and held it like I was merely taking a picture. Actually, I'd activated the Inventure app's scan mode. It was a piece of software I'd assisted in the development of and was in the Netherlands to help field test. This was as good a test as any, but I'd have to be in the office pretty early on Monday morning to make sure no one found out what I'd been up to. On the other side of Amsterdam, inside the Zurtech building, a 3-D printer had now come to life and was crafting an exact duplicate of Marengo in resin. Soon *I'd* be giving a surprise to Fenna and Roos.

They had not quite seen the last of Marengo.

CLOSE EDGE

Elinor Zimmerman

She wears a knife around her neck. I bought it for her as a birthday gift, wrapped it so carefully in the most beautiful silvery tissue paper and put it inside a little wooden box I'd made for her. Lola keeps her rings in that box now. The necklace she wears every day and keeps on her bedside table while she sleeps.

It's symbolic, the necklace. It's a little pocketknife—she has a collection of bigger knives at home—and it folds out. When you first see it, the necklace is just a pretty brass mermaid. It takes a second to catch the glint tucked up in her tail and realize there's something sharp inside. I thought of Lola the second I saw it. She's the hottest, toughest femme top I've ever met. You might look at her and see nothing but those tantalizing hips and thick, strong thighs, her fishnets and boots and those little skirts she wears with pockets she sewed on herself, the false eyelashes and smudged red lipstick. You might see her fantastic eyebrows creeping together (that she says make her look like Frida Kahlo), her big-ass door-knocker earrings, that little mermaid pointing to all that cleavage, and read her wrong. People do that a lot. A short brown girl with blue streaks in her hair, a curvy chick showing skin? You know what they're thinking. Then Lola flashes a pretty smile and glides right by. Or then Lola destroys somebody with her perfect, soft-spoken phrases, leaves some asshole blinking and stunned. On our second date Lola asked to kiss me, whispered what she really wanted to do, and when I said yes she slammed me against a wall with all her strength and knocked the wind out of me. You think she's decorative but inside she's steel.

Lola always gives me exactly what I want. Sometimes she starts as soon as I walk in the door. She greets me by pushing her fingers into my hair, her rings catching in it and pulling painfully. Sometimes she lets me think we're going easy tonight, lets me slip out of my heels and trade my pencil skirt for sweatpants and take off my bra. Then Lola rubs my shoulders and sneaks up on me. She gets me relaxed before she bites my shoulder so hard she leaves marks.

Today I think she's aiming for a slow burn, but she can't wait. She walks into the bedroom as I hang up my skirt. I'm still dressed other than that, button-down, panty hose, underwear. I've stepped out of my heels. I know the look in her eye when she comes in. I know we're already playing. She says nothing as she pushes me on the bed. She pulls the necklace off her neck. Lola flicks out the blade. My breath catches in my throat. We have a standing agreement about it—knives are welcome from five thirty to six thirty every day unless I tell her they're not—but it takes a second to be ready. Lola doesn't give me a second. She's already pressing the little pocketknife against my calf.

Lola keeps all her blades sharp, even this one. The tip slides into the fabric so smooth, so easy, and then it's just a matter of running it up the side of my leg, ripping it apart. The tip of the blade grazes my skin, a kiss that doesn't cut but promises it could. She does the left side as a straight line leaving flaps of nylon from my ankle to the waistband. On the right side she gets creative. Lola slashes, jagged and haphazard dashes going at all angles. She rubs her thumb over the exposed skin. She digs her nails under the little access ways she's created.

Then she smiles at me, a smile that says where we're going tonight. I nod. She binds my wrists with the restraints we keep under the bed. Once I'm secured, Lola goes to her desk to get her collection.

She folds the pocketknife back into the mermaid. Lola comes back with it looking like a necklace again. In her hand is her knife with the three-inch blade and the slick black handle. My tights are all cut up, but the crotch is still stitched tight. I know she brought out the bigger knife to change that.

First, though, she's going to tease me. Lola presses the dull edge of the blade to my naked skin at the slices she's made in my tights. It's smooth and cool. I shiver thinking what she will do with it. Slowly, she turns it around, skimming the so-sharp edge up my legs, curving from outer thigh to inner, high up until the blade rests, perfectly still, against the fabric covering my cunt.

"You can't move," she says, which I already know. We have done this before, so many times, but every time it is new. Every time it is unknown.

With quick, clean cuts she excises the crotch of my panty hose. The knife destroys the seams, the careful stitches. *These were new,* I think, for just a moment. *I'm going to have to buy new ones.* For that second, there's no danger, no thrill, just the crush of errands to run, panty hose that must be worn, the responsibilities of adulthood.

Lola hates that kind of thinking. She works in a bookstore where no one would blink at ripped-up tights, but probably she'd just skip the whole thing, her gorgeous legs bare under her short skirts. It's different for me, working in an overly air-conditioned office, with expectations for "professional" appearance. I hate it, hate the panty hose and the muted colors and the fact that I am thinking about this when Lola has me tied to a bed and is straddling my leg. She tells me to quit all the time, but I can't, not yet. So there's this, her greeting with a knife in her hand, helping me forget my day.

There's her bringing me back to this, right now, with the insistence of that knife. Lola tears at the hole she's made in my tights. She puts the knife on her bedside table right by the little wooden box. Lola rips that hole wide. The thin nylon gives at her ferocious tearing. She rips with fury, with glee at her destruction. She rips it so wide that, though she cut out just the small oval of reinforced fabric where the garment came together, she makes it split past the sides of my underwear, and up the front almost to my belly button.

"There's still something in my way," she says, stroking the black cotton of my panties.

We don't usually do this. Usually cutting up the tights is enough. I'm picky about my underwear and don't love replacing those if she cuts them to bits, but today I want her to. I give the tiniest nod.

Lola angles the knife against my pubic bone. The fabric here is thicker, the edges scalloped with lace trim. The trim gives at the first pull of the knife. Once she's made the incision, cutting a straight line across is easy for Lola. The knife grazes me ever so slightly, but does not break the skin. The loose flap of the now-ruined panties falls down on the bed. The waistband of the underwear stays snug while my smooth cunt is exposed. Lola scoots off me to sit between my legs and admire her handiwork.

The air against my naked skin feels chilly and electrifying. I can hear my heart pound in the silent room, the blood rushing in my ears. The look in her dark eyes, so raw with wanting me, undoes me completely. I know she sees how wet I am, how that fuels her and pleases her, and this thought makes my clit throb.

I want to beg her to fuck me, but that's not how this works. I want to tell her to yank down her tights and her underwear (is she wearing any today?) and lower herself onto my mouth. I want everything, all at once. But it's greedy. When we play with a knife, it satisfies us both in a way beyond words, but it also takes a lot. If I let go, I can soar, but when I've pushed in these scenes, we've both found ourselves drained. If I trust her to give me what I need, she does.

Lola reads me so well. Sometimes she cuts up everything I'm wearing, chops buttons off shirts—she even cut through bra straps once—before running the knife all over me. But not today. I don't have the patience today. She can see it on me. So she shoves up my shirt and bra and runs her left hand over the plane of my belly. Her right hand holds the knife. Ambidextrous Lola will not be putting it down any time soon.

"You aren't allowed to move," she says again. This time she brings the knife to the side of my left breast, resting the blade against my goose-bumped skin. "I'm going to hold it steady but if you move you might cut yourself. You don't want to cut yourself, do you?" Her voice is singsong sweet.

"No," I whisper, though of course sometimes that's exactly what I want. Not right now, but sometimes.

"Good. So you'll be very still," she says. Lola lies on me, angles her hips between my legs, and kisses me on the mouth. She's very gentle, very soft. I want to rear up and get rougher but there's the knife against my breast. I stay put, follow her lead, kiss her tenderly the way she's kissing me.

Lola kisses her way down my neck, over my collarbone, to my breasts. As she moves away from my mouth she starts using her teeth. By the time she's latched on to my right nipple she's biting and sucking hard. I want to squirm but I keep myself motionless. With the other hand, she moves the knife over my left nipple in feather-light strokes, no pressure at all so it does not cut. Then she switches, taking the knife in her left hand and repeating the motion and torturing my left nipple with her mouth.

I'm aching. I could come like this if she lets me. But just as I think that, she takes her mouth away and moves the blade from my nipple back to the side of my breast. Without a word she adjusts, straddling my leg again. Lola glides two fingers inside me, rests them there. She looks me over, considering. She's planning what to do with me. Will she take out her dull knife and ease it inside me? Will she pull out the pretty red harness and the big blue dick, hold this blade to my throat and fuck me? Will she keep the knife where it is and grind herself against my thigh until she comes? Will she get up and leave me like this while she sits in the chair in the corner playing with her knife until I break? She's done all these things to me. She might choose any of them.

But today, she's generous. Today she pumps her right hand against my cunt while her left hand holds the knife against me. She fucks me with her fingers and I clench around them. I move my hips while trying to keep my upper body still. We're both moving and motionless, both in pieces like this.

Lola trails the blade up my body. She curves it around the side of my breast and over the top to the center of my chest, puts the tip to my breastbone as she slides it up, hovers that sharp point at the hollow of my throat. She keeps fucking me the whole time. When that knife rests against my neck, I don't move anymore. I don't breath.

"Baby, you can move now," she coos. Lola pulls the knife away, sets it down on the bedside table again. "It's okay."

"Can I come?" I whisper.

She nods. Her smile is so kind. I fell for that smile, those round cheeks with the dimples, as much as I fell for how razor sharp she is. Lola eases her fingers in and out, brushes my clit slow and steady with her thumb. I rock against her wildly. I'm still tied up but my hips are free to shake and push and grind. Lola's got the weight of her body pushing against me, backing her arm as she fucks me. She's moving her own pussy on my leg. She's shaking and sweating but holding off for me. Lola always takes care of me.

She reads me like a book, every time. I'm so close, on that edge, and she knows what pushes me over edges. *Playing with edges shoves me over edges,* I think, and I laugh. She's not laughing. She's biting her lip and trying to get me off before she comes. Lola grabs that knife again. We're not being gentle. She digs it up under my breast. Both her hands are full and busy. I'm writhing and squeezing her fingers with my cunt. I'm using her thumb to rub my clit. I'm cutting myself just a little on the blade as she holds it still. I'm coming on her hand and calling out.

I can't feel the pain of the cut as I come. I can just feel the release she brings me. It rushes through my body, shakes me, makes me swear and grab at the restraints at my wrists. When I start to still, she puts the knife away on the table. Then Lola reaches under her skirt while she's pulling her other hand away from me. She touches herself as she wiggles on my thigh. Her free hand is slick from me, and she licks her fingers clean. I'm still tied up and can't reach out to her like I want to. She savors my whimpers. She moans and humps my leg, coming faster than I want her to. I want to watch her longer. I want to help. But she's coming and swearing and collapsing on top of me.

I love the crush of her weight on me. I could stay like this forever. Lola releases me, unbinds my wrists, rolls off me.

I still can't feel the cut on my breast, still too blissed out. "How is it?" I ask, lifting my breast.

She smiles. "I used the dull edge. Didn't break the skin."

"Cheater! I wanted it to scar."

"Not tonight."

I pout a little. She shakes her head. "When I cut you

like that, baby, I like to make it special," she says. She points at the new white sheets on our bed. "And I'd lay a towel down first."

No matter how punk rock she is, Lola's nothing if not practical.

"I love you," I exhale.

She kisses my temple. "Love you too. Come on, get changed. I've got dinner in the slow cooker."

I get up slowly. I open my drawer for sweatpants and there, on top, is a shiny, unopened package. A new pair of panty hose. Beneath it, a new pair of underwear.

"Lola," I say, touched. I change as she watches. "So thoughtful," I add as I slip into my new underwear.

She flashes me that smile again. "I knew you'd be needing them." She straightens the mermaid at her neck. Then she takes my hand and leads me to our kitchen.

BEDTIME STORY

Robyn Nyx

I feel her stir in our marital bed.

"Baby, are you awake?"

I laugh quietly, tempted to answer with the old cliché, "I am now," but of course I'm awake. I can feel her need, it's buzzing like a low-voltage current. I've just been waiting for her to pluck up the courage to ask me. "I am, babe. Are you okay?"

"I'm horny, baby. Are you too tired or will you tell me a story?"

"What kind of story, babe?" I'm teasing. I know exactly what kind of story she wants. I know her fingers are in position and moving in slow, circular movements over her clit. In the soft glow of the night-lights, I can see the comforter moving up and down over her hand.

"The bedtime stories you're so good at."

"And what have you done to deserve such a treat, sweet slave?"

There's a pause while she contemplates her answer. She

doesn't want to seem too presumptuous, and risk incurring my wrath. Or maybe she does.

"Earlier this evening, Sir, after I'd finished tending to your hands and feet, you said I'd done a good job. You said I could choose a reward, and to choose wisely. This is my choice, Sir . . . if it pleases you?"

I turn on my side to face her, and slip my hand onto her breast. Her nipple is already rock hard. I pinch it before I begin . . .

You're hitchhiking on a typically long road somewhere in the never-ending Texas desert. There hasn't been a car for miles. It's dusk. You came across a motel a few miles back, but it was closed down. Boarded up. You couldn't even break in to squat there for the night. It's gone dark, and all you've got is a tiny Maglite to keep you from veering into the desert and away from the road. The coyotes are howling. You don't want to admit it, but you're a little scared, so you pull yourself up tall, strong at the core. It's dropping desert-cold, so you zip up your battered leather jacket. Your trusty backpack warms you a little, but it's not much. You're wishing for a warm comforter to snuggle into.

In the distance, you see lights. You're not sure if they're moving or it's a motel. You're hoping for the latter. Nope, they're moving toward you. At speed. You're tempted to stick out a thumb, but they're going in the wrong direction. The truck zooms past you, but the interior light is on, and you catch a glimpse of the driver. You smile. She was kinda hot.

The brakes screech, and you spin around—an accident? A coyote in the road? You see the truck turning around. It's coming back to you. The window retracts, and the handsome woman leans over.

"You need a ride, honey?"

You come closer to the truck and rest on the window's edge. "I do, but I'm going this way. You weren't."

She smirks and blows smoke in your face. "I can go your way, honey."

There's something a little dangerous about her, but you can't quite put your finger on it.

"That'd be great." Looks like you're taking the risk and going anyway.

"Hop in then."

You open the door and swing yourself in. You know it's not much for safety, but you put your backpack between you and this mysterious stranger.

"Looks like you've got your whole life in there." Her voice is a little hoarse; something you always find sexy. She's observant too; another check on your list.

"Yeah, I'm just traveling."

"Traveling or getting away?"

"A little of both." Your honesty surprises you.

"Do you need a place to stay?"

"Is there a motel close?"

She laughs. "There are no motels round here, honey, but I've got a ranch just up the road."

"And you don't mind putting me up for the night?" Now your bravery is surprising you too. Or maybe you're thinking you misjudged her. She's got an easy nature, and she seems laid-back.

Another laugh. "I don't mind at all."

You take a moment to watch her hand come to her mouth as she sucks on her cigarette. Her hands don't look that rough for a rancher, but you guess she probably wears gloves. She must be hot, because you can see her veins are popping all over. You find yourself wanting to trace your tongue over them.

She's caught you staring, and you look away quickly.

"See something you like?"

Jesus, straight to the point. "Sorry. I didn't mean to stare."

"Sure you did."

She's cocky in her assumption. Cocky and totally right. You like that—you always do. She smiles, self-assured, and looks back at the road.

The silence is heavy in the air, and you want to say something, but you don't know what.

"Horses or cattle?" It's an inane question, but it's the only thing that springs to mind other than, *"Please pull over and fuck me right now."*

She smiles again. "Really? That's what you want to know?"

She's got a great smile too. Genuine. Knowing. She knows you're hot for her. You try to look away again, but her eyes are magnetic and draw you in. You have an inescapable feeling that there's a caged animal behind those eyes.

"I guess . . . I don't know."

She's got your tongue. You're never speechless. Words are your life. But words are also what you're trying to get away from.

"Why don't you ask me something real?"

The truck suddenly turns onto a bumpy track.

"Do you live alone?" It could be an innocent question. It's not. It's loaded.

"Why?"

She's playing with you. "Just a question."

"No, it's not. You want to know if I live alone because you want to know if I'm going to fuck you."

Now it's your turn to laugh. Nervous laughter that never sounds right. If nothing else, she's a straight talker. "No. No, that's not it."

"Sure it is."

Your breathing's become shallow and quick. You're not sure what's happening. You wonder if you made a mistake getting in the truck.

"Having second thoughts?"

"No. I need a place to sleep."

"Who said you'd be sleeping?"

Nervous laughter again. She makes you uneasy but somehow relaxed at the same time.

She pulls the truck into an open barn and climbs out. She's at your door before you even think about moving. You grab your bag and start to climb out, but she reaches over and stops you.

"You won't be needing that."

She pulls you out of the truck and onto the hay-covered floor with a quick tug. The truck door slams. You're stunned and start to scramble backward.

"Where are you going, honey? You don't wanna run away from me."

You stop. She's right. You want to know where she's going with this.

"I saw your tattoo. When you got in the cab, your jeans hitched up."

You look down at your leg without shame. You're kind of impressed she saw it.

"And?"

"And, I know what it means."

Your pussy jumps, throbs. "Really?"

Her laugh. You already love that laugh.

"It means 'slave.'" She's matter of fact about it. Just comes straight out with it.

"So?" More bravery. Keep going.

"So, you're in luck. I know exactly what to do with a woman like you."

Your eyes cast downward and take a moment to drink her in. Heavy black boots she could crush you with. Dark jeans tight around strong, muscular legs. A patriotic buckle on a rough, fucked-up leather belt. Tight black tank over an impossibly perfect body. Tanned muscular arms. She takes another drag of her cigarette and her bicep bulges. Your pulse races: muscles are one of your big turn-ons. Slender neck, perfect face. Hair short at the back, slightly longer on top. Bleached.

And those eyes. You could stare into those hazel eyes for hours. If they weren't so fucking intense. She practically walked out of your fantasy world and stepped on your chest.

"Why so silent? Don't you have anything to say?"

You know what you've got to say. She's demanding it. She shouldn't have to spell it out. You were speaking the same language before you even met.

"What would you like to do with me . . . Sir?"

That smile again. It melts you. Sets you on fire.

"Stand up."

You're on your feet before her in exactly the right amount of time. You've trained yourself well. "Sir."

So fast you barely see her move, she has a handful

of your hair. She drags you to the rear of her truck and throws you against it. Your shoulder jars and pain sears through you. It feels fucking great.

"Face the truck and put your hands on the mountain tops." She makes it sound poetic.

You grasp the metal bars and wait, shaking just a little with anticipation. She's behind you, and you feel her strength again. Ropes slide over your wrists and slipknots are pulled tight. You're bound to the truck faster than a cop could've cuffed you to it. She never answered, but now you're guessing she ranches cattle by the way she just tied you down.

She unzips your jacket, and her hands are all over you. Squeezing hard, grasping like she's trying to tear pieces from you. She shoves her hand down your jeans and sighs deeply into your neck when she feels how wet you are. She pulls out, and her hands are nowhere for a moment. You're already missing them.

A Bowie knife flashes in front of your face. It's huge. The barn lights catch in the blade.

"I'll buy you a new one," she whispers as she slices through your leather jacket from collar to hem, from cuff to collar.

You loved that jacket, and it falls away in three pieces to the dusty floor. You kinda don't give a shit right now. Your T-shirt follows. As does your bra. She moves your long hair over your shoulders, baring your back. Her hands dig into you all over, like she's got more than two.

"You know what I love about Texas?"

You're breathless, drunk almost. "What?"

"How we've really hung on to our ranching history."

You're not sure what she means, but you don't really

care. Her voice is so sexy. Everything she's doing is the stuff you've only dreamt about. Things you've trained yourself for, waited for your entire life. Could you be this fucking lucky?

"I'm not like most Americans. Obsessed with technological advancement and this so-called digital age. I like to continue traditions, artistic traditions. I have an antique quirt, one used on a ranch just like this centuries ago. Its core is full of lead. I've rebraided it and added a few more, heavier falls, made of buffalo hide, so you can really appreciate its weight."

Is it possible you might pass out? All the blood from your head is driving straight to your cunt.

"Would you like to see it?"

"I'd like to feel it."

She's gone from you, and the moment you know she's back is when the strike of her quirt throws you against the truck. You gasp. She's not warming you up. She's heading straight for the core of you. She's hungry. You want to feed her with your pain. She strikes you again. Your naked breasts hit the truck. Pain, front and back. This time you steady yourself and hold on to the truck for the next strike. You can enjoy this one. She's giving you time to savor it.

She brings the quirt down on your back and ass, time and again. You lose count. She's not talking to you. You can't talk to her. You can only feel. And it feels so fucking good. You've wanted something like this for years. And here it is, across your path with the luck of the Irish.

You can hear her growling and exhaling with each strike. You're weakening. You don't think you can take much more. Your knees start to give way. She stops and presses her whole body against you, her tank on your raw, beaten back. She drops the whip into the truck hold and slips her hand into your hair. Yanking your head back she bites into your neck, and you scream.

She stops. "Too much for you?" It's rhetorical. She doesn't care.

You don't want her to care. "No, Sir. Please. Use me. I'm sorry to scream."

"No need to apologize. Your scream is musical." She bites down again as her hands unbuckle your belt and open your jeans. She's away from your neck, pulling your jeans to your ankles. She kicks your legs apart, and you buckle slightly. Her fingers are inside you, easily. You're not stopping her. You couldn't if you tried. It's not that your body's taken over, as much as your mind has just released all of you into her hands to do with as she pleases. Trusting her to know you even though she knows you not.

Two quickly become three, four, inside you. Her thumb folds into her hand, and you become her puppet. Slowly, her hand becomes a fist inside you. You feel it in slow motion as if you could see it happening. Her left hand is at your neck, pushing you into the cold metal of her truck. Her right fist pumps inside you, violent but safe. Vicious but so fucking sexy. You're screaming now. Begging for her to carry on. If anyone stopped her right now, it's possible you'd consider committing murder.

Her mouth bites into your hip, your ass. She tongues the welts on your back, and her saliva burns, reawakens the pain. She twists her left hand into your hair and pulls your head back. You arch. You hear her growl again. She's watching your body so closely, taking in your reaction. She's fisting you exactly the way you love it, and your body is screaming for her to consume you. Her teeth and mouth are all over you. Her tongue slips between the cheeks of your ass and traces all the way up between your shoulder blades.

You're glad for her strength, how she's holding you up.

She releases your hair and pulls your belt from your jeans. One handed, she flicks it around your neck, through the D-ring, and pulls down. Her fist is still working your pussy. You're closing around her. The belt constricts around your neck, and you gasp for air. She pulls it tighter still.

That's all you need. You explode around her, tighten, keep her in there. But she has no intention of going anywhere. She waits out the orgasm while you pulsate around her hand. She pulls a little tighter on your belt.

"Thank you. Thank you, Sir."

Slowly, she comes out of you. As does the abundant slickness of your orgasm. Her Bowie knife slices through your bindings, and you begin to collapse, but she catches you. She picks you up easily in her arms, carries you to the hay bales close by, and lays you on a soft blanket. She hitches up on them and envelops you in the strong arms that have just taken you to the heights of your fantasies and beyond.

You drift into a thankful sleep in the arms of the Master you've been waiting for.

I feel her body shudder its beautiful orgasm, and smile. Words are our life, and I do love making her come without touching her.

"Thank you, Master."

"Sleep well, sweet slave of mine."

"I will now, Master."

ABOUT THE AUTHORS

EMILY BINGHAM (emilyerotica.com) lives and loves in Portland, OR. Her erotica appears in a number of Cleis Press anthologies. Her memoir, *Diary of a Rope Slut* has been recently published. When she isn't writing, she's playing with rope or teaching bondage classes.

AVERY CASSELL is a genderqueer writer, poet, and cartoonist. They've published a queer smutty fiction novel, *Behrouz Gets Lucky.* You can find their erotic short stories in several anthologies, including *Best Lesbian Erotica 2015* and *Sex Still Spoken Here.* They're working on another novel, a memoir, and a children's book.

KIKI DELOVELY (kikidelovely.wordpress.com) is a kinky, queer, witchy femme who has toured with Body Heat: Femme Porn Tour and whose work has appeared in various publications, including *Best Erotic Romance*

2015, *Take Me There: Trans and Genderqueer Erotica,* and *Bound for Trouble: BDSM Erotica for Women.*

CECILIA DUVALLE is a writer and lover of erotica and mysteries. She spends her time writing, knitting, reading, and loving in Redmond, WA. Her work can be found in many anthologies and links via her website at ceciliaduvalle.com.

With stories in more than forty anthologies, **TAMSIN FLOWERS** (tamsinflowers.com) has probably been writing erotica for far too long, but she isn't going to stop. Having completed her yearlong *Alchemy xii* BDSM novella series, she's now turning her attention to a new novel of a dark and twisty hue.

SACCHI GREEN (sacchi-green.blogspot.com) has published stories in a hip-high stack of erotica anthologies, including *She Who Must Be Obeyed* and eight volumes of *Best Lesbian Erotica*, and edited a dozen anthologies, among them *Best Lesbian Erotica 20th Anniversary Edition* and Lambda Award winners *Lesbian Cowboys* and *Wild Girls, Wild Nights.*

J. BELLE LAMB holds an MFA in poetry. Her work has recently appeared in the anthologies *From Top to Bottom: Lesbian Stories of Dominance and Submission* and *Best Lesbian Erotica 2017.* She's active in her local kink scene and always easily distracted by hot women.

ANNABETH LEONG is frequently confused about her sexuality but enjoys searching for answers. Her work appears in the 20th anniversary edition of *Best Lesbian Erotica*, and many other anthologies. She is the editor of *Maker Sex: Erotic Stories of Geeks, Hackers, and DIY Projects*. She is on Twitter @AnnabethLeong.

ROSE P. LETHE is a corporate copyeditor, copywriter, and avid watcher of cat videos. After completing an MFA in creative writing, she found she could no longer stomach "serious literature" and has since turned to more enjoyable creative pursuits.

ROBYN NYX is a lover of all things fast and physical. Her writing often reflects both of those passions. She is the author of *Never Enough*, and *The Extractor* series with Bold Strokes Books. She lives in England with her fellow scribe and soul mate.

MEGHAN O'BRIEN is the author of multiple lesbian romance and erotic novels, including *Thirteen Hours*, *Battle Scars*, *Wild*, *The Night Off*, *The Muse* (Lambda Literary Award winner), and *Camp Rewind*, from Bold Strokes Books. She's also the author of a veritable cornucopia of dirty stories, published online and in various print anthologies.

JANELLE RESTON (janellereston.tumblr.com) is a pansexual powerhouse whose erotica has appeared in anthologies such as *To Obey Her, Going Down, From Top to Bottom,* and *The First Annual Geeky Kink Anthology*. She loves sci-fi, sexual innuendos, and living in a lake town with her partner and their cats.

PASCAL SCOTT is the pseudonym of a Decatur, GA,–based writer whose erotic and romantic fiction has appeared in *Harrington Lesbian Literary Quarterly* and the anthologies *Thunder of War, Lightning of Desire*; *Through the Hourglass—Lesbian Historical Romance*; *Order Up, A Menu of Lesbian Romance and Erotica*; and *Haunting Muses*.

SIR MANTHER is a graduate student in biology with a wild imagination and an insatiable appetite for pain. She is training for her second marathon, has two tattoos (so far), and is working on a memoir about science and unrequited love. This is her first published erotic work.

SONNI DE SOTO has two BDSM erotica novels published and stories in *The New Smut Project* and in *The First Annual Geeky Kink* anthologies. As a kinky masochist of color, she knows how difficult it can be to accept one's own desires, but how necessary it must be to fully enjoy them.

B. D. SWAIN (bdswain.com) is a butch dyke who started writing queer smut because of a deep need to do so. Pushing her sexual expression is what makes her feel the most alive.

MARY TINTAGEL is a British writer who lives on the fringes of Sherwood Forest. Mary enjoys horse riding, rock climbing, spelunking, and walking her dogs. She has never fallen off of a horse without getting right back on it.

KATHLEEN TUDOR is currently hiding out in the wilds of California with her spouse and their favorite monkey. Her wicked words have broken down the doors to presses like Cleis, Mischief HarperCollins, Xcite, and more. If you see her, please contact polykathleen@gmail.com— approach at your own risk!

BREY WILLOWS, author of the forthcoming *Afterlife Inc.* series, has been editing lesbian fiction for nearly a decade. Her stories under another pen name appear in *Me and My Boi*, *Order Up*, *Women of the Dark Streets*, *Where the Girls Are,* and others. She lives in the UK with her partner.

ELINOR ZIMMERMAN (elinorzimmerman.weebly. com) is a queer femme writer and grad student. She's a regular reviewer for *The Lesbrary* and is currently at work on a novel about queer BDSM and aerial dance. Elinor lives with her fantastic wife in the Bay Area.

ABOUT
THE EDITOR

D. L. KING (dlkingerotica.blogspot.com) has a literary-minded cat who begs for her 9:00 treats from about 8:00 p.m., on. However, while other cats like to sit on keyboards and sleaze their way in front of your monitor, Batgirl knows how important the work of writing and editing is and refuses to bother her during those times. (No, really, it's true.) She must be a very patient cat as D. L. is almost always at the computer. D. L. King is the editor of fourteen anthologies, including a Lambda Literary Award Winner, *The Harder She Comes: Butch/Femme Erotica*, a Lambda Literary Award Finalist, *Where the Girls Are: Urban Lesbian Erotica,* and four Independent Publisher Medalists, (two gold and two silver) *Carnal Machines: Steampunk Erotica, The Harder She Comes: Butch/Femme Erotica, Under Her Thumb: Erotic Stories of Female Domination*, and *The Big Book of Domination: Erotic Fantasies*. Her short stories have been published in close to a hundred anthologies, including six volumes of *Best Lesbian Erotica*, as well as titles such as *Say Please: Lesbian BDSM Erotica*, *Girl Crazy: Coming Out Erotica*, and *Girl Fever: 69 Stories of Sudden Sex for Lesbians*. D. L. King is also the editor of *Best Lesbian Erotica of the Year: Volume 1* and *She Who Must Be Obeyed: Femme Dominant Lesbian Erotica*. She has a couple of novels and a few novellas in print, as well as a collection of twenty-one of her favorite femdom short stories.